REIGN

BEHOLDEN TO BALANCE, BOOK 2

CILLA RAVEN

Cover art and design by
Nichole W. - Rainy Day Artwork

Get new release updates and exclusive content when you sign up for my mailing list!

✽ Created with Vellum

I dedicate this book...

To everyone who read Initiate and jumped on board for this one too, I love the hell out of you!

To everyone who's like, "Cilla, you wrote a book?!?!" It's two now, bitches!

And of course, to my great amazing, fantastic, wonderful, awesome husband who inspires me each and every day.

Oh! And to every snowflake that got offended by book one, you're not gonna like this one either!

Also, please just skip the bad words and dirty parts, Mawmaw, I love you!

CONTENTS

PROLOGUE

LEANDRO

"What are you doing here? Were you following me, you piece of shit?" Mikeal asked as he stood from his attack crouch. His bright blue eyes cut across the room, narrowing in on me. The initial alarm painted across his perfect, ancient features retreating quickly, his fangs and claws retracting since my presence was obviously not something to be alarmed by.

"Of course, I am. You're the best elder to follow when shit hits the fan. We all know how you like to hide," I goaded him, twisting my lips into a smirk as I made my way down the stairs into the grimy basement our coven had forgotten about a long time ago.

"Watch it," he warned, then under his breath, he added, "Weird fucker."

His reaction was priceless. His distaste for my words, and me in general, was so thick in the air around him that I took a deep, subtle breath to savor every drop while it lasted. The centuries of mistreatment at his hands and those of every other elder in my coven were finally about to come to their inevitable and inexplicable end. They'd had no clue they were in danger when I visited them, and Mikeal had no inclination, even now, that I was finally the biggest threat in the room.

He was going to pay. Everyone else already had. His was the last name on my list, and I was going to enjoy every fleeting second of his distress, knowing it would never make up for everything they'd put me through.

"I am not hiding out for the foreseeable future with you, Leandro. Get the fuck out. Find your own spot to die," Mikeal said, slinking back onto the cot behind him, making his lack of worry painfully apparent. He threw one long leg over the other and laced his fingers behind his head, eyes closing lazily, his body relaxing.

He expected me to listen and follow his orders, just as I had every single day since I'd woken up as this malformed and barely functioning bag of genetics, fangs, and venom. But today was going to end all of that. Today was a day to beat every previous day. A day where I finally got what I'd wanted for so long: a love that made it all worthwhile.

I'd endure a thousand centuries more of their torment if it meant I could be with my mistress, my future queen. However, that would be unnecessary since I had the key to our freedom hidden right in my pocket, the cap still on the needle, so it didn't stab me as I moved.

I ran my hand over the shape of the syringe from outside my pants, making sure it hadn't gone anywhere, silencing my irrational fears that I might've dropped it somehow as I raced to stand over Mikeal's ignorant form.

"Don't rub yourself when you look at me, you sick fuck. I told you to get the fuck out!" He'd opened his eyes and seen me move but didn't even have the decency to take his hands from behind his head as he yelled at me. He was so confident I wasn't a danger to him that he didn't even bother trying to sit up as I towered over him.

"Disgusting, how little you think of me," I thought in my head as I answered out loud, "Okay, Mikeal. I won't rub myself when I look at you. But, please do let me stay. I don't want to die. Please?" I pitched

up my voice at the end like someone would if tears were prickling the backs of their eyes. He wouldn't be able to tell whether it was a real emotion I was feeling or not since none of our species could cry anyway, but he could hear it in my voice, and I knew his weaknesses.

I knew all of their weaknesses.

It was how I was able to get to every one of the elders and infect them, playing on their basest desires until I found a moment of opportunity.

And Mikeal proved no different than any of the others.

My plea got his attention immediately. His eyes narrowed, and his lips parted as he sat up slowly, swinging his legs off the cot with practiced ease.

I took a step back, giving him room to stand while I lowered my head in submission, taking in his jean-clad legs and bare feet, small tendrils of hair poking out the bottoms of his pant legs to trail down the tops of his feet.

Unable to resist a plea of any kind that played to his need to dominate, whether it came from a male, female, vampire, or a human, Mikeal rose to the occasion as I'd hoped, asking lowly, "You want me to keep you safe?"

"Yes, sir," I said, letting false lust enter my voice thickly, even as the thought of what was about to happen made me want to curl in on myself. I had to keep my mind on the payoff and my focus clear on what I needed to do.

Mikeal circled me slowly, taking his time as he examined his prey.

"And what are you willing to pay for my protection?" he asked as he continued his steady walk, a growing bulge evident at his crotch from his own words.

Letting my breath shake audibly before I answered and ensuring he heard it, I filled my gaze with unease and peered up at him, pretending to seem pitiful as I sighed, "Anything," in a breathy whisper.

Using his preternatural speed, he came around behind me and put his mouth right next to my ear. "Beg me, slave."

I could taste his arousal on my tongue as its smell permeated the space around us, nearly smothering me with its intensity. There's nothing like the taboo to cause extreme arousal.

I was this misshapen, laughable example of an elder vampire and had always been deemed too unworthy to be allowed to act as one. I was 'officially off-limits' to anything and everything the coven members would've happily done to anyone else simply because I was so outwardly broken.

However, that never stopped any of them from taking what they wanted in the dark, out of the way place no one ever went because the room belonged to me. At some point over the centuries, each of the elders had visited my room in secret. Every. Single. One of them.

'If they'd known how broken I was on the inside, it would've been a lot worse,' I thought sarcastically as I finally brought myself to answer Mikeal.

"Please protect me, sir," I pleaded. "I'll die without you."

The next few hours passed by excruciatingly slow, but I paid the price for my happiness and future selflessly, going through the motions until I had my chance.

Eventually, Mikeal was utterly spent and dazed from our escapades, and I furtively pulled the needle from my pants pocket where they lay forgotten in a heap on the floor. I removed the cap carefully, and while pretending to have one last sip of Mikeal, I injected him with the serum that was my salvation.

He barely felt the prick of the needle with how high he was on my blood, and he never even noticed when I slipped out from under him and escaped up the stairs.

The only thought in my mind at that point was reaching my mistress to tell her the good news. We'd waited such a long time for this day to come, and despite the price I'd paid many times over, I felt nothing but exhilaration as I rushed across the continent to reach her as quickly as possible.

~

"IT'S DONE, MISTRESS," I said proudly as I strode into our secret meeting place.

She was there waiting for me, just as I knew she would be, just as she'd been every week for the past five and a half years, the abandoned ruins around us providing the perfect atmosphere for our passion-filled liaisons.

She released a heavy sigh and turned to face me in all her beautiful glory, her bright red velvet dress flowing around her ankles as she stepped tentatively toward me. "All of them? You're absolutely sure?" she asked sweetly, her smile growing.

"Yes, mistress. All the vampire elders, other than myself, have been successfully infected with your serum. It's taken years, but I've finally infected each and every one of them. We can be together now."

"Oh, Leandro, I knew I never needed to doubt you," she said, wrapping her dainty arms around my middle.

Her hunter blood called to me and filled my lungs as I breathed her in deeply, the smell intoxicating and heady. I slid my hands over her back and nuzzled at her neck playfully (she knew I wouldn't bite her), and her resounding giggles dissolved into a full-on belly laugh. The sound was rare to hear from her, but it always brought joy and happiness to my dark and immortal soul like nothing else ever could, and I reveled in it for as long as she'd let me.

Slowly, a tingling sensation began to spread through my body, and I knew she was teleporting us somewhere new. Satisfaction and contentment settled deep inside my chest as I savored the smell of her hair, the tenderness of her touch, and I closed my eyes so I could enjoy our new surroundings that much more when I opened them up again.

I imagined we'd land in her home (wherever that was), and that she would finally let me into her world, into her life, without fear of repercussions from disrupting the balance with our plan to be together. I'd pictured our lives with one another countless times, me reigning as king of a new order of vampires, and her as the queen of all hunters.

We'd create a new line of descendants once the previous lines had all died or killed each other off. We'd be formidable, unstoppable even. Nothing would ever be able to call a halt to our new empire, and I laughed into her shoulder as my thoughts ran away into *happily-ever-afters*, one right after the next.

When I opened my eyes as she released me, I took in our surroundings with confusion. Cold, dark, and dank, the smells of the dungeon cell were repulsive enough to make me gag if I'd had a reflex for such a thing. Luckily, I didn't.

"Where are we, mistress?"

She took a step back from me and looked up into my eyes, her long lashes batting sinfully at me. "We're in my dungeon, where you're going to stay until I need you again."

"Stay?" I asked.

Mounting apprehension began to take hold of me as her face contorted from the sweet and loving one I'd grown so used to and morphed into something else entirely.

Something sinister was lurking behind her eyes, and I couldn't help the fear growing inside me for what she might have planned. As sweet as she could be, my queen was not someone to take lightly or disappoint. There were severe consequences for those that failed her, and as I watched her teleport outside the cell, leaving me alone behind bars, I knew I'd messed up somehow, though I couldn't for the immortal life of me figure out how.

"What did I do wrong, mistress?"

"You've actually done almost everything right, Leandro," she responded coolly as she plucked a piece of fuzz off her shirt, discarding it without thought.

Not willing to wait and see what her motives were, I walked over to the bars and tried to pull them apart, grabbing them tightly in my hands and pulling with all I had in me, but they wouldn't budge despite my vampiric strength.

The cell was probably spelled. She was a working hunter, after all. With everything she dealt with daily, I was sure the cells were created to keep the worst supernatural creatures under lock and key, stripping them of their freedom when it was necessary. I didn't stand a chance of breaking out by force. But I wasn't the worst creature in the world. Far from it, actually.

"Then why are you leaving me here, mistress? I thought I'd done well. I sought out and infected every elder, exactly as you requested." I was keeping my temper in check, but not without difficulty. It would only make matters worse if I let my anger seep into our conversation. She hated it when I got angry.

She stood up straight with a disgusted look on her face and said, "You didn't infect yourself."

I chuckled some because I knew then that this was all just a big misunderstanding. She could be laughably forgetful sometimes. "Mistress, you know I've never sired another vampire. The other elders would never allow it. They thought my genes were defective, so there's no need to infect me. I'm not a problem. We've talked about this before, don't you remember?" I asked, smiling as I reached out a hand to cup her face lightly, but she sidestepped my reach before I could make contact with her skin.

"Of course, I remember our little talks," she said before she crinkled up her face and changed her voice to one of mocking disrespect. "Poor and overlooked, Leandro. The weakest vampire elder who'd be so great if only someone in your coven would give you a chance. Sad Leandro, who isn't allowed to sire new vampires because everyone hates you."

My grip on the bars tightened, and my fangs elongated as I stared my mistress down, her words cutting through me like a knife.

"You whine and complain about your circumstances so much I might die if I have to hear another word. God, I am so sick of hearing about you and the plight you've made for yourself!" she spat, making my heart hurt inside my chest.

I knew I had to do something to calm her. She simply wasn't making any sense. She'd always listened to me when things in the coven were going wrong. It was part of why I loved her so much: she was the only one who'd ever taken a genuine interest in me.

"Mistress, please hear me," I said slowly. "I didn't know I was

7

annoying you by talking about myself. I'll stop, I promise. We can talk about whatever you want from now on, you'll see. Just let me out of here."

"You're so naive," she said as she rolled her eyes. "I don't think you understand what's going on here, Leandro."

"What don't I understand, mistress? Tell me. I'll learn, and then we can be together like you always talked about. It'll all be okay, just tell me what I need to know," I pleaded without an ounce of self-respect, the fear of losing her outweighing even my love for myself.

"You still think I want to spend the rest of my life with you?" She started laughing then, and I couldn't understand what she found so funny; my heart was cracking inside, shattering into a million tiny pieces at her words. "There are a few thousand reasons why that would never happen."

I attempted to bury my pain and laugh off her madness again.

"But, my queen, that's why we were infecting the elders in the first place: to eliminate the reasons that were keeping us from being together." Again, I reached out to her, but she just stepped further away from me.

"Here's the truth you're too small-minded to see, Leandro," she said, her menacing smile sending a shiver up my spine. "I needed your help to kill off the vampire species. I needed someone they would never suspect or see coming, and with how they treated you like a court jester, existing solely for their entertainment, you fit the bill perfectly. The other elders probably never even knew what hit them. I don't love you; I've never loved you. All I had to do was whisper a few sweet nothings in your ear every now and then, and I had you eating out of the palm of my hand like the bottom feeder you and your species are."

"Mistress, no," I barely heard my voice say.

"Now that they're all infected, I just have to wait until they kill each other off. So, thanks for that," she said as she turned on her heel and started walking down the long hallway toward the dungeon's door.

"Mistress, wait! You can't possibly mean what you're saying. What we have is special. You do love me, and I love you! Come back, and we can talk about this! I can make you feel better about everything. Mistress!" I yelled, sinking to my knees as the door slammed behind her, leaving me alone in my despair.

CHAPTER 1

BECKS

"Good job, Becks. One more round to go. You've got this," Adam said as he curled two one-hundred-pound kettlebells in each of his hands without breaking a sweat or moving a single blonde hair out of place.

In charge of combatives and weapons training, Adam usually took a very aggressive approach when training the members of Dragon team. During my first few days with them, he'd yelled and been as aggressive with me as he usually was with the guys. However, today, he was taking a lighter, more uplifting approach, for which I was grateful, but that's not to say his training regimen had suffered in any way.

"Uh-huh," I managed to say between panting breaths, sweat seeping out of my pores by the gallon as I made my way over to the stairs to start the stupid circuit again for literally, the tenth time. Fortunately, it was the last round I had to get through before I could call it quits.

Ten sprints up and down the safe house stairs, fifty jumping jacks, forty push-ups, thirty mountain climbers, and twenty ten-pound kettlebell curls later, I was exhausted, my body completely depleted of its energy reserves. When I dropped the weighted bells to the sand, I laid my body down beside them and eyed the sky while I tried to get my breathing back to normal.

'This is torture!' I thought, my extremities feeling more like sore, limp spaghetti than limbs at that point. 'There is no way I'm going to be able to do this every day, and Adam is batshit crazy if he thinks otherwise.'

'It's not torture, Becks, it's training. Adam knows what he's doing. The more you work at it, the better you'll get, especially after you go through the gauntlet and get the rest of your powers. After that, this'll seem like a cake-walk,' I heard Brax, my familiar, respond to me telepathically from where he'd laid down beside me.

Hunters are charged with maintaining the balance between good and evil, so the world doesn't end in an apocalypse, making bad things good and good things bad wherever their interventions are needed. The gauntlet is a series of tests in Heaven and Hell that every initiate has to pass to become a true hunter. It was designed to determine if a hunter initiate was balanced enough to find the imbalances that could cause an apocalypse.

I only had seven months left before I would have to enter the gauntlet or die; the prospect of both ideas chilling me to my core despite how hot I was from training.

Brax's bat-like wings were outstretched under him, his tiny hands resting behind his blonde head as he relaxed in the afternoon sunlight. *Just look how easy it is for the guys. It'll be that easy for you too if you make it through,'* he thought.

I sat up to see my teammates and wasn't disappointed by the view. Derrick, Adam, and Tyler moved way faster than humans; it was almost comical to watch. It was like they were moving in fast forward, blurs of muscles and tattoos moving from one area to the next at breakneck speed. I couldn't even imagine moving that fast, but I trusted Brax and his predictions about my future.

With a foul-mouth and a fiercely protective demeanor, my two and a half foot tall, half-elf, half-gargoyle familiar had been with me from the beginning, since before I was even born. I was unable to see him for a long time while I was growing up because the medications I was forced to take in the insane asylum stopped me from seeing the supernatural. However, once I was out on my own, I stopped taking the pills, and Brax was there in the flesh, or stone-like skin, as it were.

He saw every terrible thing that had ever happened to me, plus all the terrible things I'd tried to do to myself because of them. He stayed by my side through all of it, waiting for the day when I could see him again, for when he could help, even if I didn't know he was there.

The consequences of interfering before then were *end-of-the-world* steep, so despite how much I'm sure he'd wanted to prevent my horrible childhood, he'd remained invisible until I stopped taking the pills and the supernatural world opened back up to me. The whole experience felt like I'd found a long-lost key to the most treasured safe in existence.

When that day finally came, and Brax placed his tiny little hand in mine, our connection came back with an extreme force, branding and binding my soul to his, solidifying our link, so it was nearly tangible in our minds.

A burst of energy passed through me then like a strong gust of air that threatened to knock me backward, snapping my thoughts out of the recent past, the guys all feeling the blast as well.

They stopped where they were and scanned some distant part of the beach we were on. Brax jumped into the air, taking off in the direction the force came from without a word, and I stood up to watch him go.

"Someone's trying to get through the barrier. Stay with Becks," Derrick commanded Adam and Tyler before he took off after Brax, running faster than I'd ever seen him run before.

Adam and Tyler never took their eyes off the far end of the beach as they each started backing up to stand in front of me, blocking me from seeing anything.

Immediately, I was angry they felt they had to protect me from whatever was happening. Though I wasn't quite sure whether it was anger at them, so much as it was anger at myself for needing to be protected in the first place, not carrying my own weight on this team yet. I was closer to being a human than a hunter right then, and I wasn't too happy about it.

However, their freak-outs were for nothing. The chief was stopping in for a visit.

I saw Otto's shiny head with its ring of white hair and his signature calf-length socks, watching in astonishment as he hurried toward us, matching Derrick and Brax's speed as they ran and flew over to where we stood in the sand. Derrick and Otto were talking while they ran, and I wondered how these hunters seemed to be able to do anything they wanted without their bodies stopping them.

I couldn't wait until my body didn't stop me by needing to do things like, I don't know... breathe? 'The world better watch out,' I thought with a chuckle.

"No need to be alarmed, Dragon team," Otto said with a smile on his slightly weathered face as they all came to a stop before Adam, Tyler, and me. "It's just me." Then moving his blue eyes to mine, he said, "Hello again, Rebecca."

Noticing he was still refusing to call me Becks, I responded in kind, choosing not to call him Chief. "Hello again, Otto. What are you doing here?" I asked as I looked him up and down. "Or is this a regular thing I haven't learned to expect yet?"

Otto had a big grin on his face at my words and responded kindly, "I don't usually check in on teams personally, no, but I thought the matter I'm bringing to you required a bit more delicacy than is normally required."

He tugged on the satchel he carried and opened it up, displaying a few folders that looked remarkably similar to the ones that still lay unread on the dresser in my room for each of the guys on my team. I mentally made a reminder to read those whenever I got a chance and waited for an explanation.

"We were about to go clean up and have some lunch. Would you care to join us, or do you need to speak with Becks now?" Derrick asked. We all turned and headed back to the safe house, talking as we walked the short distance.

"I need to speak with Rebecca alone, but I don't see why it couldn't wait until after lunch," Otto said with another smile. Nervousness crept through my belly at what he'd need to talk to me about, but I slid it to the back of my mind for the time being.

"What are we having?" Otto asked as we closed the distance to the stairs that were the bane of my existence.

"Probably just sandwiches and chips," Adam said. "If we'd known you were coming, we would have prepared better."

"All the more reason not to tell you when I'm coming over," Otto laughed as he patted Adam's shoulder in good-natured familiarity. "I don't know the last time I had a good ol' sandwich and chips. My mouth's watering already."

We were all smiles as we walked into the living room, the cold air-conditioning a welcome relief from the heat of the beach, but I could also feel an uneasiness flowing through each of my teammates from my connection to Brax and his connection with them. The chief popping up out of nowhere was not something he did regularly, maybe ever. That much I was sure of if what I was picking up from Brax and the guys was correct.

"We're going to shower and change, then we'll be back to make lunch," Derrick said as Otto nodded and took a seat on the couch in the living room.

'What do you think all this is about?' I asked Brax in my mind while I showered.

'No fucking clue,' he responded from his spot on my bed where I'd left him. 'The chief does some weird shit sometimes, but it all seems to work out later. Just go with it.'

'Have the guys talked to him about everything that happened last night yet?'

'I don't think so,' my elf-goyle responded. 'But it'll probably come up now that he's here.'

'No, no, no! What do you think he'll do?' I asked, considering that the night before, I'd murdered my rapist with the dagger Adam had given me. 'Do hunters have any kind of jail? Am I going to spend the rest of my life in another institution? Oh my God, oh my God, oh my God!' I started freaking out, but honestly, who wouldn't in my circumstance?

'Pixie titties! Chill the fuck out!' Brax thought-yelled at me, effectively pausing my worry for a few seconds to hear him out.

'Look Becks, you're allowed a certain amount of... leeway and understanding as a hunter. Sometimes you're going to have to off somebody to get the job done. Really, it's almost expected of you to have a few casualties along the way. No one is judging you for it. We all understand why you had to do what you did. If the chief is going to be mad at you at all, it would be for not informing your team of what you had planned. But you've already learned your lesson in that regard, so I'll stick up for you if it comes to that.'

'Okay, I'll calm down. This is all just so new to me. Thank you,' I thought towards Brax as I walked out of the attached bathroom and through my bedroom to my closet. The new clothes I'd bought the night before were already hanging up when I woke up that morning, and I didn't know who to thank or yell at for the intrusion into my personal space.

Knowing we were heading into a cold crypt to meet with a coven of vampires later that night, I decided to go with something I could move around in comfortably. I thought a tight-fitting black t-shirt that said, 'Fuck off,' and some stretchy jeans that could hold the utility belt Derrick had given me would work nicely for what I was expecting. Though I really had no idea what to expect since this was going to be the first time I'd been around vampires other than when they were trying to drain me dry a few nights ago.

'Are you ready yet?' Brax soon asked with exasperation from his spot on my bed as I finished brushing my wet hair out. *'They're all ready and waiting on us.'*

"I'm going, I'm going," I said as I made my way back to the kitchen with Brax flying behind me.

~

THE EVENTS of the previous night were the first topics covered over our lunch, as I had a feeling they would be. However, Otto's response to hearing about how and why I killed Rick awed the hell out of me.

"Sounds like he got what was coming to him," he chuckled as he reached out and patted me on my shoulder. "The world is better for what you did."

I nodded at him and tried to cover up how fast my heart was still racing with worry by taking another bite of my sandwich.

Once the whole night had been relayed to the chief, he focused on Derrick and asked, "You still have the fairies' gem, right? May I see it?"

Pulling the tiny, bright red stone from his pocket as if he'd expected to be asked to produce it, Derrick handed it to Otto, along with the note that accompanied it when Ava had given it to me.

The chief held the gem up to the light and smiled. "Just as I thought," he said elusively. "Look," he instructed as he handed the gem to me.

I held the stone up to the light like Otto had, noticing the inside of the gem seemed to have millions of moving particles traversing the space inside it.

"What is that?" I asked as I placed the gem in Brax's outstretched hand so he could examine it too.

"What do you think it is?" Otto asked with a smile that reminded me of how a child would act if they'd discovered superheroes were real.

I glanced around the table hoping Brax or one of the guys would pipe up to help me, but instead, they were focused on passing the gem back and forth amongst themselves to get their own glimpses into its secrets.

"Magical dust?" I hedged.

Otto laughed at my answer, and his cheeks turned pink. "Close, Rebecca. You're close," he said. "Inside that little gem there is the entire ancestral line of the fairies, dating all the way back to the beginning of their species," Otto said.

You could hear a pin drop with how quiet the guys became as all of their attention turned to Otto.

"How's that possible?" Adam asked before he held the gem up to the light again with renewed effort.

"Have you guys ever noticed there aren't any fairies or pixies in Heaven or Hell?"

Shifting in his seat, Tyler leaned forward and placed his elbows on the table in front of him. "Well, yeah, but there's a lot of creatures that don't make the cut."

Adam handed the gem back to Derrick as Otto spoke, "That may be true for some species. But for a select few, they do win an afterlife, just not in the traditional sense."

"Why weren't we ever taught this?" Derrick asked.

"Hold on," I interrupted, "You guys have been to Heaven and Hell other than when you were in the gauntlet?" My mind was churning with questions, but that one had to be asked first.

Everyone turned to face me with different expressions. Otto was still smiling, while Tyler was shining his best *are-you-serious* face. Derrick and Adam looked like they couldn't comprehend why I'd asked the question, and Brax wasn't doing a good job of hiding his laughter from beside me.

"Yes, we go there fairly regularly," Otto answered. "It's our job to ensure the five realms maintain balance. We couldn't do that very well if we were denied access."

"Five realms?" I asked.

I knew I probably sounded dumb to them, but there was no way around the fact that I lacked a substantial amount of information due to my unorthodox upbringing. Being raised in an asylum, instead of by my hunter parents, placed an insane handicap on me in nearly every facet of my new circumstances. No matter where we went or what we did, I was constantly feeling like I was stupid and uneducated, naive, and unworthy of my place on this team. In reality, I wasn't any of those things, I'd just been prepared for an entirely different life than the one I was living.

"Ugh," Tyler said as he wiped a hand down his face in exasperation before he leaned toward me, some of his dark hair falling in his eyes, gesturing with his hands as he talked. "Okay, look. You know that hunters have to keep the balance between good and evil, so the world doesn't end, right?"

I nodded my understanding so he would continue.

"Well, here's how it works: there are five realms. Earth, the Veil, Heaven, Hell, and the Void."

I interrupted again, "What's the Void?"

"I'm getting to that," Tyler said quickly. "Earth is where all humans live, and they are to be protected and kept unaware of magic at all costs, so they are free to exercise their free will without magic's influence."

"Because when people know about magic, they can do all sorts of terrible things," Otto interjected conspiratorially toward me. "They can get power-hungry, selfish, territorial, and evil with only a hint of magic." He leaned back in his chair and raised his eyebrows as he said, "That's not to say they can't do those same things without magic, it's just almost a guarantee whenever magic is allowed in the human world."

"I guess that makes sense."

"But we don't stop everything from influencing humans," Adam spoke up. "Angels and demons are a couple of the species that are allowed to influence humans, for example, but only within reason. If anyone steps out of bounds or goes too far, we'll stop them as well."

"Anyway," Tyler started again, and I could tell he was getting irritated with everyone speaking while he was trying to get something across to me. "Yes, all that goes for humans on Earth. There's also the Veil. That's where most magic is kept. Some species are allowed to travel between Earth and the Veil, but some are not allowed to leave either one."

"Imagine the portals between Earth and the Veil as a sort of border crossing," Derrick said from the other end of the table, "and we're border control."

Smiling at his obvious simplification of what was probably a very complex system, I nodded my understanding before Tyler spoke up again.

"Then you've got Heaven and Hell. Hunters, angels, demons, and the dead make up most of their populations, but we're the only ones that are allowed to come and go as we please."

Otto turned somber as he said, "Well, it should be clear that we can't go everywhere." His tone gave me pause, and I looked to him with concern. "Anyone, no matter the species, can go *to* the Void, but no one and nothing ever comes *back*."

"It's where souls go to die," Adam said. "If a soul goes to the Void, there's no hope left for an afterlife or reincarnation or anything. From what we understand, the Void rips a soul apart for eternity."

I studied the solemn faces around the table and nodded again as I swallowed, the entire concept of the Void terrifying me.

"Yeah, so, those are the five realms," Tyler said, getting back to his forgotten chips.

"So how does the gem play into all that?" I asked Otto.

Smiling again, he said, "Well, there are some supernatural creatures that have souls, but they aren't quite right for Heaven or Hell. In those instances, afterlives were created for them that are neither good nor evil; they just are. We've found a few, but it's a tightly guarded secret. We hide this information from everyone, even other hunters, because we aren't immune to corruption either, as we all know too well."

I knew he was talking about the traitor at Binaria West, whose identity had remained elusive since before I was born. My real parents died trying to protect me and the world from whoever the traitor was by making a deal with a jinn named Absinthe. However, from what I could tell, the deal and their deaths had done nothing but lead to me being raised in an asylum.

"I can trust this team to have the utmost discretion in this regard, correct?" Otto asked, looking pointedly at everyone in turn.

I couldn't imagine any one of us putting an entire race of souls at risk for any reason whatsoever. We all resolutely nodded in response, and I could tell it was enough to appease Otto's worry.

"You guys need to return the gem to the fairies and find the pixies' sacred seed as soon as possible. I have a feeling the pixies' seed is just like the fairies' gem, another entire afterlife stored in a small, easily lost, or destroyed artifact. And if I'm not mistaken, souls that die and aren't promptly sent to the artifact holding their afterlife will be lost forever. We can't have that," he said.

'So, every fairy or pixie that has died while their artifacts have been missing has been sentenced to the Void?' I wondered, my eyes going wide.

'Pretty sure that's what he means,' Brax responded telepathically to me as his wings twitched behind him a few times.

"Then we'll go there before we head to the coven tonight," Derrick decided.

"Ah, speaking of which, I've been wondering how those vampires knew where to find Rebecca in the first place," Otto said before he took a sip of his soda. "Brax and I did a lot of work to keep the world unaware of Rebecca's existence. How they knew to find her in exactly the right place, and right when Brax wasn't there, isn't sitting right with me."

I hadn't thought about it, but now that he'd mentioned it, it did seem a bit too coincidental to me as well.

"If the fuckers had been watching her apartment, they might have known where she lived, but they wouldn't have known I'd headed back to Binaria since I teleported from inside her apartment. I don't see how they would've known I wasn't there," Brax growled.

Everyone seemed to be thinking about Brax's words, but then Adam said lowly, "Brax, who saw you in the time it took you to find the chief?"

The room quieted then, and I don't think anybody missed what Adam was implying.

Brax squared his shoulders, lowered his head some, and said, "I only talked to a couple of hunters on my way, and they were mainly worried about me busting in on your team's meeting with the chief. Otherwise, there were probably a few others that saw me on my way." Brax took a breath and crossed his arms over his chest. "You think the traitor saw me and called in the hit on Becks?"

"That's what I'm thinking now," Derrick said as he leaned back and brought a hand to his chin in thought.

"Who has vampires on speed dial?" I asked. "And why would they want me dead anyway?"

No one spoke, and that was an answer in and of itself. They didn't know, or they weren't willing to talk about it yet. Either way, I still felt left in the dark.

"This note here might have something to do with it," Otto said as he picked up the note that had been attached to the gem.

The note had been meant for me and said ominously, 'Start at your beginning,' though I had no idea what it was talking about.

"Adam, have you gotten any visions from it?" Otto asked our resident psychic, but Adam shook his head in response, his blue eyes meeting mine across the table.

"In that case, Brax, you might want to start by taking the team everywhere Rebecca was as a child. Start with where she was born and work chronologically from there looking for clues as to the meaning of all this," Otto said, lifting the note in question, the list of things we needed to do growing by the minute in my mind.

"Sounds like as good a plan as any," Tyler said as he crossed his arms and started bouncing his leg, eyes downcast to the table in front of him.

We all sat in silence for a minute or so before Otto stood, the motion causing all of us to rise as well. "I'm almost out of time for chit-chat," Otto said with a sigh. "Rebecca, let's take a walk on the beach before I head back to Binaria West."

Steeling myself for whatever else we still had to talk about, I stood up, put my dishes in the sink, and started to wash them, but Derrick came over and stopped me. "I've got this. You go ahead."

THE SUN WAS on the other side of the hidden island we were staying on, casting shadows from the tree line where we walked along the water's edge, careful not to get our feet wet. Otto was silent for a time, but eventually, he pulled his satchel off his shoulder.

"Here, take this," he said, and I reached out to take the bag and carry it while he talked.

"That there holds most everything I have on your parents. Their histories..." he paused. "Well, your history, too, I suppose."

I didn't say anything, only nodded, but I don't think he saw the movement since his eyes were so focused on the distant horizon.

"They really were wonderful hunters. Just good people put in a bad situation, I think."

Again, I nodded for no one but myself.

"Read up on them when you get a chance. See all they did and make your own assessment. I know making a deal with Absinthe had to have been a last-ditch effort, a last resort for them. I don't think they would have done it if they hadn't felt it'd been necessary. Whatever deal they made with him, killed them and orphaned you, so I know in my heart they did it for the greater good. Probably to protect you over everything else, if I had to guess."

Sighing, he said, "I wish I knew what they knew. We might be able to stop this looming apocalypse threat if we discovered that information." Otto looked thoughtful; his eyes distant as his pace unintentionally slowed.

"Do you think my real parents figured out who the traitor was?" I asked after a few silent beats, venturing the only guess I could come up with from what little I knew.

"Quite possibly. But something doesn't seem right about it. If they knew who the traitor was, why didn't they simply oust them and clear their names? Why'd they go to Absinthe instead? Something doesn't add up. I'm prone to paranoia, though, so I might not be the one to ask," he chuckled and winked at me.

I smiled up at him as we walked, the safe house almost out of sight behind us, "Growing up in an asylum, I know paranoia pretty well. She can be a bitch, but I'll talk to her for you."

He laughed at that and said, "I'd appreciate it. I really would." The humor fell from his face slowly, the mystery of everything that was going on seeming to leach the happiness from his face right before my eyes. "In all honesty though, the files aren't all I was here to talk to you about."

More unease spread through me at his words, and I gripped the satchel tighter.

"Normally, hunters are raised by their parents wherever they work as hunters, be it here on Earth, or in the Veil. If they live in the Veil, hunter children go to their version of school to learn how to go through the gauntlet successfully. If they live on Earth, it gets a bit trickier, where one of their parents or one of their parents' team members with teleporting abilities takes the children back and forth to the academy every day.

However, you are an adult that missed all the opportunities that normal hunter children are given, and are too old to begin going to the academy now. Plus, I don't think your team can complete their missions without you at this point. You've become a vital part of their team, and despite how unlikely it may seem, everything that is going wrong is somehow leading back to your and your parents' pasts."

Otto took a breath and said, "What I'm getting at here is that I'm going to take some time every day to teach you since you can't learn everything from your teammates in the amount of time you have left before you have to enter the gauntlet."

Taken aback slightly at his words, I asked, "You're going to teach me? Are you sure you have time for that? Why would you want to invest that much into me? I'm probably just a lost cause at this point, right?"

Otto stopped in his tracks and turned to face me, a hostile look in his green eyes as they shone down from where he stood. "You are not a lost cause, and please don't ever speak that way again. Every hunter child deserves a fighting chance, and it's not your fault what happened in your life that led you to this point. Your life and the troubled past you've had is a reflection of a failure on behalf of our leadership at Binaria, not you. And I personally take responsibility for not coming up with a way to get you into better circumstances before now. It pains me greatly, everything you went through, and I'm going to do everything in my power to see that you not only succeed in the gaunt-let, but as a hunter, and in your life as well."

His words shocked me, the conviction in his tone bringing tears to the backs of my eyes. I swallowed past the lump in my throat and nodded, peering down at my feet because I couldn't look him in the eyes.

Turning as if nothing at all was wrong, Otto continued with his plan, "Every day, I'll need you to have Tyler bring you to me at Binaria when you get the chance. I don't care what time you get there, or what I'm doing when you arrive, just as long as you see me for an hour every day. I know you guys have a lot on your plate right now with the missions you have already, but I can't understate the importance of having you ready to face the gauntlet when the time comes."

Nodding and smiling to myself, I said, "Sounds good to me."

It was a commitment I was actually excited about agreeing to. Time with the chief? Questions finally answered? The supernatural explained and not dying in the gauntlet? All of those things had been building up and plaguing me since I first met Brax and was placed on Dragon team. I'd have agreed to just about anything to get all the answers I'd been seeking and not finding.

Otto smiled and stopped to consider me once more. "My powers are hard to explain, but I know when something is meant to be. Like when I knew that your parents needed to be on the same team, or when I knew that adding you to Dragon team was the best option. Call it intuition or whatever you like, but I know better than to ignore what I know and feel in my gut. I might not be able to tell you how I know, but I can tell you are very special, Rebecca. You matter. Your existence matters to more than just Brax, the guys, and me. Whatever you end up doing in this world is going to be monumental. I can feel it."

"No pressure, right, Otto?" I asked with a smile.

"None at all," he said. "I'll see you tomorrow sometime."

And just like that, Otto disappeared, leaving me to stare at the crashing waves before me.

~

WHEN OTTO WAS GONE, I took the files out of the satchel and stared at them with a mixture of feelings. My whole life, I'd wondered about my real parents. Things like who they were, what they were like, or how they'd treated each other. However, the answers to those questions and a million others I'd wanted to ask throughout my life had always remained elusive. I was beyond excited to know more about my real parents, but something in me was making me hesitate. When I took stock of how I was feeling, I was a bit shocked to realize I was actually scared to open the files, afraid that I might not like what I found.

I couldn't let that small fear stop me though. Time alone, I was learning, was hard to come by in this new life I was leading as a hunter initiate. The guys were almost always around, and when they weren't, Brax was most certainly by my side. I couldn't let this time alone slip by without taking advantage of it.

The first file was labeled simply, "Amanda Woodridge."

Inside the front cover was a picture that made my heart skip a beat and another lump form in my throat. A beautiful woman that was strikingly similar to the face I saw in the mirror every day stared back at me. She looked like she knew a secret she wasn't willing to share, her thick lips pulled up on one side in a sassy smirk. Her hair was long and brown like mine, eyes the same shade of blue. Even her expression reminded me of myself, and I found that fact hard to reconcile.

I didn't have any memories of my real parents. Not even fleeting glimpses of life from before I was adopted at two years old. Seeing someone that looked so much like me was incredible and a little weird, too, if I'm being honest. The resemblance was uncanny. Eventually though, I kicked myself for wasting precious time and started inspecting the rest of the inch and a half thick file.

The information on my mother was in list form, extremely clinical, and familiar to me from the ten years I grew up in an asylum, so I read it like the story it was.

Amanda Johnson, her maiden name, was raised in the Veil and did so well in the hunter academy that she went to the gauntlet early at the age of only seventeen. She made it through with scores of four out of seven in both Heaven and Hell.

'Whatever that means,' I thought as I kept reading.

She was classified as a top-level spellworker when she passed the tests that turned her into a true hunter and was placed on Essence team with four other individuals: Malcolm Woodridge, Brandt Rivers, Logan Howell, and Benjamin Razner.

There was another picture in the file showing her whole team together in what looked like a desert of some kind, but it wasn't labeled with their names, so I had no idea who was who. My mother stood in the center, at least a head shorter than each of the four men surrounding her.

The guy on her left had his arm wrapped around her waist from behind, and the smile she was casting as she looked up at him was infectious. I found myself smiling at the picture, shifting my focus to the man who I immediately assumed was my father because of their body language. He smiled a lopsided grin down at her, his short blonde hair whipping in the wind as he pulled her close to his side.

The other men in the photo were all laughing, eyes trained on the couple between them. From left to right in the picture, one man had really pale skin, long blonde hair, and stood imposingly taller and bulkier than the others. He reminded me of what a Viking would look like in real life.

Next to him was a dark-skinned man with his hair cut short. I could just make out the faintest hints of tattoos running along his arm, where it was draped playfully around my mother's shoulders.

The last guy on the far right of the picture looked native in my undereducated opinion. His skin tone was tanned deep like mine, but with long black hair that nearly reached his lower back. He had his hands planted on his hips as he smiled a toothy grin in the direction of my mother.

Once I looked closer, I noticed the men weren't looking at who I thought was my father at all. They were all staring at her, my mother.

'She'd probably said something funny as the picture was taken to make *them all look at her like that,'* I thought as I brought my attention back to the here and now.

I'd been walking back to the safe house as I poured through her file, but when I glanced up, I saw I'd already made it back. If I hadn't looked up when I did, I might've kept on wandering around the island until my legs gave out, or I ran out of things to read. Whichever came first.

I trudged up the wooden staircase and slid the files into the satchel carefully. I hadn't delved into everything they had to teach me yet, but I knew those files were already some of my most prized possessions, just as precious to me as the dagger I'd gotten from Adam, the utility belt from Derrick, and even the lacy underwear sets Tyler had given me.

All the talk of souls and afterlives coupled with the new images of my mother and her team, the thoughts surging through my mind at an alarming speed. However, when the next idea formed, it nearly paralyzed me as I froze halfway up the stairs.

'Hunters have souls, and they must go somewhere when they die, so where are my parents' souls?'

My heart felt like it'd stopped, my breath jerked inward and stayed in my lungs while my stomach let loose a million butterflies and tingles. I gripped the railing tightly with my hands, so I didn't fall down from the impact the thoughts had on me, my nails sinking subtly into the wood as sweat beaded on my forehead and the most significant dose of excitement I'd ever felt in my life spread through me. *'If I can go freely between the realms, does that mean I could actually still meet my parents?'*

Nearly bubbling over with joy and nervousness, I ran up the rest of the stairs and burst through the doors, taking in the guys as they all considered me with curious expressions on their faces from where they stood in various spots around the kitchen and dining room.

"If we can go to Heaven and Hell and if my parents' souls are in there somewhere 'cause they're dead, in either place I mean, that means I could still actually meet them, right?" I barely got a comprehensible sentence out with how emotional I was, but from the way they all gawked at me, they grasped what I was trying to get across instantly.

However, it took my brain a few seconds to process the fact that their faces looked forlorn and somber, not happy and enthusiastic. They weren't matching my elation like I'd thought they would for making the connection and possibly finding a way to solve almost all of our problems in one fell swoop. Instead, their faces shifted as they eyed me, all of them looking scared and worried before they started moving toward me slowly, timidly almost.

Brax reached me first, hovering right in front of me about a foot away from my face as his stormy, sandy-colored eyes captured mine and held them there. I barely even noticed each of the guys coming up to surround me, standing a few feet away as if they were afraid to get near me.

"Becks, I need you to take a breath and calm down," Brax said, confusing the hell out of me.

'Why would I need to calm down? This is the best news I've ever heard in my life! Why isn't he answering my question? That was probably the most important question I've ever asked, and right now is when Brax doesn't want to tell me what he's thinking? What the fuck?' My thoughts raced away, questioning everything.

Trying to ignore what he'd just said, I asked again, "Can I see them? I mean, I know it might be hard to find them or whatever and we've got a lot of shit to do. And Hell, especially, might be super fucking scary. I mean, it's not like I've ever been to Heaven or Hell before, but like, it's possible, right? I could talk to them? And if we *could* talk to them, we could find out what they knew, why they made a deal with Absinthe, and that should tell us how to stop the apocalypse! It's a win-win situation all around!"

"Becks... babe, look at me," Tyler said, pulling my focus to him. Concern was lacing his handsome features, but I still had no idea why they were all acting so weird. He stepped toward me with his hands raised somewhat in front of him, almost as if he were bracing for an attack or something, which only confused me even more.

"What?" I asked, my anger at the situation leaking out in my voice more than I'd meant it to. "Why are you guys acting like this? Answer me. Please," I said, hope seeping away from me by the second as the inkling that I might have been wrong about all this started to snake its way into my psyche.

"Babe, can you let go of your power for a second so we can talk?" Tyler asked softly.

"What are you talking about?" I asked as I glanced down at my body and saw I was literally glowing the purple-ish blue color of my power.

"Oh!" It shocked the fuck out of me, and I jumped back some seeing it, but shortly after realizing what I was doing, I let my power go, and my body felt like it was getting back to normal pretty rapidly; until my knees got weak and my eyes got heavy. Releasing that much power at once seemed to have a very detrimental effect on me since, in the next second, I stumbled over my own two feet and nearly face-planted into the carpet.

Tyler grabbed me before that happened though, catching my body in his arms as he picked me up easily and carried me over to the couch where he laid me down gently. My head was a little dizzy, and as hard as I tried, I couldn't steady the world around me.

'Hunter rule number seven: don't fucking glow,' I thought sarcastically.

"Don't close your eyes either, it'll make it worse," Brax said as he came over and sat on the back of the couch with his feet dangling down near my belly, staring at me pointedly.

"The fuck just happened?" I asked and watched the guys as best I could, where they stood around me.

Derrick shared a look with both Adam and Tyler, their expressions changing as if they were having an entire discussion without saying anything, and I knew whatever they were thinking had to do with me, and they weren't willing to talk about it in front of me.

Instantly, I was pissed off all over again and rolled my eyes as I looked to Brax for an answer. "Well? Is anyone going to answer anything I've asked? Fuck!" I said as I brought a hand to my forehead where an ache was starting to form.

"You just got too excited, I think," Brax said dismissively, but his thoughts seemed elsewhere as if he were listening to the guys' conversation rather than paying me much mind.

"Dammit! If you guys don't answer me right now, I'm going to pull my power out again and turn you all into llamas or some shit!" I knew I couldn't do what I was threatening to do, but it felt good to yell at them, given how uptight and depleted I felt right then.

It got their attention though, so it was a win in my book.

"I'm sorry, Becks. Yes, I'll answer you," Derrick said as he reached behind him and pulled the coffee table closer so he could sit on it and explain.

Once he was comfortable and the other guys had found their spots around the room, Derrick said, "This may be tough to hear, given how happy you were by the idea of meeting your parents, but I've got to tell you anyway." He paused to take a deep breath, anxiety growing in my chest as I waited. "We don't know where your parents' souls are."

"What do you mean?" I asked.

Adam placed his elbows on his knees and sat forward as he answered me. "The hunters have been looking for their souls in both Heaven and Hell since the day they found out your parents passed. No one has been able to find them anywhere. We have to assume, given all we know now, that Absinthe probably sent them to the Void as payment for their deal, whatever that was." His face squinched up some, making it obvious he didn't want to tell me that little nugget, so even with how the information made me feel, I found myself somewhat relieved because he'd actually told me what I needed to hear.

I didn't know how to process the hurt that built inside my chest at his words, rapidly tightening my throat and forming tears that fell unchecked down my cheeks in two silent streams of pain and unrealized hopes. It was crushing, feeling like I was losing my real parents all over again, while at the same time, feeling like I'd never had them in the first place.

I closed my eyes and wiped angrily at my face with my hands before crossing my arms over my chest as I tried to get the tears to stop and the pain to subside. Ignoring the gasps my body wanted to take in, I forced my breathing to stay normal, focusing on that rather than letting the sorrowful thoughts and their images from the file take hold of me.

A warm hand started rubbing my hair away from my face in a soothing, repetitive motion that almost made me want to cry anew for how comforting the feeling was, but I couldn't bring myself to open my eyes to see who it was yet. I knew if I opened them, the tears wouldn't stop for a long time, so I squeezed them shut tighter, and breathed deeply a few times.

After a few minutes and a bunch of angry tear-swipes to my face, I felt like I finally had control over my rambunctious emotions. My body seemed completely recovered from my power surge or whatever it'd been, and I sat up slowly, opening my eyes to take in the room. Everyone was watching me with pity, and I hated it.

Needing to focus on something else and get those expressions off of their faces, I stood up and walked over to where I'd dropped the satchel Otto had given me, picking it up and carrying it over to the kitchen table where I sat back down.

"What did the chief want?" Brax asked, knowing I needed to talk about something other than my parents' souls being ripped apart for eternity. The elf-goyle smiled a little at me, folding his arms across his chest, the toddler-sized collared shirt and overalls he was wearing bunching up some with the motion.

I took a breath and glanced at the satchel before I looked back to Brax. "He gave me files on my parents. They're in the bag."

The guys started moving in then, coming to take their seats around the table. Tyler sat on my left, Adam on my right with Brax on the corner of the table between us, and Derrick directly across from me.

"Do you want some time to look through them on your own?" Adam asked with his velvety smooth voice and sweet demeanor. I had come to really appreciate his thoughtfulness in the short time I'd known him. It was as if Adam just thought about others more than he thought about himself, and with the life I'd lived before joining this team, his consideration for what I needed was a breath of fresh air.

Whether I needed distance, a fresh perspective, or a dose of reality, he wasn't afraid to give them to me.

Admiring his sapphire eyes, I responded, "No, that's alright. I looked through some of my mother's file on the way back already. I can wait until we have more time to go through them." I paused for a beat, then said, "Thanks for offering, though."

Adam smiled at me in return, and my belly did that little flippy thing it does whenever these guys are nice to me despite the somberness I still felt, but I tried to ignore it as Derrick leveled me with his brown-eyed stare.

"Was that all he wanted to talk to you about?" he asked, arms crossed on the table in front of him, his intricate black tattoos poking out of his short-sleeved shirt to trail down his forearms as his forehead crinkled.

Derrick, I'd come to realize, needed to be taken with a grain of salt. Though he could initially come off as hostile and cold, inside, I was beginning to think he was a very passionate person that had a lot on his plate.

He was the leader of a hunter team that'd taken on an initiate that didn't know what all of her powers were, much less how to use them. That would make anyone more severe and stern, I'd think. However, if his kisses from last night were anything to go on, the man had passion in spades, and I couldn't help the small smile that formed on my face as I thought about it.

"Otto knows you guys are training me, but he wants to train me too," I started. "He said he doesn't care what he's doing or what time we get there, as long as Tyler teleports me to him every day for an hour." I tried to sum up my brief conversation with Otto for the guys and Brax.

"What? He doesn't think we're good enough to teach you what you need to know?" Tyler asked hostilely from beside me. His brown hair was falling in his eyes again, and his leg was bouncing as he leaned back in his chair, legs spread wide, with an elbow draped on the back of his chair leisurely.

Clearly the angriest of the bunch, Tyler was the one that felt the most deeply out of our group if I'd had to guess. I didn't know anything for sure, but I did know he was constantly battling the beast that lives inside him for control over the body they shared. Where I'd initially thought he was just a cocky asshole, I'd quickly realized he was anything but.

In the short time we'd known each other, I'd discovered he could be funny and playful, as well as sexy and smooth. My first kiss, Tyler surprised the hell out of me with the amount of affection I felt from him. He was a puzzle I wanted to figure out, a lock I wanted to know the combination to.

In fact, they all were.

Pulling myself back to the present, I attempted to calm Tyler's worries, "No, it's not that. Otto said there was just too much that I needed to learn in too short a time period for you guys to be able to teach me everything yourselves. I think he's only trying to help out since we've got a lot going on with the missions we have already."

Tyler nodded at me before Derrick spoke up again. "Alright, we'll make sure you train with him every day." He took a deep breath and stretched his arms above his head, his t-shirt pulling taught against the muscles underneath, and I held my breath until he was through.

Apparently, my never-before-used libido had a 'fuck sadness' approach to life, and honestly, the erotic thoughts that flowed through my mind were a very welcome distraction from everything that'd just happened.

"Speaking of missions, it's nearly time to go," Adam said as he stood up, the reality of our situation assaulting me like a splash of cold water on my heated skin. I was excited to check in on the fairies and pixies, but I was still really nervous about meeting vampires face-to-face.

Brax took to the air on his rubbery wings and read my thoughts. "Becks, you don't need to worry about anything. The vamps know better than to fuck with hunters. It'd be suicide for them to even try." My familiar was trying to calm my steadily growing uneasiness, but it wasn't working as well as I thought he wanted it to.

"But I'm not a hunter yet, I'm just an initiate," I said as I stood, grabbing the satchel to take to my room and get ready for what we were about to do.

Adam spoke up from behind me as we made our way to our respective rooms, "Yeah, but they don't know that, and it might be best to keep it that way."

His words didn't help, but I tried to ignore my fears and focus on the task at hand. I plucked the utility belt off my nightstand, strapped it on, and slid the dagger into its sheath on my side.

Brax handed me a stake as he flew into my room, and I didn't need to ask what to do with it. I took it from his outstretched hand and placed it on my other hip. Reaching down, I grabbed the duffel bag Tyler had brought me from Otto and gestured to Brax questioningly.

"Will I need any of this stuff?"

He walked over to the bag on my bed and opened it up, eyeing what was inside. "Nah, not this time, I don't think. Tyler is teleporting us, and the coven we're going to is still in the U.S., so you shouldn't need a passport even if some weird shit does go down. Unless you're planning on buying something, I'm pretty sure you won't need the cash either."

"Okay, what about the gun?" Nervousness crept through me at the thought of wielding such a weapon, which was kind of ironic since I'd slit a man's throat the night before. *'Why didn't I shrink away from the dagger?'* I wondered.

"You should only need the stake tonight."

"Okay."

"If I've got anything to do with it, you won't need that either. Those fuckers better not try anything else with you. I've had just about enough of their shit," Brax said, making me smile as I left the duffel and met everyone back in the living room.

"I second that," Tyler said with a wink in my direction that made my stomach do that flippy thing again. I smiled and moved toward him, looking him in his eyes.

I slid my hand up his chest slowly as everyone else placed a hand on him somewhere, the intensity of Tyler's gaze making me giddy as I felt him teleporting us away from the safe house.

～

RIGHT AWAY, my nostrils flared with the stench surrounding us as we materialized on some railroad tracks under a bridge in a forgotten part of Atlanta. Derrick stepped over the rails and down the packed rock until he was standing at the foot of the slanted concrete structure where people were driving right overhead, utterly unaware of our presence. He reached out his hands and started twirling them before him, chanting some incomprehensible words as the portal to the Veil opened like a shimmering curtain. We all walked through, and I breathed a sigh of relief as the smell of fresh flowers, recent rain, and earth filled my lungs.

The first time I'd come through this portal, it'd been right in the middle of the fairy/pixie war. A fight that was centuries old, the original cause of the war forgotten but still defended, was basically my first mission with this team. We had them sign a treaty to work together rather than against each other, and in return for their cooperation and cease-fire, we'd agreed to find their missing heirs and artifacts.

If I'd thought the forest was beautiful then, I was astounded by what I saw now. The entire forest seemed to have blossomed tenfold since I last saw it. Where before there were only white blooms of the pixie's flowers growing throughout the forest, now there were flowers of all colors growing thick and bountiful everywhere I looked. The exquisiteness of it all nearly took my breath away.

"I've never seen anything this beautiful," I heard myself say softly, hardly aware I was speaking at all, lost as I was in the sights around me.

As if I were being summoned or hypnotized, my eyes locked on a purple flower as big as my hand that hung down with others like it from the trees surrounding us. I found my feet moving forward of their own accord as I drifted toward the beautiful bloom, everything else around me forgotten.

With every step I took, a sound I couldn't name, grew louder in my ears, a soft ringing melody that spoke to my soul in a way it had never been spoken to before. It drew me in closer, made me long to hear the flower's song more clearly. I couldn't stop myself from answering it's call, nor did I want to.

When I finally reached out and lightly grazed my fingers along one of its perfect petals, it was as if my mind had succumbed to the flower's power entirely. All I could hear was its serenade, all I could see was its flawless shape, and all I could feel was utter happiness, through and through. I'd never felt pleasure like that in all my life, and I never wanted it to end. I stepped closer to the flower to breathe in its intoxicating smell, and I decided then it was by far the best decision I'd ever made.

"Becks," Brax's voice sounded concerned when I felt his little hand pulling on my shoulder to make me turn around and face him. "You okay?" I heard him ask.

When I looked at him, Brax's shape started to morph, blending in with the shapes around him, his worried eyes bleeding into the background of the forest. Colors began swirling through my consciousness as tingles flowed through my whole body, and I felt my pulse slow, feeling like I was drifting away on the most beautiful and fluffiest of clouds. I knew I was smiling as my body fell to the ground, Brax's weird face twisting in my thoughts as I reveled in the precious high, and I couldn't have cared less.

CHAPTER 2

ADAM

*T*he forest around us had more blooms in it than I could count, and I knew instantly that our interference with the fairies' and pixies' affairs had changed something dramatically for an effect this drastic to have taken hold in such a short period of time. We were only here yesterday, giving them copies of the treaty they'd signed. Yet somehow, magic had spread exponentially over the forest during the night. I was taking in the plethora of new plants around me, noting the absence of our flying friends when Becks started easing away from us.

Something about the way she was walking didn't seem natural for her. I turned to watch her go, trying to identify what had piqued my awareness as being off or unusual. Brax flew behind her while Derrick and Tyler were still planted firmly where they landed on this side of the Veil.

I heard a small giggle from Becks, and I watched her as she reached out to touch one of the flowers hanging overhead. Then when Brax asked if she was okay, it only took one look at her dazed face to make me move.

She started falling swiftly, her legs crumbling beneath her. But with my speed, I was able to reach out and catch her before her head hit the ground. I landed hard, my knees slamming into the forest floor, sending a shock up each of my legs as I caught Becks at just the right angle to lay her head gently in my lap. I breathed a sigh of relief because luckily, she didn't seem hurt at all, just unconscious.

As soon as I stared down into her beautiful face, a vision slammed into my consciousness so hard I felt my head tilt all the way back, and my muscles lock up with the intensity of it.

"Where are we?" I heard Becks ask from beside me, and I noticed our surroundings had changed drastically.

I glanced over to her and knew right away; something wasn't right. This didn't feel like any other vision I'd ever had.

I tried moving my body, bringing my hands up to my face, turning them this way and that, unable to understand how I was able to do such a thing.

I'd never been able to control what was going on in my visions before. It was just another part of having psychic abilities that I hated, not being able to change what they showed me. Typically, if I felt my body move or heard myself speak in a vision, I wasn't consciously controlling it. I saw the future from my perspective, but I wasn't able to change anything. It was just something I could watch that may or may not come to pass at some point in the future.

This was different, though.

This felt real.

"What are you doing?" Becks asked with a raised brow in my direction, snapping me out of the perusal of my physical form. "You're acting weird," she said with a smile that warmed me, given how she had looked earlier with tears on her cheeks. I dropped my hands from in front of my face, knowing that if this was real and not a vision, I probably seemed like an idiot.

Heat flooded my cheeks, and I heard Becks giggle again as she inspected me, her gaze as distracting as the vision/not vision we were in.

She looked around for a second, and I followed her lead, taking in the stone walls surrounding us and the intricate tapestries that lined them. We were in a medieval-looking bedroom of some kind. Eleventh- or twelfth-century if I had to guess from the furniture populating the ample space.

In the corner opposite where we stood, there was an overly large bed with intricate engravings carved into its thick wood, and woolen blankets tucked in neatly over its mattress. Purple fabric draped from the head of the bed and spread down the length of it to easily be pulled across for privacy or warmth, and at the foot of the bed was a crib, empty except for the plush blankets that laid inside it. There were two tall arched windows on the wall farthest from us with stairs leading up to each one, and a fireplace with a rounded-out mantle roaring to life between them.

"Um, the last thing I remember, I was sniffing a flower, Adam. Can you please tell me where everyone is and how we got here? And where here is exactly," Becks said, unconsciously stepping closer to me, her arm brushing up against mine as she took in the room, and the fact that she moved closer to me rather than farther away in this confusing situation wasn't lost on me.

I took her hand in mine and knew for sure this wasn't a vision. At least not like any I'd ever experienced before. Everything was too real to be a vision since there wasn't the shimmery effect that usually accompanied them.

Becks squeezed my hand and looked up into my eyes. "Would you answer me already? I'm starting to freak out," she said. "I can't feel Brax."

The worry on her face was unmistakable, and as I searched through my mind, I realized I couldn't feel him either. After becoming accustomed to his connection with me, I realized the absence of the little guy was actually somewhat painful.

"Sorry, Becks. I thought this was a vision at first, but now I'm pretty sure it's real. I don't know what's going on or where we are," I said, but seeing plainly on her face that my words were doing more harm than good, I added, "Don't worry. We'll figure it out."

Still squeezing her hand as tightly as she was squeezing mine, I took my other hand and pushed a stray lock of hair behind her ear, taking my time as I slowly ran my finger down the side of her jaw and down her neck before I dropped it back to my side. "You're always safe with me," I promised.

Becks smiled as the large metal and wooden door to the room opened.

Both of us turned to watch a lady with a long apron walk in, staring down at a baby she was cradling in her arms. Unaware of our presence, she walked right past us without a glance and made her way over to a chair by the fire to begin breastfeeding the infant.

"Um, excuse me," I said gently, not wanting to startle her, but still wanting to get her to take notice of us before the whole situation got weirder. But the woman didn't even acknowledge I'd spoken. She started humming a slow melody as the baby latched onto her breast greedily.

'She must not have heard me,' I thought. 'How do I get her attention without scaring the hell out of her?'

Apparently unburdened with societal niceties, Becks said louder and more sternly than I would have, "Ma'am," as she let go of my hand and walked over to stand in front of the woman. But, again, the woman didn't even look up.

Obviously annoyed, Becks reached out to touch the lady's shoulder, but surprisingly, her hand passed right through the woman's form as if she were a ghost.

"Woah," Becks said as she stepped back, her widened eyes focused on mine. "Am I projecting again? I don't remember falling asleep. And usually, I stay where my body's at when I'm projecting," Becks barely paused for a breath.

"Hold on, how am I able to touch you? And how can you see me in the first place? You've never been able to see me projecting before.

What the fuck is going on?" She was getting really worked up, and I couldn't blame her. I was feeling and wondering the same things.

I looked around just as Brax flew through the door dressed in a red, long-sleeved dress of some kind, his tiny feet covered with white stockings, which was not at all what he was wearing before in the forest.

"Brax," I said with a sigh of relief to the elf-goyle, hoping he could explain everything that was going on, but instead of answering me, he flew over to sit on the bed, staring at the woman and the baby, ignoring us as well.

Undeterred, Becks walked right up to Brax and tried to touch him too. Her hand slipped right through him though, and at that point, I was thoroughly confused.

'What could possibly be going on right now?' I wondered. *'Why can't Brax see us? And where the hell are we?'*

Taking a second to look around again, an uneasiness started to spread from my chest. *'Fuck,* when *are we?'*

It took a minute for my mind to wrap around the only logical conclusion I could come to, but the more I examined everything, the surer I felt about my determinations.

"Why can't I feel Brax, and why can't he see us? That's the part that's really fucking with me," Becks said, voicing my thoughts precisely and making a valid point. "And why the hell is he dressed like that anyway? Where are his overalls?"

"Becks," I said as I walked over and pulled both of her hands into mine, making her look at me. "I think we're in the past. Brax's past if I had to guess."

Stepping back a little, but still holding my hands, Becks asked, "What do you mean Brax's past?"

"I've never seen those new flowers you were smelling. There's no telling what magic they possess. I think the one you sniffed did something, and since I was touching you, I was pulled along with you to wherever we are right now."

"You're saying a flower is somehow showing me the past?" she questioned smartly, her tone indicating she might have actually thought I was losing my mind.

The soft snore of the woman jerked my focus away for a second. Her head was dropped to her chest, fully asleep as the baby kept suckling in her arms. A bit of worry slid through me, but I turned my attention back to Becks.

"I know it doesn't make sense, but somehow we'll find our way back."

Brax was smiling at the child in the woman's arms the same way I'd seen him smile at Becks before when he didn't think she'd notice. When I glanced at the baby too, I saw the woman's arms go limp, watching helplessly as the baby tumbled to the floor with a dull thud.

My breath caught in my throat, and Becks made a small squealing sound as we both rushed over to see if it was okay.

However, Brax beat us to it. He looked down into its face as Becks unsuccessfully attempted to pick it up. She huffed in frustration as she realized she couldn't help, and the baby cooed while the lady who'd fallen asleep woke with a gasping start.

The woman reached down and picked the infant up gently, saying, "Oh, I'm so sorry, miss," in a thick accent I couldn't quite place.

"Why didn't she cry?" Brax asked, and I assumed he was talking to the woman.

She didn't respond, just studied the baby with tears in her eyes.

"Milady, I'm so sorry," the woman said again as her eyes glanced to the door and back to the child's face with worry written over each of her plump features. She was bouncing the child gently where she stood, looking like she couldn't decide what to do.

I spared a glance at Becks, and she seemed just as concerned as I felt. *'What in the hell are we watching?'* I wondered.

Finally seeming to come to a decision, the woman lifted her chin, wiped her eyes, and started heading out of the room.

"Well, this should be interesting," Brax said as he flew after the woman who seemed completely unaware he was there following her.

"Do we go after them?" Becks asked.

"I think we have to." I grabbed Becks' hand, and we followed the weird apparitions. '*Or maybe we're the apparitions,*' I thought.

The woman walked us through an ancient-looking castle, and everything I could see confirmed my fears that we were indeed in a very distant past. This kind of authenticity just couldn't be accurately portrayed even in the best of museums.

Heading into what seemed like the kitchen of the castle, the woman holding the baby slowed, easing toward another woman who stood with her arms crossed and a scowl on her face as she watched an elderly woman roll out some kind of dough.

"That last batch will be coming out of your pay, Helga. I shouldn't need to tell you not to burn the food for our guests," she said before turning and seeing the woman with the baby. "What is it this time, Gertrude?" she asked with derision dripping from her tone.

"Sorry, milady," Gertrude said with a bow to the woman who was evidently in charge. "I dropped the babe, milady." Her voice came out weakly, but as the other woman started rushing toward her, she cowered some and sputtered, "I'm so sorry milady! I didn't mean to hurt the babe, I fell asleep, and when I woke, she was on the floor."

The woman in charge harshly stole the child from Gertrude's arms and glowered down at her with anger as she pulled this way and that on the child's wrappings.

"I don't think I hurt her, milady. She hasn't cried a wink," Gertrude said with a gentle hand reaching out to touch the infant softly.

Jerking the infant away from Gertrude, the woman said, "Don't touch her again, you doltish ne'er do well. Of course, she cried if she fell to the floor. You're dismissed. I want you out of this house, right this very instant."

"Milady," Gertrude began but was cut off by the woman.

"Now! Get out!" The woman screamed, causing everyone in the room to flinch, including Becks and me.

Gertrude bowed and turned promptly, fleeing from the room with tears streaming down her face, a sob barely contained as she escaped down the corridor.

"Well, now who's going to feed Philippa, you mewling crone?"

Brax yelled with the same enraged scowl I'd grown used to seeing on him marring his features.

The woman didn't answer Brax. It was as if no one could see him either, and that was somewhat concerning to me. We were obviously watching his past for some reason, but I thought familiars were only assigned to hunters. Why was he worried about a human baby?

"Helga, go find Phillipa another nursemaid before she dies of starvation!"

"Yes, Countess," Helga responded as she wiped the dough residue from her hands, bowing as deeply as her elderly knees could handle before she turned and scampered away through the corridor.

"Maybe if you could be bothered to feed your own child, this wouldn't be a problem," Brax growled from where he hovered in front of the countess.

The countess sighed heavily and carried the baby back up to the room we'd landed in initially, with Brax, Becks, and me following behind her every step. She walked over to the large bed and hastily began unwrapping her without the gentle touch I thought the task warranted.

I wasn't an expert, but I didn't think the way she was handling the child was at all how someone should treat an infant. And if the tiny, barely perceptible bruises showing on the baby's skin were any kind of indication, this woman should not have been allowed to touch another human being, much less a defenseless infant.

"This woman is a cunt," Becks said, anger lacing her tongue from beside me, arms crossed over her chest as she glared at the countess.

Brax didn't respond, but he obviously held contempt for the woman as he watched her.

The countess checked Phillipa out, lifting her arms and legs roughly to examine them. After not finding anything concerning to her, the countess wrapped Phillipa back up and nearly dropped her in her crib, saying, "What's wrong with you that you don't cry when you are hurt? Hmm? What kind of devil are you?" The last part, she said under her breath as she wrung her hands in front of her.

"She's not a devil, you are! She's barely a week old, and already I've

45

been more of a mother to her than you have, and she can't even see me!" Brax yelled, his tiny fists balled at his sides where he hovered above Phillipa's crib, the countess completely unaware of his presence.

The room started to spin then, colors and shapes blending with one another at a dizzying speed. I was aware long enough to grab hold of Becks around her waist before blackness took over my mind.

CHAPTER 3

TYLER

"*What* the fuck?" I yelled as I ran over to Adam, Becks, and Brax, where they'd frozen in place, a smoky purple mass beginning to swirl around them thickly. Adam was on his knees with his head leaned all the way back. The muscles in his neck were pulled tight and taught, his eyes were squeezed shut, and his teeth were bared to the heavens as if he were in excruciating pain.

Becks' head was in his lap with her eyes closed, her legs situated in an off-putting tangle resembling a rag doll that'd been thrown to the ground. Hovering above them, Brax's wings were frozen in midair, and he had a worried and scared look on his otherwise scary-handsome face. The entire scene left no question in my mind as to whether they were in danger or not.

"Stop!" Queen Agatha warned, right as I was about to reach my hand into whatever the purple shit was and pull my teammates out.

Derrick had been moving beside me with the same intention, I'd assumed, but at the fairy queen's cautionary voice, we both stopped to look at her.

"What's going on? What's happening to them?" Derrick asked, fists clenched at his sides as he stared her down.

Queen Agatha flew over closer to us before she spoke. "They will be fine as long as you don't move them. They're on a journey right now that nothing could've prevented," she said as she clasped her hands behind her back with a smile while her butterfly-like wings beat as fast as a hummingbird's above them.

I turned her words over in my mind, but I couldn't comprehend her meaning, and my beast bucked within me at the non-answer explanation the flyer had given. I'd never seen anything like what was happening to my teammates, and the worry I felt for their safety was almost too much to handle.

"What the fuck does that mean? I swear, if they're hurting in any way, I will burn this entire forest to the ground with you in it," I warned, taking a step toward the flyer, concern for Becks, Brax, and Adam taking over my ability to rationalize. My anger was a problem Derrick had always had with me, and I knew without looking he wasn't happy about me threatening the flyers, but in this circumstance, he'd just have to get the fuck over it. I wasn't playing around.

"Calm yourself, shifter," King Preston of the pixies said as he flew over from somewhere off in the distance, his dragonfly-like wings bringing him to us quickly.

"The magic that has been released from calling a halt to our war has brought back plants and animals we thought were completely extinct!" the queen stated happily. "It's wild and untamed, completely untarnished. We haven't eaten this well in centuries," she laughed as she did a little twirl in the air, arms spread wide, indicating the lush forest around us. A growl escaped my throat since my beast and I were getting more pissed off with every second she wasn't telling us what we needed to know.

The fairy and pixie flew back some, eyeing me warily, but luckily for them, she continued speaking.

"This flower," she pointed to the purple one emitting all the smoky swirls, "is very powerful. Its magic is old, timeless even. We call it the timekeeper. Until early this morning, it hadn't been seen in this forest for decades. When you entered the Veil, I saw the reaction Hunter Becks had to it. Timekeepers don't speak to everyone, only those lucky enough to hear its song, and it was calling to her strongly. She couldn't have avoided it any more than you could have. Her friends just happened to be standing too close, so they were brought along on her journey."

"What kind of journey is it taking them on, and how long is it going to take?" Derrick asked with irritation as he rubbed a hand down his face.

"We can't know that until they wake up having seen everything the timekeeper wanted to show them," King Preston said. "It could be hours or even days if the visions are really juicy."

"Days!" I said, exasperated. "We don't have days!"

"You don't have a choice," Queen Agatha stated. "The magic has already taken effect."

I breathed deeply, shoving my beast and my anger deep within me so I could ask the questions that needed to be asked. "Are you sure they aren't in pain?"

Queen Agatha smiled and lowered her head as if she were talking to an errant child, "If they are in pain, it would only be from what they are witnessing, not from any physical harm."

"Well, as long as nothing hurts their bodies or moves them while they're in the trance, that is," King Preston explained further.

Derrick sighed beside me. "What happens if we move them? Pull them out of the fog?"

A worried expression fell on the queen's face. Still, she responded coolly, "If you were to somehow pull them out of the cloud without being taken into its magic yourselves, you'd risk leaving their minds wherever the flower has taken them for all eternity. It's your call to make, but I would strongly advise against it."

I huffed as I crossed my arms over my chest and battled with myself, trying to accept the situation we were in.

Derrick, ever with the mission in mind, switched subjects quickly. "Fine. We'll leave them be... until we can't. Now, we've found this," he said, reaching into his pocket and withdrawing the sacred gem of the fairies.

The queen looked like she was nearly salivating at the mouth to get her hands on the artifact, but reined in her eagerness, hastily calling forth another fairy dressed in battle armor to her side.

"Fovy, take the gem to its sacred ground, please. Tell no one what you are doing along the way."

"Yes, your majesty," Fovy said quietly before he carefully took the gem from Derrick's outstretched hand and flew off.

We watched the fairy as he disappeared through the forest, and Queen Agatha said, "I can't thank you enough," with a relieved sigh, bringing her hands together in front of her in a praying position, meeting Derrick's eyes with sincerity.

"We're going to need some answers," Derrick said sternly as he squared his shoulders and stood up straighter. I knew what he needed to ask, and I was hoping she'd be willing since we didn't have any other leads to follow.

The queen nodded. "I'm sure."

"I know you don't want to show us where the gem was taken from, but we're going to need to see that place to look for clues. We only found the gem by happenstance, and if you still want us to find your daughter, we're going to have to get more information to do it. The same goes for where your sacred seed and son were taken from, King Preston."

Agatha and Preston shared a weighted glance with each other, which was a weird prospect given the two hated each other only a couple of days ago. "Give us a second," the king said before they flew away to where we couldn't hear them.

I turned to Derrick but kept Adam, Becks, and Brax in my line of sight while we waited. "What do you think they're seeing?" I asked him, gesturing to our team.

Swiveling his head to stare at them as well, Derrick said, "There's no telling. I wish it'd hurry up though, or we're going to miss our window to meet with the vampire elders."

"We've come to a decision," King Preston said, pulling our attention back to the monarchs. "We will show Hunter Becks our sacred ground, and no one else." He stated this like it was a hard and fast rule that couldn't be argued.

"Why the hell would you do that?" I asked. "We're on the same damn team. Whatever she finds, she's going to tell us about, so you're not preventing anything with this fuckery."

Scoffing some, Queen Agatha said, "Be that as it may, we don't trust you hunters. What's to keep you from wiping out both of our races if it befits your idea of balance? I don't know how or why, but Hunter Becks is different from your lot, even though she's a hunter as well. She sees us. I know I can trust her to keep us safe."

"And you think we won't?" I asked, my anger seeping out more. "The reason she's different is that she isn't a full and true hunt..." I couldn't finish what I was saying because Derrick pushed me backward with one arm and stepped toward the queen with a placating tone, cutting my words short.

"What Tyler means is, Becks is special. We agree with you whole-heartedly on that, but what he said is true. She will tell us about whatever she finds, so hiding your knowledge from us is a waste of everyone's time. Especially since Becks is otherwise indisposed at the moment," he said, motioning to Becks. He was trying to be diplomatic, but the way he'd cut me off pissed me off, and I had to work a bit harder at not lashing out at him.

"Again, our word stands. No one is to see our sacred land except with explicit permission from us. And you guys do not have it. Only *Hunter* Becks has permission, and that will not change," she said, accentuating the word 'hunter' and looking pointedly at me while she said it, just proving that Derrick didn't need to cut me off. She knew what I meant.

Sighing, Derrick agreed. "Fine, we'll wait here until they wake up, and then you can show Becks where your gem was stolen from."

The monarchs both nodded and flew off to wherever they'd come from as Derrick turned his sharp gaze to mine.

"What do you think you're doing? We don't want anyone knowing Becks isn't a true hunter yet. They could hurt her, attack her, take advantage of her human weaknesses," he spoke softly through gritted teeth in a whisper so as not to be overheard by the flyers that were still, no doubt, within earshot.

"Becks doesn't have any weaknesses that we know of since she killed Rick, and these guys aren't going to do anything to her," I said with annoyance. "The flyers love her, and you know it. You've seen the way they only really talk to her when she's around, and how dismissive they are of us. Open your eyes, dipshit."

"Let's just hope your mouth doesn't get her killed," he said, crossing his arms over his chest.

"She can't die, remember?" I goaded him, knowing I was pissing him off more, but I didn't care. He needed to get off his high-horse.

Derrick turned then, dropping his hands to his sides as he got in my face, lowering his voice. "We don't know that's true, and until I've proven otherwise, we're going to walk on eggshells if we have to. Her life could depend on it. Do you understand me?"

He wasn't giving me an alpha order, but I could tell he wanted to so he got his own damn way. This was just like him, to paint me into a corner where his bravado made me feel like I needed to defend myself, but by doing so, I'd be defending something I didn't agree with.

If I argued with him about protecting Becks, I was the bad guy. I didn't want to endanger her, not at fucking all. But if I didn't defend my opinion about the flyers loving Becks, he'd still believe they were a threat when they weren't, putting us in an unnecessary state of high alert.

I hated that I always ended up in this position, and before Becks had shown up, I might've bitten his head off without a thought. However, since Becks joined our team and I'd promised the chief I'd do my best to make this team work as a unified unit, I'd found myself biting my tongue more than usual, hiding what I actually felt and thought. "Yeah, I understand," I said through gritted teeth.

Derrick looked amazed by the fact that I wasn't putting up a fight, but didn't say anything more. He walked over and took a seat on a thick tree limb that was growing close to the ground facing our incapacitated team members. He stared them down as if through sight alone he could wake them up, and I rolled my eyes as I walked over to sit next to him, arms crossed over my chest, thoughts of Becks beginning to roam through my mind.

There was just something about her that called to me. To me and to my beast. A feat other girls had never even come close to achieving before.

She was beautiful and sexy as fuck, yes, but she was also easy to talk to and nonjudgmental. Becks was reasonable, considerate, strong-willed, and sarcastic. A deadly combination in my book.

But there was also pain in her eyes that matched my own, even when she smiled, and that might've been the most beautiful thing about her. She saw things differently than most because she knew what real pain felt like, how it felt to be completely alone, and afraid, but she hadn't been jaded by it. Instead, it was as if she was thriving because of it, rather than in spite of it, using what was done to her to make her better and not as an excuse to get worse.

The kisses we'd shared were like a single drop of water to a parched throat in the desert, nowhere near enough to satisfy me. I wanted more.

I wanted her.

I knew how she felt through our shared connection to Brax, but I was having a hard time deciding how I felt about it. She liked all of us; that much was certain. However, it seemed as if she wasn't willing to choose between us. Like she'd rather not be with anyone than hurt one of us by choosing another. It's not as if any of us had asked her to choose, but she was smart enough to know at the outset that her feelings could do some pretty serious damage.

I mean, I could comprehend what she felt, but the only way I could have her in that situation would be if I was willing to share. And I didn't know if I was okay with that.

I knew that kind of thing worked out sometimes for other people, Derrick specifically with his dads and all, but usually, the guys in those kinds of relationships were all friends, sometimes even brothers. I'd consider Adam a friend, but not Derrick. He hated me, and I just barely tolerated his overbearing ass. If Becks refused to choose between us and instead decided she'd be with all of us, that would mean I'd have to be okay with watching her be with them, and I wasn't sure my beast or I could handle such a thing. Simply imagining her with someone else made my blood boil.

But the simple fact remained... I wanted her more than I'd wanted anything else in a really long ass time.

I looked beside me to Derrick, imagining a life with Becks that was tainted by him, and anger surged through me. When he glanced back at me with a questioning glare, I said, "Fuck you," and got up to find somewhere else to sit and wait on the timekeeper to get done with its shit.

CHAPTER 4

BECKS

*a*s soon as my vision started to clear, I knew we still weren't back in the forest with Derrick and Tyler. Instead, we were standing inside the big front foyer of the castle. This time, it was daylight out, and a bunch of people could be seen milling about right outside the open doors of the castle, all dressed in old-timey clothing I couldn't put a date to. Cauls and cloaks, tall and triangular-shaped hats with veils covering ladies' faces, and dresses undoubtedly from a different time caught my eye as I peered outside.

Adam was holding me tightly around my waist, and when he tried to let go to stand beside me, I grasped his arms compulsively and held him in place. I don't know what possessed me to do such a thing, but his touch was soothing, and I didn't want it to leave yet. His warmth was seeping into me, and I wanted nothing more at that moment than the comfort his presence offered.

He didn't seem to mind though, since in response, he squeezed me a bit tighter and leaned the side of his face against my head for a beat.

I couldn't explain why I was okay with the guys touching me since

I'd held a strict 'no-touchy' rule since childhood, but for some reason, I didn't get that cringy feeling when it was one of the guys. They were slowly growing on me... *'Okay, maybe not slowly... I've known them for a little over a week, and already I've kissed two of them. Come on, Becks, get your shit together.'*

Just then, the countess came into the foyer from somewhere in the castle holding a baby on her hip, and Brax flew in behind her dressed in the same style he was before, except this time he was in a blue toddler-sized dress instead of a red one.

"Is that the same kid? Philippa?" Adam asked from behind me, and I took a closer look to see what he was talking about.

The child indeed had the same head of white-blonde curls, though it was a bit longer than before. However, it was surely the same girl because her features were the same, if somewhat plumper than they'd been before. "I think so," I said, eyebrows drawn down in the center of my forehead as I tried to wrap my mind around what the hell was going on.

"I do not see how it is so difficult a task for you to have her ready when I call," the countess distracted me with her harsh voice as another woman followed her, Philippa, and Brax into the foyer. "You knew very well Philippa would need to make an appearance at this gathering. I'll give you one more chance, however, if this keeps happening, I'll send you right back to being a scullery maid in no time."

"Yes, Countess," the girl replied with a bow. She was about my age, I noted.

"I'll have her ready next time, I promise."

The countess was sweating and looked like she was exhausted, but the way she sauntered around carelessly swinging the baby this way and that had me on edge. I found myself hoping she didn't get too near any walls or something because she might just run poor Philippa into one without a thought.

"It's time," the countess said, almost to herself as she stood by the open doors that led outside where all the guests were waiting, squaring her shoulders and lifting her chin in the air before she walked out into the sun.

Brax flew behind her, and I reluctantly stepped out of Adam's embrace, capturing his hand instead, so we could follow them.

The countess shrieked a few yards from the door as she gaped at Philippa, and I rushed over to see what was the matter.

When I got over to them, nearly everyone around us was freaking out, yelling, and otherwise losing their minds. I looked at the baby and realized her skin was smoking as if she were the last remnants of a fire that'd just been extinguished, and a gasp escaped my throat as I heard Brax yelling over the crowd's hysterics.

"Get her back inside, you flea-bitten fool! Go!" Though the countess couldn't hear him.

Philippa wasn't crying despite the noticeably severe injury that was continuing to get worse on her skin by the second, and the thought scared the hell out of me. Bright red splotches were starting to form on the child's exposed face and head right before my eyes, and all I could do was watch in horror as those red splotches began to slowly bubble up.

"What the fuck?" I heard myself say in a horrified whisper.

A man dressed smartly in a pair of form-fitting breeches, and a tailored cloak came over and took the girl from the countess in haste, tucked her into his chest, and started running the short distance back inside the castle. Brax flew after them, and I started following after him, Adam still at my side, though I'd dropped his hand when I'd seen the child and reached up to cover my mouth.

As soon as the man was inside, he rushed through the castle to the kitchen we'd been in before, placed Philippa on a long stone counter, and leaned back to look at her with concern on his face.

"Is that her father?" I asked Adam.

"I think so," he replied as I watched the man try to comfort her even though she didn't seem like she cared at all.

The countess came storming in the kitchen then, cornering the girl she'd been yelling at before who'd followed us in all the ruckus, passing right by her child, not even sparing her a glance.

"What did you do to Philippa, you witch?" she yelled in a high-pitched squeak.

"Nothing, Countess, I swear!" the girl whimpered as she made her way over to see the baby in question.

As soon as the girl saw Philippa's skin, which was no longer smoldering, but was still very badly burnt, the girl let out an audible gasp. "Devil!" she cried as she backed away briskly. She almost stumbled on the stone floor, which seemed to be her breaking point because she immediately turned away and ran out the back door.

"You little devil!" The countess turned her anger toward Philippa, who was still being fussed over by the man with the beard. "Now, I'll have to find yet another wet nurse to keep you alive! I wish you'd never been born! It's not as if I didn't have enough children already," she screamed.

My eyes flashed at her in fury, her antics reminding me all too vividly of my adoptive mother, and straight away, I was worried by the implication that others had been raised by this piece of shit.

The man rounded on her then with a deep voice and a tone that garnered no arguments. "Enough. I'll handle the child. Ye go see to our guests." His accent was different from the very proper English one the countess spoke with, but I couldn't place it correctly.

He picked Philippa up and carried her off as Brax asked, "Why don't you do this every time the countess acts like a bespawling goblin on tree sap?" But again, no one heard him.

'This must be a terrible existence for him,' I thought as I looked at my familiar. 'Brax seems so lonely. And tired.'

"I think we should follow them," Adam said softly beside me in that velvety voice of his as we watched Brax begin to follow after the man and the baby.

"Alright."

The man took to the stairs and unknowingly led us through the castle back to the bedroom we'd been in before. Once in the room, he took Philippa to a chair by one of the windows. He filled the air with a sweet melody he hummed softly as he cradled her in his arms and stared into her eyes. Brax sat on the stairs in front of the window and rested his face in his hands. It was a sweet and painful thing to watch as I took a seat on the floor near Brax, and Adam sat down beside me, but I couldn't look away from the trio.

"Why'd her skin do that?" I asked Adam, entirely at a loss for what could've caused such a reaction.

"I've heard of this before in a couple of humans. I think it's called solar urticaria, or something like that. It's where she's allergic to sunlight," he answered, and I was surprised that he knew the random fact.

"What a horrible disease," I said. "So, she's got to live in darkness? That's so incredibly sad." My thoughts kept playing over the scene outside. "But does she even feel it? I mean, she didn't even cry as her skin was literally about to burn off."

Adam shook his head. "There's also another disease in humans that makes them unable to feel pain. If she has that on top of the solar urticaria, she's got one hell of a life in front of her." And almost as an afterthought, he added, "And so do the people that have to care for her."

I considered the father holding Philippa, and a warm feeling spread through me at the tenderness in his touch and love in his eyes. If he were to watch Philippa and raise her, I had no doubt that she'd live the best life possible given her issues, whatever they may be. But if the countess downstairs had anything to do with it, I imagined her life would be hell.

I was pondering Philippa and why Brax was here when the world shifted again, and blackness took over my sight for a second time. However, this time it didn't last nearly as long as the last one had.

When I could see again, we were in the same positions we were in before, and so were Brax, Philippa, and her father, but the light from the windows was nearly completely gone. The sun had set a while ago from the looks of it, so barely a hint of its existence lingered.

Philippa's father was playing with her while she sat on his lap. He was cooing at her and making her smile light up her damaged face. But after a minute, he sighed deeply since she seemed to be getting fussy. When he stood and let Philippa cling to his hip, Brax woke up from his snoring slumber with a start that pulled a giggle from me.

I'd seen that reaction a couple of times from my familiar, and it got me every time. His eyes going wide as if he had no idea where he was or what century he was in.

'He might actually wonder that,' I thought with amazement as I put two and two together.

Philippa's father strolled out of the room, and we all followed him as he walked downstairs. At the bottom, he met a woman who bowed deeply to him when he nodded to her.

"She be needin' milk, sir?" the woman asked.

"Yer the new wet nurse?"

She bowed deeply again, and he made a come here motion for her to follow him. He led her into a library or old-timey office of some kind and had her take Philippa in her arms.

"Yer stayin'?" the woman asked the man with large eyes.

"Just do yer job," he said hostilely. I noticed they both had the same accent, and I was kicking myself for not knowing where it came from.

The woman seemed flustered, but whipped out a boob anyway and had Philippa suckling in no time as if she were a seasoned pro. I didn't know much about breastfeeding, but from the looks of it, this woman knew what she was doing.

"Why are we here watching all this, Adam?"

He stood next to me with his arms crossed over his chest and answered, "I have no idea. But I think it's happening for a reason." He didn't elaborate further, and I figured that was all he was willing to say about his thoughts on the matter.

Once the woman was done feeding the baby, Philippa's father took her from the nursemaid and told the woman he'd no longer be needing her. She looked put out by what he'd said, but left the room anyway.

"What did you do that for?" Brax asked huskily from where he was still clearly trying to stay awake.

Philippa's father bounced her in his arms and patted her back, trying to get her to burp, I assumed, and once she did, he held her back so he could examine her face.

It was a significant moment. It seemed like he'd decided something as he stared into her eyes, and uneasiness began to creep through me. He walked to the large chair and grabbed his coat, careful not to shift Philippa too much while he put it on.

"Where are you going?" Brax asked.

We all followed as the man walked through the castle, picking up random things: two small blankets, a metal rattle that Philippa clung to tightly, and his hat that he placed on his head before he stepped out of the castle.

"What are you doing?" Brax asked, his voice coming out sounding worried.

The man grabbed a torch from the handle by the door and started walking out onto the property, Philippa happy in his arms as he hummed in her ear. We followed behind the man, and Brax flew near us as he walked and walked. The darkening night was seeping in close to us, but we continued on our journey, winding first through sprawling gardens, then down a gravel path in the woods.

When the man wandered off the gravel path and into the forest, Brax asked again, his voice low and dangerous, "What are you doing?" His fists were balled at his sides, and I could practically see the rage building up inside him.

Not too far off the gravel path, I saw our destination. A cave entrance loomed ahead of us, lit only by the torchlight. I knew then, I wasn't going to like what was about to happen.

"If he hurts her…" my words drifted off because I realized there was nothing I could do if he did anything. My presence was utterly useless, and my stomach turned with the thought, worrying about what I was going to have to witness.

"You think he will?" Adam asked, and I looked at him as if he were missing something obvious.

I could feel it. So could Brax if his demeanor was anything to go by. "I don't know, but I don't have a good feeling about this." Adam nodded and grabbed my hand again, giving it a gentle squeeze as we followed Philippa's father into the cave.

He laid his torch down and held her out where he could see her face. "I love ye so, though devil ye may be."

I knew right away what his plan was, and horror spread through me, a thick and prickly feeling of fear for the helpless baby in his arms.

He laid Philippa down on the dirt floor of the cave, covered her with her blankets, gave her the rattle he'd picked up from the ground where she'd dropped it, kissed her forehead and both cheeks gently. Then he stood up and left, walking out of the cave without glancing back.

"You can't leave her here!" Brax screamed from the entrance to the cave as reality sunk in, and I felt like I needed to puke.

'Who could just leave their child, their baby in a fucking cave? He might as well have gone ahead and killed her. At least then she wouldn't have to suffer. Now, if he doesn't come back, she's got to feel the cold and hunger of starvation until her little body gives out.' I thought as I swallowed hard a few times, trying to get my senses about me. Somehow, I felt connected to Philippa, the similarities too drastic to ignore.

The man's actions hit too close to home with my own demons from being born in a cave, going days without eating as a child, freezing in my toddler bed because I didn't have a blanket, being abandoned at the insane asylum, growing up basically alone because not one human on this planet loved me. And even though Adam rubbed his hand down my back to comfort me as my breath came in quick little panting gasps and my heart raced, it was too much.

I started dry heaving, my stomach rebelling hard against what Philippa's father had done, and when the blackness began to creep in again, I welcomed it with open arms.

My thoughts were still swirling around the visions I'd seen when something that felt like it weighed a metric fuckton landed roughly on my belly and made me open my eyes with a grunt of pain.

We were back in the fairies' and pixies' forest, and Brax had fallen from the air to land right on top of me. He was passed out, it seemed, but I could just about feel my internal organs rupturing if I didn't do something soon to get him off me. Brax could weigh a ton or change his weight to be as light as a feather with a single thought, and I figured out right then that he needed to be awake for his weight-changing power to work.

I tried pushing him, but I couldn't budge him. I tried rolling to the side, but that motion was useless too. With no other option, I called my power, remembering intention was everything when it came to harnessing them, and I focused it into lifting Brax off me.

With a whoosh, he was airborne, fresh air finally reentering and filling my lungs once more.

I watched Brax sail upward to a tree branch with so much speed the limb broke against his back before both he and the limb started falling right back toward me where I laid with my head in Adam's lap.

Lightning-fast reflexes I didn't even know I possessed had me scampering away from what was coming and getting out of the way just in time, even with grabbing and pulling Adam along with me in my haste.

The jolt of being jerked out of harm's way didn't seem to faze Adam though, since he smiled at me proudly and squeezed my hand in his.

"You know I'm going to require that you move that fast in training from now on, don't you?" Adam asked as he inspected me in wonder.

"I don't even know how I was able to do it in the first place," I said honestly, but if I had to guess, it probably had something to do with being in touch with my power when I'd dragged us out of the way.

Looking back at where we'd moved from, I didn't know if it was his back hitting the tree branch or his head hitting the ground, but one of the impacts had woken Brax up, and he took to the air quickly with an expression like an angry dog that'd been cornered. His sandy colored eyes searched everywhere around him before they finally landed on me, and the sigh he released at seeing me was loud.

"Girl, if you ever do some dumbass shit like that again," the elf-goyle warned as he took a deep breath and ran a hand through his blonde hair, trying to relax.

I smiled at my familiar because he could finally see me, and he was finally in the here and now with me. What he'd said still struck a chord though, so I had to ask, "What did I do that was so dumb?"

His breathing now somewhat under control, Brax cocked a bushy eyebrow up and regarded me with incredulous anger. "You don't go around sniffing random ass things in a magical forest, crazy!" he yelled at me, and my smile only grew wider at his words.

"If I have a choice next time, I'll definitely avoid it," I said as I released Adam's hand and walked over to where Brax was hovering. I wrapped him up in a tight hug that he returned with no questions, and our connection solidified, strengthening with the contact. It warmed me and made me feel genuinely safe, inside and out.

"I'm sorry you guys had to see all that," Brax said when we separated. He seemed worried like he was ashamed of the memories we'd seen, and I couldn't think of why he'd feel that way since it wasn't like he was the monster in his memories. I also didn't know how he knew what we saw in the first place since he wasn't in the visions with us.

"How do you know what we saw?" I asked.

"The timekeeper called to you, Becks. And when you looked at me, all high and shit, it decided to show you things from my past. It could've shown you anything, but since you were looking at me when it took you under, it chose to show you shit from my past. The only reason Adam was there with you was because he was touching you when you went under. I watched everything you did in the visions, but I wasn't 'in' them with you because I wasn't touching you," he tried to explain, but I was utterly lost as to what he was talking about.

"The *what* called to me?"

"They call that flower the timekeeper," Derrick said as he and Tyler walked up from wherever they'd been this whole time.

Derrick explained about the magical flower and everything else that had gone on while we were under the timekeeper's influence, but before I could even begin to try and unpack the whole 'we-won't-show-anybody-but-Becks' shit, I had to ask, "Hold on, let's back up. Do all of these new flowers do something weird?"

Tyler sighed and rubbed a hand down his handsome face before he answered me. "Probably, so let's not take any chances. Brax is right." Then, in a smart-ass sarcastic tone, he said, "Hunter rule number four hundred and seventy-six: don't sniff magical shit." He had that sexy as fuck smirk on his face that caused heat to rise in my belly, and I couldn't stop myself from smiling at him.

"Good to know."

"Well now that that's been covered," Derrick said with an eye roll, "We need to get a move on with all this if we still want to have a chance at meeting up with the vampire elders tonight."

In a booming voice that startled me some, he screamed, "Queen Agatha! King Preston!"

"Pixie titties! Did you have to do that right next to my earholes? Fuck," Brax said as he grabbed at his pointy ears and flew over to hover beside me instead of Derrick.

All serious-faced and unapologetic, Derrick said, "Yes. I did."

A few seconds later, the king of the pixies and queen of the fairies showed up with relieved looking smiles directed at me.

"Hunter Becks, we're so glad you're awake. How did you enjoy your trip?" Queen Agatha asked, making it sound like my 'trip' through Brax's past was more like a backpacking trip through Europe than the horrible worry-fest it'd turned out to be.

I smiled back at her though, and said, "It was… enlightening."

"Good, you know you're the first person to have partaken in the timekeeper's secrets in a few decades," King Preston said furtively toward me from where he hovered beside the queen.

"I did not know that," I said with a glance back at my team before I turned my attention back to the monarchs. "I heard you will let me see where your children and artifacts were taken from." I didn't want to divulge any of my experiences with the flower or Brax's past with them, so I segued smoothly into why we were there in the first place.

"Yes, right this way, Hunter Becks," Queen Agatha said, holding her hand out beside her.

Brax started flying behind me, but both monarchs stopped and leveled him with a glare. "Only Hunter Becks is allowed," King Preston said sternly, and Brax scoffed at the tiny pixie.

"I'm her familiar."

"It doesn't matter what you are to her, she's the first person who isn't a fairy or pixie that's being shown our sacred grounds. We're not taking any chances," the queen said before she turned around and started leading the way for me.

'I'm sorry, Brax,' I thought toward him. *'Maybe now we can test out this telepathy thing and see how far it reaches,'* I offered.

'That's a good idea. I'm going to see if I can open up a link between all of us, so we stay in the loop. It was pretty hit or miss in my last life with my last familiar, but I've been wondering if it would work better this time around. Either way, you stay safe, you hear me, girl?' Brax thought, and at first, I was excited by the idea of being able to talk to all the guys at once, but then fear started to creep in by the same prospect. I'd definitely have to watch my thoughts if my familiar was successful in setting up that kind of link.

The king and queen led me through the forest that I'd been dying to explore since I'd first seen it, and the sights didn't disappoint along the way. The woods were lively and beautiful everywhere I looked, and I found myself wishing the whole world felt as good as their forest. More and more fairies were showing up the further we traveled, little sparks flying and zipping this way and that, all over the place. A few tiny ones, children perhaps, even landed in my hair and on my shoulder, giggling in my ears as I walked.

"Who are you?" one of the tiny fairies who'd landed on my shoulder asked with a smile.

I turned my head to see her as best I could, smiling back as I answered. "I'm Becks, what's your name?"

"I'm Saleem," she said. "Have you seen the new creatures in the forest yet? They all showed up this morning! Little baby ones everywhere! Mama said we have to help raise them and show them how to be what they are. I'm so excited!"

"That's so cool!" I said sincerely as I scanned the forest for all these new creatures she was talking about, but I didn't see anything other than more fairies than I could count.

The tiny fairy girl barely even let the answer come out of my mouth before she gushed to me about her great morning. "Yeah, when I woke up, there was this fuzzy thing with big gray eyes just staring at me! It scared me so bad!" she laughed. "Mama said we had to get to work, so I didn't get to play with him much, but oh, Becks! I'm so happy! Aren't you?"

"I sure am," I said genuinely as I thought about the fact that we'd done some real good here the other day.

I'd had my doubts about the hunters from the beginning since one of the first things I'd heard they could do was start a plague, but seeing the benefits of ending the fairies' war with the pixies, I realized hunters did a lot of good too. And I'd been a part of it. Somehow that made it all that much better.

"Saleem," Queen Agatha called, not stopping in her flight to wherever she was leading me. "Don't you think you should be helping with the animals now instead of harassing our guest?"

The small fairy laughed at her queen and said, "You're right, Mama." Then turning to me, she said, "I'll see you later, Becks! Bye!"

"Bye!" I yelled after the princess, but she'd already flown off at a wicked pace.

When I'd first come to this side of the Veil a few days ago, Queen Agatha had said her sacred gem was stolen from her castle's vault. Call me naive, but I'd imagined an actual castle like what you'd find ruins of in the human world.

I couldn't have been more wrong.

"This is…" my voice came out all breathy, "amazing!" I had to make myself close my mouth since it'd fallen open as I stared and tried to see everything at once.

The fairies' 'castle' turned out to be what looked like the most giant tree in the forest; it's base as broad as a bus is long, and its height nearly unimaginable in my mind. There were hundreds of small holes dotting all the way around and up the tree base as far as I could see, entrances to the inner workings of their 'castle,' I assumed.

An abundance of new flowers bloomed thickly on long vines that interwove themselves around each of the holes and up the sides of the trunk. Fairies were flying everywhere around it, going from one small fairy hole to another, sparkles following every flap of their little butterfly wings.

"Thank you, Hunter Becks," Queen Agatha said with a blushy smile. "We do love our castle."

"I do, too," I giggled, still trying to wrap my mind around what I was seeing.

We skirted around the base of their tree castle, heading toward the backside (if any part of a round tree could be considered the back), but when the queen started heading away into the forest on the other side, confusion set in.

"I thought you were taking me to see where your gem was taken," I asked the queen, and she nodded her understanding at me.

"I know I told you it was stolen from our castle's vault, but in reality, we don't really have a vault in there."

"Okay?" I asked, hoping for an explanation.

"I lied because I hadn't really met you yet, but now that I know you aren't going to kill us all, I'm going to show you where we actually keep our sacred gem."

I nodded and followed her as she led me through more and more thick and hilly forest, and I noticed there was no visible trail we were following. I knew right then I'd never get back to my team if I didn't have a guide, but I was strangely unafraid of the prospect. Probably because even if I did get lost in this forest, I didn't think I'd mind. The place was filled with magic. Happy and soul-lightening magic. I don't think I could've been angry if I'd tried as I nearly skipped along behind the queen, King Preston following beside me.

I've gotten the link to work, we can all hear you,' Brax thought at me then.

'*Hey, Becks,*' Adam said, his voice in my head sounding exactly like it did when he spoke out loud.

'*Hey, Adam,*' I thought back with a smile I couldn't avoid.

Some kind of animal whimper echoed through my mind, sending a powerful surge of emotions toward me, and I instantly knew I was hearing Tyler's beast in my mind. The sound was mournful but happy, and without much thought, I sent some happy feelings right back at him.

'*Where are you now?*' Derrick's serious voice broke into my thoughts.

I looked around and thought-answered him as best I could, '*No idea.*'

'*Alright, just let us know what you find,*' he commanded, and I nodded even though I knew he couldn't see me.

As we got closer to wherever they were taking me, King Preston said, "This is where I'll wait until you're done with Queen Agatha. I'll take you to the pixies' sacred grounds when you get back."

"Alright," I said as I kept walking around the base of a tall hill.

Queen Agatha came over and sat on my shoulder then, and though I was surprised by her closeness, I didn't say anything.

"We're about to pass through the barrier that hides our gem. You need to either be a fairy or be touching a fairy to get through. If I weren't here with you, you'd be confused and start heading in another direction. It's how we've kept everyone away for so long. Well, until someone broke in, that is." She sounded disappointed that their barrier hadn't worked, but motioned for me to keep walking anyway.

A short distance later, I took a step that made me feel like I was walking through water. Any movement took a lot more effort, but after a few more paces, everything went back to normal, and I could move about freely.

The queen and I traveled for a while in relative silence, but after a bit, she paused and turned to me.

"This is it," she said, and I was more confused than I'd been before.

I surveyed the area around us quickly, but nothing made this spot any more distinguishable than the others we'd already passed through.

"Um," I said, not really knowing what to ask.

The queen flew down to the forest floor and pulled back some of the foliage to reveal the sacred gem I'd held that morning. It was floating about an inch off the ground, turning slowly as little blue and golden curls of light encased it.

"Why do you keep it here, all out in the open?" I asked as I knelt down to look closer.

The queen said, "This is where it has always been. My ancestors thought we'd only be drawing attention to it if we marked its location somehow, so we've always left it here. All we've really done is set up the barrier which had been working well up until recently when someone broke in and took it."

'You guys see this?' I asked as I sent a mental picture through the link to my team, and not seconds later, I was answered with a few, *'Yeses'* and an, *'Uh-huh.'*

'What is it you guys want me to find? It all just seems like a normal fairy forest to me,' I thought toward my team.

Derrick's voice sounded in my head as he thought, *'Check the ground around that area for anything that looks out of the ordinary. Footprints, animal tracks, anything that doesn't seem to fit. Find what's not supposed to be there.'*

It didn't take a rocket scientist to figure out that this was a large part of the new job I was expected to perform, finding the imbalances or the things that didn't belong. *'Okay,'* I responded as the importance of finding something the fairies had missed settled inside my chest.

"We've combed all through this area since it went missing, but have come up empty. I'm hoping you can find something we missed," Queen Agatha said, then almost under her breath, she added, "It would make trusting the pixies a lot easier if I knew for sure they weren't the ones who took it."

"I'll do what I can," I replied, knowing the alliance between the fairies and pixies was a new and unsteady one that could be shoved away and forgotten in an instant if I didn't do something to prove the pixies weren't at fault. They'd only agreed to work together under the assumption that each side was telling the truth when they'd said they hadn't stolen the other species' artifacts or kidnapped their heirs. If I didn't solidify that bond with fact, I knew their treaty would fly out the proverbial window.

I started wondering how I was going to find anything in the thick undergrowth but knew that if the fairies had already gone over everything, they'd probably already ruled out or found any footprints that might've been there.

I knew I had to think outside the box, and I stood up, placing my hands on my hips as I tried to work my brain in a way it'd never worked before.

'Remember your powers,' Brax thought at me, and I sighed with the obviousness of what he was saying.

I really needed to live by that mantra now that I had powers, whatever they might entail.

Closing my eyes, I imagined my power, that purple-ish blue orb that lived inside me, wrapping around my soul, waiting on me to tap into it. I touched my power with my mind intending to see what was out of place, and immediately I felt a pull on my chest.

I opened my eyes and started moving where my power was guiding me, stepping over and through the plants at my feet. The further I walked, the more right my path seemed, and I started speeding up my pace with excitement.

The queen was following me, and as I got to the barrier, she jumped onto my shoulder so I could continue, and we passed through it swiftly before I kept going. The pull on my chest got stronger with every step I took, and I knew I was headed in the right direction. Suddenly, the pull stopped, and I knew I didn't need to go any farther. I'd reached my destination.

When I glanced all around, I spotted something shiny amongst the foliage below me and leaning down, I picked up the tiny piece of metal.

It was shiny and silver, small like a quarter, but thinner. It had a beveled shape with intricate designs carved everywhere on its surface, even on the backside. The etchings appeared to be elaborate letter A's connected to one another, and there was a tiny hole at the top of it, reminding me of something I could slide onto a necklace easily.

Distracting me from my examination of the charm, Brax's thoughts rang through my head, *'I've seen that kind of charm before.'* His voice sounded weary and almost scared, a new emotion I hadn't felt from him before. *'It looks like a piece of Absinthe's armor.'*

CHAPTER 5

BECKS

'*You* mean Absinthe like the evil genie that killed my real parents and shredded their souls, Absinthe?' I asked with my mind and a shaky breath, the metal object in my hand feeling remarkably more substantial than it had before I'd known its owner.

'*Get back here, now,*' Derrick thought, and the emotion lacing his thoughts caught me off guard. The guys had explained how dangerous and powerful Absinthe was to me before, so I already had a healthy dose of fear spreading through me at the implications the metal piece held. However, the fear in Derrick's thoughts increased my anxiety exponentially. He wasn't one to get scared from what I'd gleaned about him thus far. However, it was evident in his thoughts, so I knew whatever was going on had to be taken seriously.

"I need to get back to my team ASAP," I said to the fairy queen.

She looked surprised but answered anyway, "Okay, I can lead you as fast as you can keep up."

She took off then, leaving a trail of sparkles behind her in her wake, and now that I knew I'd move faster if I tapped into my power, I grabbed hold of them and tried to keep her trail in my sights. It actually wasn't hard with my power helping me out, and in no time, I was matching her speed as I ran, and she flew.

At some point, King Preston joined back up with us, and even though I was running scared, I was also running happy, having nearly forgotten how wonderful it felt to run with the magical creatures. The last time it'd happened, I was around seven years old, and it had been one of my most favorite things to do. Reliving that feeling was nostalgic and heartwarming despite everything else that was going on, so I tried to enjoy it while it lasted.

Eventually though, it came to an end when I could see my team off in the distance. Adam was running a hand through his blonde hair, Derrick was standing with just the tips of his fingers in his pockets, Tyler was pacing back and forth as he watched me move toward them, and Brax was hovering in front of my team, locking eyes with me as soon as he got me in his sights.

"I apologize, Queen Agatha, King Preston," Derrick nodded at both the monarchs when we came to a stop before them. "We need to investigate that as soon as possible," he said, motioning to the charm clasped tightly in my hand.

King Preston didn't look like he understood what was going on, but Queen Agatha responded in a sympathetic tone, "By all means. Do what you need to do to find out who did this."

Derrick nodded again, then opened the portal for us to go back to Atlanta. Once we all stepped through to Earth, no one wasted any time.

Tyler came over and placed his hand in mine, and I was surprised to feel the sweat on his skin. Derrick, Adam, and Brax put their hands on Tyler, and within a millisecond, we were back in the living room of the safe house.

It was way after sunset when we got there, and after noticing how late it'd become, a wave of sleepiness swept over me, but I tried to ignore it when Adam spoke up. "What does this mean?"

"Well, it obviously means Absinthe had something to do with the fairies' and pixies' having their shit stolen," Tyler said with an eye roll.

I handed the charm over to Derrick when he asked for it, and once he examined it for himself, he said, "Ava said the gem was meant for Becks. It can't be a coincidence that it ties back to Absinthe."

"Well, no fucking shit," Brax huffed in disgust with his chest puffed out as he paced midair. He moved his hands as he ranted, big wings flapping carelessly behind him. "That cuntsucker, Absinthe, is probably fucking with us. What? Taking Malcolm and Mandy wasn't enough for him? Was being the cause for Becks growing up in an asylum, not enough? What does he want now? Becks? Well, that shit isn't fucking happening, I can tell you that right now! Over my cold dead statue!"

I could feel the rage, frustration, anger, and fear spreading through my familiar, and with one glance around the room, I knew all the guys felt it too.

"Why would he have kept Becks alive back when she was two if he was planning on killing her now? That doesn't make sense, Brax," Derrick said in a visible effort to calm my elf-goyle, but it was no use.

"I don't fucking know! Pixie titties and fairy farts, he's a jinn! He doesn't need a reason!" Brax was thoroughly pissed off. I didn't know what to say to get him to see a silver lining of any kind, mainly because I couldn't find one myself. I knew he needed to chill out, but call me crazy, something about his freak out was funny to me, and I tried to stifle the giggle that wanted to erupt from my mouth.

"I'm getting a drink," Brax said with an exasperated sigh as he flew to one of the kitchen cabinets and pulled out a little airplane-sized bottle of whiskey. "Fuck going anywhere else tonight. We're staying here until we can figure out what our next move should be. Those vampires can fuck all the way off." He opened the bottle in his hand aggressively and tipped it back, gulping all of its contents down his throat in one swift motion.

"When did you stash that?" Tyler asked around a smile.

'At least I'm not the only one that finds Brax's antics funny,' I thought to myself, still smiling.

Glaring at Tyler with fury in his eyes, Brax said, "I've always got some whiskey lying around somewhere for times like this, don't you?"

I peered around the room, wondering what they all thought of my familiar's words, taking in mixed expressions on the guys' faces. Tyler was smiling at my familiar as he leaned back against the couch, Adam's eyebrows were raised in shocked surprise, and Derrick looked just as stern as ever.

"Brax is right. We should stay in tonight and deal with the vamps tomorrow. It's not like they're going anywhere," Tyler said as he made his way over to another cabinet and pulled out a big glass bottle of shiny blue liquid.

"Damn right, I'm right! And I want some of that," Brax said somewhat belligerently, pointing one of his tiny fingers at Tyler, the pace of his wings skipping a beat every now and then, so he'd drift downward some and have to compensate by flapping them faster to stay afloat.

Derrick rolled his eyes and walked over to Tyler, snatching the bottle out of his hands rudely. "We might not be going to see the vamps, but we're definitely not getting drunk on fairy wine instead."

"Don't take shit out of my hands, Derrick," Tyler spat as he got right in Derrick's face, fists balled at his sides.

"Don't make dumb, rash decisions, Tyler. We need to have clear minds to handle all of this," Derrick said in a low and stern voice that sent an unexpected shiver up my spine.

"Fuck you, I'll do what I want. Try and stop me. See what happens," Tyler's voice turned colder than I'd ever heard it, and I couldn't for the life of me understand why they were all so on edge.

Yes, I knew we... no... *I* was probably in danger from Absinthe, but that didn't mean everybody had to get so worked up.

"Fight, bitches! Fight!" Brax yelled, fists raised in the air above his head as his eyelids started to droop. "Knock him out!"

I tried to figure out who he was talking to or rooting for, but there was really no telling.

"Yeah, I don't think that's going to help anything, Brax," I said with a small chuckle, eyes glued to the two men in front of me who were having one of the sexiest stare-downs I'd ever seen.

"It will help!" Brax said as he swiveled his head to face me. His voice got real low as he came over and attempted to whisper in my ear, "Let 'em duke it out. I'll call dibs on fighting the winner, and then they'll stop fighting because they'll know I'll kick all their asses."

Adam walked up and carefully pushed the two men apart, taking the bottle of fairy wine from Derrick's hand as he went. The two backed up slightly, and I noticed there was something about Adam that gave both Tyler and Derrick pause.

"Look," Adam said. "It's been a long day. Go clear your heads or something and come back when you can both keep yourselves in check." He wasn't overly stern, nor was he giving the order lightly. He sounded confident and understanding at the same time, and I respected Adam more for the way he'd handled the situation. He wasn't one of those guys that always had to prove himself by showing off in any way. He didn't need to push others around, and he didn't cower when he was confronted. He just acted. And people like that almost always deserve to be respected.

Brax's gravelly snore cut through the tension like a knife through butter, and a round of giggles finally escaped me as I took in the sight of him. I raised my hand to my mouth as I laughed, looking at my familiar where he'd laid down with his body draped limply over the back of the couch. I think it was the twitching in his wings with every snore that did me in, though. I laughed like crazy at the image, tears forming in my eyes before I turned back to the guys.

"What? He has a stupidly low tolerance for alcohol. It gets me every time," I tried to explain as I gasped breaths deeply enough to get my laughter under control. They were all staring at me, completely overlooking Brax and how funny he was.

But after my explanation, they seemed to snap out of whatever trance they'd been in. I saw the heat rise in their cheeks as they turned and started walking down the hallway to their rooms to change. I didn't know what their problem was, but I decided I didn't care as I made my way to shower and change myself.

A short time later, I walked into the kitchen to see Adam at the stove cooking something with a glass of the blue liquid in one hand, spatula in the other. He smiled at me as I entered, and I smiled back in response. Derrick and Tyler each had a glass of the stuff, too, where they sat around the dining room table, but I wasn't about to bring up how that came about.

'I'll take my wins where I can get them, thank you very much,' I thought to myself.

"What are you making?" I asked as Adam poured out another glass of the pretty blue stuff even though his was still full.

"Burgers. Is that alright?" he asked as he handed me the drink he'd poured.

I answered, "Yes," as I took the glass but eyed it warily. I remembered the guys' story about waking up in some random field in Oklahoma the last time they drank fairy wine, and I was still very hesitant with alcohol, given my experience with Rick.

"It's delicious," Tyler came up beside me, wrapping an arm lightly around my waist and looked down, his bright green eyes locking me in place for a moment.

Glimpses of memories from the night I was raped flashed through my mind, and I closed my eyes tightly to get the images out of my head.

'I'm safe now. Rick is dead. I killed him. These guys aren't going to hurt me.' I repeated the self-confidence boosting words over and over again to myself before I could finally open my eyes, and when I did, I was met with concerned gazes from each of my teammates. Derrick had come to the kitchen island where I was standing and leaned against it with his drink in his hand as he looked at me, concern evident in his handsome features.

"You don't have to drink if you don't want to," he said, and I relaxed some at his words.

However, when I peered over at Adam, his face reminded me of the proclamation I'd made on the beach. I'd said that I wasn't going to allow what happened to me to keep me from experiencing everything life had to offer. I wasn't in the same unfortunate situation I'd been in the last time I drank. I was surrounded by guys that were as tough as nails, and for some strange reason, they all seemed to care about me.

They weren't going to hurt me or let me come to harm in any way as long as they could help it, of that I was sure. Today had been so full, and all I wanted to do was relax and unwind, maybe even get to know my teammates a little better. And with those thoughts dancing in my head, I took my first sip of the most delicious drink I'd ever tasted in my life.

～

ONLY A COUPLE of minutes and a few sips later, the fairy wine was already beginning to warm me, starting by sending a tingling feeling first through my thighs, then down my arms, where it eventually coalesced and leveled out, leaving me feeling truly relaxed for the first time all day. Since our training session this morning, it'd been revelation after revelation, and I knew I needed time to process everything I'd learned. Everyone had gotten quiet when they started eating the incredible burgers Adam had made, and I used the moments to sip more fairy wine and go over what all had happened since I woke up.

I was getting better at Adam's physical training; the fact that I'd made it through everything he'd tasked me with this morning proved that much, at least. But Otto and the guys wanted me to train a hell of a lot more to be ready for the gauntlet and life as a hunter in general. I knew Derrick was really wanting to work on bringing out more of my powers while Tyler wanted to see if any of my new abilities were like his.

After my chat with Thomas about which powers I possessed the other day, I was under the impression that the ones he'd mentioned were the only ones I had. So, after my glowfest and my increased speed showed up out of nowhere today, the guys' thoughts on the matter were confirmed.

They thought more of my abilities were going to show themselves as time went on, but hadn't explicitly said anything about it yet. I'd seen their thoughts about my powers and their plans for me through my connection to Brax when we were getting ready to work out, but with everything that'd happened after, we hadn't been able to get to anything else like they'd wanted. The other night over dinner, Derrick had said we'd have to slide training in wherever we could work it in between missions, and I completely understood that now after the day we'd had.

Our missions weren't turning out to be as cut and dry as I'd first imagined them to be in the beginning. It wasn't like, *'Go here, start plague, go home.'*

It was more like a bunch of little threads that wove together in a weird and complicated way that we had to unravel one string at a time, a puzzle that could only be put together with the picture side face down. After today, there was no denying Absinthe was one of those threads, one of those upside-down puzzle pieces.

His name popped up everywhere I turned. From being the one that killed my parents, shredded their souls, and put me on the path to living my terrible upbringing, to the person who stole the fairies sacred gem, the jinn was playing a substantial role in my first real mission on Dragon team. I just couldn't figure out why... or even how Absinthe was so intertwined with my life. It was starting to seem like the only way to get the answers I needed would be to go and get them from the infamous jinn himself, but I doubted my teammates would be down with such a thing.

The pictures of my mother and her team were still in my parents' folders in the satchel in my room, right next to the files on my team-mates, and they were all burning a proverbial hole in my psyche with how badly I wanted to read through them. I wanted to know as much as I could about everyone who was playing a role in my life, but like I'd realized this morning, time wasn't on my side when it came to figuring out the past.

Speaking of pasts, today I'd also been infected or whatever by that fucking flower, the timekeeper. *'What the hell was that, anyway?'* I could hardly wrap my mind around everything I'd seen from Brax's past, much less why the timekeeper felt those visions were so important to show me. I knew the elf-goyle had lived a few lives, but we hadn't talked about them yet, and I didn't think he was going to be waking up anytime soon to start, seeing as how he was millimeters from falling off the back of the couch in his drunken comatose slumber.

Seeing the potential for injury, or at least a loud crash, I got up from my spot to go save him, ignoring the small dizzying feeling I had when I stood. As I walked over, I thought, *'At least the fairies and pixies seem to be getting along. And that forest... it seems to be doing very well.'* The sheer number of new plants was astonishing, and Brax's worries and Tyler's rule floated back through my mind, making me smile as I rolled Brax onto the couch. He fell on his back, wings tucked tightly behind him with his arms splayed out on either side while his mouth hung open, and I caught a glimpse of his little fanged canines. They weren't that obvious when he talked because of the way his mouth moved, but they were evident now, and I smiled when I saw them.

"Who wants to walk on the beach?" Derrick awed me with the happy tone in his voice.

'The fairy wine must be working on him too,' I thought before I agreed, and we all took off out the back door, leaving Brax to sleep it off.

The night was cool, but not chilly, and the moon was so bright with such a clear sky, I could see way farther than I usually could at night. The lightness of the sand reflected the moonlight, brightening up the night in a way that felt peaceful and serene. The sand was getting between my toes, and I wiggled them, enjoying the feeling as I waited for the guys at the bottom of the stairs.

"Here, I refilled your wine for you," Tyler said as he handed over my glass, fairy wine dancing around close to the rim. I had to take a few sips before I felt comfortable walking with the drink, but once I did, I felt its effects almost straight away. Warm tingles spread throughout my body, and my head felt light, but again, I ignored the impact it was having on me since the guys were handling their alcohol consumption better than I thought they would. I wasn't going to be the first one to show how drunk I was getting. I wanted the guys to respect me, which wasn't something I thought they'd do if I was wandering around like a floundering idiot.

Trying to play it cool, I walked beside Tyler and pressed my hand gently to his bicep. "Thank you for this," I said, indicating the drink in my other hand.

"Don't worry about it," he said as he pulled my hand into his, interlacing his fingers in mine and flashing me a wicked smile that had the little hairs on my skin rising up and my belly swimming with butterflies.

Derrick was on my left and every few steps, our arms would brush by one another, even though there was plenty of room for each of us to walk without bumping into each other, and some part of me said he was walking so close because he wanted to be touching me. The thought mixed with the fairy wine, Tyler's smile, and the way he was holding my hand, building me up far too much for my own good.

'Slow your roll, Pimpin',' the self-deprecating voice that lives inside my head said, reminding me that I shouldn't read too much into what these guys say or do when it comes to me.

'Bitch,' I thought back in retaliation. I didn't know what these guys felt for me, but I did know how I felt about them. I wasn't strong enough to reject any of them or the things they did that set my skin ablaze and my insides quivering. I just couldn't do it. That voice could go fuck herself.

"So, what's our plan, then?" Adam asked from Tyler's other side where his bare feet were wading through the water.

"Do we always have to make a plan?" Derrick asked in frustration, letting out an audible sigh, and I looked up at him in shock. He was always the serious planner that wanted to know every detail about something before he made a move. What he said didn't fit his normal personality.

"Woah, is stern ass Derrick breaking away from all of his rules?" I heard myself ask, and I almost sent my hand to my mouth when I realized what I'd said, but that would've meant letting go of Tyler's hand, and there was no way I was doing that.

A playful gaze I'd never seen on Derrick before met mine, and my stomach started doing that damn flippy thing again at the sight of it.

"Rules are good sometimes, but we've all got to learn how to chill the fuck out!" He was definitely not himself right now, and I couldn't say I wasn't enjoying it. A playful Derrick that could also be kick-ass and stern was an idea I could get used to. Once the words were out of his mouth, he shook his arms out and bounced around, turning to walk backward as he talked.

"We need to have some fun, become friends, instead of whatever this shit is," he said as he gestured with his arm between him and Tyler. "I'm so tired of it."

They'd been aggressive and standoffish toward each other since we'd gotten back to the safe house, neither one willing to back down from whatever they'd done to piss each other off. But Derrick was undoubtedly sending out an olive branch, and I watched Tyler with wide eyes, hoping he'd take it.

We'd all stopped to watch our team leader's shenanigans, shocked by his actions and words.

"I'm tired of it too," Tyler said with narrowed eyes staring Derrick down. "Let's just solve whatever's been going on with us for the past four years because you decided to lighten up and have some fairy wine. Go ahead. Fix it," Tyler dared, releasing my hand to cross his tatted arms over his chest, and instinctively I backed up from him some, taking a few steps to the side.

"I was trying to be nice and let shit go, but that's apparently not something you'd ever even think about trying. I'm not the only one who's made mistakes here. It takes two to tango, bitch," Derrick said, his happy demeanor gone like the rest of the fairy wine I'd inhaled at the onset of the conflict before me. "How about you start by apologizing for all the unnecessary shit you've gotten us into, then we still might be able to work something out."

"Fuck off with that," Tyler said as he took a menacing step toward Derrick, dropping his hands to his sides. "Why don't you start by telling Becks the truth about what you think she is!"

"Hold on, I'm not in this at all," I said as I heard my name, holding my hands up in the air beside me, and it took a second for my fuzzy brain to work through the rest of Tyler's words.

"Hey, we all need to calm down. We can't fix four years' worth of problems in one night. You're right Becks, this has nothing to do with you," Adam said as he slipped between Derrick and Tyler, but I wasn't too far gone to see that he was trying to shift my focus from what Tyler had said.

Getting pissed off faster than I usually would and blaming it on the fairy wine, I stepped up to Derrick, my face near his chest as I leveled him with a glare all my own. "What is he talking about?"

Derrick actually looked somewhat scared, and something told me not to back down, not to give an inch until he told me what he knew.

"What am I?" I asked.

"It's not that important," Adam said as he tried to place a soothing hand on my shoulder, but I smacked it away without a thought, never letting my gaze slip from Derrick.

"See? This is what I mean, Tyler! You and your beast are always stirring shit up that would be better left alone," Derrick said to Tyler over my shoulder. "You need to learn to keep your mouth shut about things I've told you in confidence, asshole. This is why I never tell you anything; you use it against me."

'Is this motherfucker dismissing me and what I asked him? Oh, hell no,' I thought right before I pushed Derrick in his chest, sending him back a few steps. I wasn't in touch with my power, so it wasn't too forceful a push, but it was enough to get his attention back.

"Tell me what you know right now," I said, power seeping out of my words unintentionally, the alpha order sending visible shivers throughout Derrick's body.

"It's not something I know, so much as it's something I suspect," Derrick answered through gritted teeth, locking his irritated eyes on mine.

I nodded and crossed my arms, waiting for him to finish. He looked like he was having some sort of internal battle, but after a few seconds, he relented.

"I don't know for sure, and I told these guys as much, but some people can't let sleeping dogs lie," Derrick started with a quick and resentful glare at Tyler. "There hasn't been one in centuries since the last of the sorcerers and sorceresses died off," he took a deep breath before he continued, "but I think you might be destined to become the hunter's next queen."

~

"THE HUNTER'S NEXT *WHAT*?" I asked, knowing my eyebrows were nearing my hairline in bewilderment.

Derrick deflated, and his brown eyes softened as they met mine. I could see the wheels turning in his head, probably deciding how much he was willing to tell me again. It was as if these guys thought I could only handle so much information at a time, and it pissed me off to no end. He blew out a puff of air and shoved his hands in his pockets before he said, "Our queen." He might have wanted to say more, but Adam interrupted him.

"Let's not worry too much about it right now."

Turning my heated glare on Adam this time, I said, "No. We *are* going to worry about it now. I'm tired of you guys holding information back from me. And didn't you just say this had nothing to do with me? Well, you must be a liar, because if I am supposed to be the next hunter queen, it has everything to do with me. And I don't fucking like liars."

"I wasn't lying," Adam began. "The issues between these two *don't* have anything to do with you." He gestured between Derrick and Tyler. "At least, they didn't use to, anyway. They've been at each other's throats from day one. You joining our team just changed the dynamics," he said as he glared at the other guys. "Whatever problems they have should've been settled a long time ago, but they're some of the most stubborn people I've ever met."

Derrick and Tyler both scoffed in response, but Adam continued undeterred. "Derrick suspecting that you might be our next queen does have some merit, but it's nothing we can prove until after you've gone through the gauntlet, so there really is no need to worry about it right now, at this very moment."

"How does it have merit? Since when do the hunters have a queen? I thought they were ruled by chiefs, one in this hemisphere, another in the eastern hemisphere," I said. Dammit, they were going to answer all of my questions tonight if it killed me. I couldn't take not knowing what I needed to know any longer. It seemed like every time I got used to a particular idea, they would come and throw another monkey wrench in the mix, just to confuse me. I was done wandering through this new life without knowing what was going on and what was at stake.

"It's the only thing that makes sense," Derrick said, and I turned to him. "You have more power than any other hunter initiate has had, and more are becoming evident every day. The way you were raised, in the asylum, could have affected that, but not to the degree we see in you now. You shouldn't be able to do all the things you've been doing."

"What exactly have I been doing that's so different from others like me, other than having more power than them?"

"Solving a centuries-old feud between the flyers is one. Something no other hunter has ever been able to accomplish. Today, Queen Agatha said you were different because you could 'see them,' which doesn't make any sense at all to me," Derrick said with an attitude. "Enhanced speed is another. No initiate gets that specific power until they've gone through the gauntlet. You shouldn't have it yet, but today that power showed up, and you used it as if you've been using it your entire life. Not like someone who just got it today. It normally takes at least a few weeks to use that power well enough to do any good."

"Glowing with power is another, and you touched my beast. Those can't go unmentioned, either," Tyler joined in. "No one has ever touched my beast. Never even tried. He scares everyone away, but for some reason, he calms when he's near you instead of trying to bite your head off like he wants to do to everyone else. And I've never heard of anyone's power making them glow. There's no telling what you were capable of right then."

"The fact that you can't die is pretty indicative of you being our next queen, too. At first, I hadn't known what to think when I heard about your inability to die, so I did some research. Turns out the last hunters to have that specific power were the sorcerers and sorceresses of old. The old kings and queens," Adam said, thoroughly blowing my mind.

"And there's a bounty on your head from somewhere," Tyler said. "I've never heard of any initiate posing so much of a threat in that phase of their life that someone would try to kill them before they've even gone through the gauntlet. There's no need to. You're not dangerous until then. But with everything we learned from Dorian, the vampire that was paid to kill you, you've got a pretty big target on your back. Nobody puts out a hit on someone unless they're worried about what that person can do."

"So, all of that is leading you to think that I'm going to be queen?" I asked.

"Pretty much," Tyler answered.

"How does having a queen maintain balance? Why'd they all die off? *When* did they all die off? How could I possibly be the next one? I mean, I understand what you guys are saying, but my real parents were just normal hunters, right? How could they birth a queen?" The questions I had were rolling off my tongue almost as fast as I could think them.

"Let's sit down and talk about this," Derrick offered, hand outstretched, indicating a spot in the sand away from the water's edge. Once we all took a seat in a square-type formation, he said, "It looks like we've got to give you your first real history lesson for you to understand what all's going on."

Derrick glanced around at the guys, but after seeing them nod their heads at him, he started in on his lesson.

"Heaven and Hell agreed to make hunters so they could maintain the balance between all the realms and prevent the apocalypse because neither side wanted all of this to end. They did that by having angels and demons come together to make the hunter race. They figured the combination would make the most well-balanced species ever created. Then they instituted the gauntlet to make doubly sure that each individual hunter was balanced enough to do their jobs."

"So, we're half-angel and half-demon?" I asked dumbfounded.

"Technically, yes. But, once enough hunters were created, the angels and demons left, encouraging the hunters to breed amongst themselves, continuing the species without needing any more help from those that created them," Adam explained.

"Well, that's pretty cool," I said as I thought through their words and tried not to let my mind wander into angel and demon sex, and how that must have gone down.

Seeming to ignore my statement, Tyler said, "While they were raising the first generations of hunters, the angels and demons lived on Earth and established the two-hemisphere system. Binaria East and Binaria West. When that first generation was grown and had passed the gauntlet, they put the best ones in positions with the most power. There were five sorcerers and one sorceress that became the kings and queen of all the hunters. And they ruled over both hemispheres, maintaining the balance between them."

"Why were there so many guys and only one woman?" I asked, not understanding how that constituted balance. If anything, it was very *un*balanced.

"Well, our first queen was the most powerful of all. She got all of the power from her angel side and from her demon side as if her blood wasn't diluted at all by one or the other. However, because she was so powerful, she had to have others around her to anchor her and her magic. From what we understand, the first queen could sneeze, and power would burst from her, but she would have no control over what that power did," Adam said.

"That is until she bound herself to her kings. They were like the second-place finishers in their gauntlet trials if that makes any sense," Tyler said. "When they bonded to the queen, their power somehow anchored her magic so she could finally control it. From what I understand, without her kings, her powers would have destroyed her, and everything else."

"Okay, well, was it their offspring that became the next kings and queens?" I asked, trying to make sense of it all.

"No," Derrick answered. "In every generation after the first, a new sorcerer or sorceress would be born, and as they grew up, their powers marked what they were meant to become. Once they'd passed the gauntlet, they would fill the roles of their predecessors at just the right time, as if divine intervention knew the deaths of the reigning monarchs were about to happen, so they planned ahead.

It worked out that way for a long time. And the dynamics always changed with each generation. So, where the first generation had one woman and multiple men acting as her anchors, the next generation had one man and multiple women acting as the anchors for his magic. Back and forth, for centuries, this pattern continued. Until one day, the reigning king and his three queens all died in the same fiery explosion that nearly burned Binaria East to the ground almost a thousand years ago."

"Every hunter began looking everywhere for their replacements, but none ever showed," Adam said as fear started to spread through me, and I couldn't understand why. "And so, since there were no more kings and queens, the hunters reorganized and rebuilt to keep the apocalypse at bay. They created the chief's position at Binaria West and another position just like it for Binaria East. They compartmentalized the two groups of hunters by their abilities, breaking down the entire structure of the hunters to its bits and pieces and regrouped them from scratch.

It made it easier to manage that way since there was no way a regular hunter, even a powerful chief, could do the same jobs that the kings and queens were able to do. So, for example, we have teams that are nothing but assassins, those that are really good at infiltrating hidden places and taking out those in power. There are teams of psychics that sit around all day trying to predict the future, and shapeshifting teams that complete their missions by turning into whatever species would be best to get the job done. There are even a few teams that their only responsibilities are to watch the human leaders of Earth and report their findings back to the chief. They never *do* anything other than watch."

"Then why are you guys on the same team?" I asked. "Derrick's a spellworker, you're a psychic, and Tyler's a shapeshifter. And who knows what I am," I said sarcastically as I rolled my eyes at myself.

"Oh, there are plenty of teams with a mixture of hunters with different abilities. Sorry if I confused you. Teams like ours are actually most prevalent," Adam clarified. "We're the ones that really get stuff done and are given the hardest missions because it takes all of our strengths working together to tackle them," he said with a pointed glance at Derrick and Tyler.

I looked down and absentmindedly played with some sand as I thought over everything they'd said as best I could with how my fuzzy brain felt in its current state. It was a lot to process, but I wasn't going to complain since I didn't want them to stop talking and letting me into their world... well, my world, too, I guessed. "So, what does this mean that I might be the next queen?"

There was a pregnant pause before Derrick spoke up, concern written into his features. "I don't know. It's just a hunch from everything we mentioned before, but if I am right, this isn't something we need to take lightly. We also need to keep it to ourselves," he said, and a chill sprinted up my spine.

"Why's that?"

Tyler growled a little across from me, and though he seemed irritable, he answered anyway. "We can't tell anyone because you already have a hit out on you when most people don't even know you exist. If Derrick is right, imagine how many more people are going to want to kill you once they find out."

Fear widened my eyes and sped up my heart as I asked, "Why would they want to kill their queen?" I wasn't accepting what they were saying, that I was the next queen, but I also wasn't dumb enough to ignore the fact that if Derrick could think it was true, then others could as well.

"For a thousand years, hunters have been running things a certain way, and I'm pretty sure they're not going to take very well to someone coming in and changing everything they know. We're a volatile group by nature. A new queen coming in right when everything's going to hell in a handbasket is only going to spark a fight. One I am not looking forward to if you are the next queen," Adam said.

"Wouldn't the hunters think the queen could come in and fix

things instead of making things worse?" I asked, trying to find a silver lining of some kind.

Derrick ran a hand through his hair again and said, "No. More than likely, they're going to think the birth of a new queen is what started making everything go wrong in the first place." He sighed and placed his elbows on his knees, sitting cross-legged and turning his gaze to mine. "They'll blame her for everything that has gone wrong recently, and are more likely to retaliate and kill her, rather than face the fact that she's probably their only hope."

CHAPTER 6

BECKS

"I'm going for a swim. Anybody wanna join me?" Tyler asked after we'd fallen into silence for a few minutes, their important disclosures needing time to fully seep into our minds.

"That sounds good," Adam said.

"I'm down," Derrick responded, already standing up and pulling his shirt over his head. I remembered swimming was what Derrick said he liked to do for fun, and suddenly, I wanted to see him doing something he loved more than I thought I would. But despite how much I wanted to see it, my anxiety started acting up again. I'd never been swimming in my life, and I didn't think night time in the ocean while I was somewhat inebriated was the best time and place to learn even if they were willing to teach me. However, I didn't want them to think any less of me, so when it was my turn to answer, I tried to play it off as less of a big deal than it was.

"You guys go ahead; I'll sit here and watch."

The guys all smirked at me as they stripped down to their under-wear, overwhelming me with the sight of their smiles, bodies, tattoos, and muscles everywhere I looked. I tried really hard to keep my eyes on their faces instead of letting them drift downward like they so badly wanted to, but my periphery still got an eyeful, and I tried not to let my libido's reaction to seeing them show on my face. They all wore black boxer briefs that accentuated their thick thighs and the stuff in between. I'd never been so attracted to another person, let alone three men at the same time who were way too supermodel worthy for their own good.

"Oh, come on," Derrick said. "The water's not even cold this time of year."

"Nah, it's okay. I'm just going to lay here and relax. Seriously, you guys go."

A playful smirk turned up the edges of Tyler's lips, and before I could even think about what he was doing, he swooped low and picked me up, carrying me bride-style as he trotted toward the water. An unattractive little squeal tore through my lips as I started squirming and trying to get out of his grasp as he neared the water.

"Put me down! I don't want to swim!" I said, trying unsuccessfully to buck up my hips to loosen his hold, but it was useless. The man was stronger than I wanted to believe, and none of my efforts seemed to make a difference at all. Well, except for bringing sexy chuckles out of his chest.

"We've got a squeaker, Adam!" Tyler called out on a laugh over his shoulder to the psychic that was right behind us, and who didn't seem at all inclined to help since he laughed right along with Tyler.

"I still have my clothes on!" I screamed, grasping at the only reason I could think of to get him to stop, even as my own giggles betrayed me and the fact that I loved this playful side of the guys.

I thought of it just in time too. Tyler stopped right at the water's edge and put me back on my feet, smiling down at me, the moonlight creating a halo effect behind his head. That damned piece of hair was falling in his eyes again, and I had to look away, so I didn't start drooling or some dumb shit like that.

"Well, that's a simple enough fix," Derrick said smoothly, coming to a stop beside me.

I was boxed in, Tyler in front of me, Derrick on my right, and Adam on my left. I could feel the heat radiating from their bodies, and that little flippy feeling in my belly wasn't so little anymore. It spread out and consumed all of my consciousness. Excitement was spreading through me at an alarming rate in more ways than one, but I couldn't stop it. And honestly, I didn't want to.

"Do you need some help with that task?" Tyler asked like a smartass, and what he was suggesting made more heat come to life inside me as I stared into his eyes.

"I am fully capable of undressing myself, thank you very much," I said, trying to scoot by them and head back to our spot in the sand, but they wouldn't let me through. When I tried to slip between Tyler and Derrick, they stepped closer together at the same time, making my attempt futile. When I tried to step between Tyler and Adam, they did the same thing, and I sighed as I stopped trying, crossing my arms over my chest.

'At least they're working together as a team,' I thought sarcastically as I stared them down.

"It'll be fun, I promise," Adam said in that sexy ass voice of his, a playful smile wide on his thick lips.

Finally deciding the only way they'd let me out of this situation would be for me to tell them the truth, I sighed and said, "I can't swim. I've never even been close to a pool, much less been swimming in the ocean where the waves might actually kill me."

I was mad at myself for not having a normal childhood where my parents taught me how to swim or at least paid someone to give me lessons. It was just another reminder of what I'd missed out on growing up, and it made me a little bitter, but there was nothing I could do about it.

Tyler's belly laughter caught me by surprise, and when I heard him laughing like that, I couldn't help the smile that spread on my face despite how mad I was that he was laughing at me. Sometimes my body did its own thing, not caring at all about what my brain wanted it to do.

"What's so funny?"

Tyler reached out both of his hands to cup my face and lowered his head down, so his eyes were staring into mine, his face mere inches from me. "You can't die, and you are adorably clueless," he said before he released me and laughed some more. Thrown by his words, I didn't know whether to be pissed off, turned on, or amused, which probably just highlighted what he was talking about.

Adam had one fist balled in front of his mouth, his other arm wrapped around his middle as he tried to keep himself from laughing as well, and Derrick was standing there smiling, but otherwise, not moving or saying anything.

"What are you talking about?" I asked when no one seemed keen on explaining what Tyler had said.

Recovering from his laughter, Tyler said, "You're a hunter, Becks. You can breathe underwater."

"No the fuck I can't," I said as I dismissed what he said immediately, thinking he'd lost his mind entirely.

"It's true. How else would we be able to keep the balance with the mermaids and other creatures of the deep?" Adam asked, and I stared at him like an open-mouthed idiot.

"Mermaids? Fuck off. There's no way I can breathe underwater. You guys are just messing with me 'cause I'm new," I searched my mind for any instance to prove myself right, but somehow, drowning had never even been a possibility in my past. Sure, I'd seen it on television, and it looked like it hurt like a bitch, but I'd never experienced it, so I had no real clue as to whether they were right or not.

"We can show you," Derrick offered, softer than he'd spoken before, reaching out a warm hand to my shoulder, and I was having a tough time trying to come up with a reason to deny him.

I glanced at the water behind me and then back to each of the guys. I knew they wouldn't let any harm come to me since it was one of the most endearing traits they all shared and weighed my options. Eventually, I decided nothing too bad could happen, so I started taking off the t-shirt and shorts I'd put on after my shower. Once they were in hand, and I was standing in nothing but the light blue lacy underwear set Tyler had given me, I said, "Don't worry, my bra is staying on, so your precious double standard will stay in place. Can I go put my clothes up there, so they don't get wet, at least?" It was a useless, last-ditch effort to get out of learning to swim, but I tried it anyway.

Tyler chuckled again, catching my reference to the other day's misunderstanding and took the clothes from my hands, tossing them back over his head where they landed some distance away near their discarded garments. "Come on," he said as he picked me back up, another squeak tearing through my throat as he headed into the water, my legs wrapped around his middle and my arms squeezing tightly around his neck as I tried not to panic.

Once we were out past the breakers, Tyler stopped, still holding me in his arms, and stood where my head was above the water's surface, as long as I clung tightly enough to him when the small swells came slipping by gently. Carefully, he set me on my feet, not letting go of my hand until he was sure I was on steady footing. I had to jump every time a new swell came in, but after a few harrowing tries, I seemed to get the hang of it and was actually starting to enjoy myself. Until I remembered things live in the ocean, and a new fear gripped me.

"What about sharks?" I asked as I tried to see through the water around me and spot one of the creatures that could bite me in half. The night was bright, but not nearly bright enough for me to see through the surface of the water. The ordinarily pristine blue water around the safe house's island was almost black without the sun's presence to shine through it. There was no way I could see what was lurking underneath.

A deep rumble of laughter hit my ears from where Derrick was standing on my other side, and I focused on him. "Sharks aren't going to mess with you as long as you don't mess with them. Yes, they're curious creatures and might bite you to see what you are, but they rarely like what they get in that bite enough to come back and finish you off," he said, and I gasped at his description.

"I don't want to be a chew toy for a shark, Derrick," I almost yelled, instinctively keeping my limbs as close to my body as possible while still keeping my head above water.

"Why not? Even if you did get bitten, you'd heal before tomorrow," Derrick said.

His smirk told me he was joking, but that didn't stop me from playfully slapping at his shoulder one good time as I said, "I'd rather not if you don't mind."

He chuckled some more, and I smiled at the horizon in front of me. It was so dark I couldn't tell where the ocean stopped and the night sky began, but it was so beautiful I didn't want to look away.

Coming over to stand in front of me, Adam said, "Alright. We're going to take this slow. Okay, Becks, I'm going to teach you the same way they teach every hunter child at the academy. Just promise me, if you feel like you're going to puke, let us know so we can all get out of the way."

"You're joking, right? Why would I throw up?"

"Taking that first breath underwater can be difficult for some initiates," Adam said. "It's all psychological, there's nothing hard about it, but still, some initiates do freak out enough to puke. It's happened enough times, I felt like I should warn you."

I was already scared of what they wanted me to do, and his warning wasn't helping me at all. However, I was going to face this challenge with an open mind as I tried to meet every challenge they threw at me, and I just had to trust that they knew what they were talking about.

"Here, hold my hands," Adam said as he pulled my arms from where they'd wrapped themselves around my middle in some kind of self-preserving embrace. His hands felt smooth in mine, and as soon as our skin touched, my anxiety started to slip away. "Alright, when you're ready, I want you to squat down and bring your head below the surface. Once you're down there, keep your eyes open and take a deep breath. I promise your mind will be blown by how easy it is."

I didn't know what to say at that moment because as soon as I nodded at him, two hands found purchase on each of my shoulders. Tyler and Derrick both placed a hand gently there, offering support without me having to ask for it, without me even knowing I needed to ask for it. But when all three of them were touching me, something shifted on my insides, steeling my resolve and empowering me with the willpower I needed. It felt insanely good, and I ducked below the surface with barely a second thought.

Once underwater, I opened my eyes and stared at Adam's chiseled face where it floated before me, blue eyes captivating in the water surrounding us. I watched as he opened his mouth and visibly breathed the water into his lungs and back out again. Determined not to disappoint these guys, I mimicked his motions, breathing in a lungful of water.

It didn't even hurt, which I was surprised to learn. Actually, it felt pretty damn good when I thought about it, like a muscle that was finally being stretched after a long stint of stillness. Once I did it the first time, I practiced inhaling and exhaling, looking around at each of the guys in turn.

Adam was smiling, his short blonde hair swaying with each swell that passed over our heads. Derrick was smirking at me again, his brown eyes appearing black in the moonlit water while Tyler was surveying the world around us, paying me no mind whatsoever, other than the hand he still had clasped to my shoulder.

"Ready to swim, little fishy?" Derrick asked, and I was astonished he was able to speak, and by the fact that I could hear him too.

I just kind of floated there and watched with big eyes as he started swimming backward under the water.

"We can talk?" I asked, amazed that even though no air was moving over my vocal cords, the sound was still coming out, the science I knew failing terribly to explain what was happening right then.

Laughing the chuckle I was slowly beginning to love to hear from him, Tyler said, "Of course we can talk underwater," as if my question was amusing as well as dumb.

"Okay, the way to move is by kicking your arms and legs like you saw Derrick do," Adam said, hands still holding mine until that moment when he let them go and filled Derrick's vacated spot to my right so I could swim through where he'd been floating in front of me.

I took a deep breath of water and used my feet to push into the sandy bottom of the ocean floor, the motion propelling me forward, a rush of adrenaline dumping into my veins as I felt the water around me gently slide over my body. It seemed like it didn't take any time at all to get used to and adapt to my new environment, and I couldn't help but laugh like a kid in a candy store because it was all so beautiful. I could see astonishingly well under the water from the moonlight streaming in, and everywhere I looked there was something new to see. I had never felt that free in all my life, and the absolute happiness that overtook me was something I never wanted to live without again.

I followed and swam with the guys, trying to keep up before I remembered how well tapping into my power worked with running, and once I grabbed hold of it with my mind, I was speeding through the water as fast as my teammates. Tyler had started what was basically a game of tag, and as he patted my arm making me 'it,' I tried to turn in time to tag him back, but I missed and had to go chasing after him. But I didn't mind at all; I could see the definition of Tyler's backside with every kick of his feet, and I had a hard time pulling my eyes from him.

Derrick thought he was being sneaky, hiding around some of the coral that was growing down below me, but when I saw him, I changed my target and started heading in his direction. When he noticed I'd seen him, he took off in the other direction, but I was still able to barely run my hand down his forearm when it swam close by me. He turned in the water extremely fast and tagged me back, but I was just as quick as I got him again, this time on the same hand he'd used to tag me.

With no warning, he was suddenly swimming toward me and wrapping me up in his strong arms, pulling me in closer to his body as my arms went around his neck naturally. "You're it," he said in that deep husky voice of his, and little butterflies were shooting through my belly spastically at his words.

His embrace was light, but the intensity of his eyes boring into mine was anything but. I found myself gulping in water like I'd gasp a breath of air as I took in his five o'clock shadow and strong jawline. I spared a glance at his parted lips, and the next thing I knew, he was kissing me senseless beneath the waves. His tongue danced lightly with mine as my legs wrapped around his hips before I even knew they were moving, but once my feet were locked behind him, I had no intention of letting go.

My long brown hair was being whipped around in the current, but before it could smother us, Derrick took both of his hands from my waist and ran them gently over my scalp, taming the wild locks as he cupped the back of my neck. A moment later, he broke the kiss and started trailing kisses down the side of my face and down my throat, one hand still holding my hair, the other sliding lightly back around behind me. My emotions were going haywire, every nerve ending in my body alight with nervous anticipation.

Right when Derrick ran his hand down my back and slipped the tips of his fingers into the waistband of my lacy underwear, a shock-wave passed through us, flinging us away from one another with its intensity. Dazed and confused, I saw the fear in Derrick's eyes from a few yards away and concern for whatever the blast had been spread through me like lightning. I searched for Adam and Tyler, finding they weren't too far away and were already swimming toward us.

"We need to go see what that was," Tyler said as he grabbed my hand in his possessively, but I don't think he realized he was doing it.

"It felt like it came from the portal, can you take us there?" Derrick asked, all signs of our previous encounter gone without a trace from his stern face.

"Yeah," Tyler said as Adam and Derrick placed a hand on Tyler so he could teleport us wherever we were going.

"Stay close, Becks," Tyler said as he squeezed my hand so tightly it was almost painful before we started fading from our spots.

Milliseconds later, we were still underwater, but like *way* underwater. There was hardly any light around, but surprisingly, I could still see well enough not to smack into any of my teammates, at least. Derrick swam in front of where we'd come back into existence, twisting his hands in front of him like I'd seen him do before to open the portal to the Veil for the fairy and pixie forest. However, after a few minutes of waiting for the entrance to open, Derrick seemed to be getting frustrated.

"Someone or something has closed off this portal," Derrick said.

I didn't know much about this world, but I suspected this new development wasn't a good thing.

"That's not possible," Adam said from my left as he swam forward a bit.

Derrick shrugged and said, "Well, that's what's happening. Tyler, can you take us to another portal? Maybe we can get there another way."

Everybody joined back up, and we went to the next underwater portal, though I couldn't tell one from another. The vastness of the ocean looked exactly the same here as it had at the previous portal.

"Fuck!" Derrick screamed when the second portal didn't open at his command, and he swam back to us quickly, anger seeping out of him as he ordered Tyler to take us to yet another portal.

However, even after three more attempts, Derrick still couldn't get us through, and finally, Adam said, "Let's go back to the safe house, get changed, and go to Binaria West. The chief needs to know about this if he doesn't already. He'll be able to tell us what our next move should be."

Level-headed and understanding, Adam knew what we needed to do, and once the plan had been made, there was nothing to discuss before we were dripping wet in the living room of the safe house. I walked over to the couch, cringing at the watery trail I was leaving behind me and went to wake Brax up. Only, he wasn't there where we'd left him.

"Brax!" I called, using my power to pull him to me, and after a second, he came into existence with a huff of frustration.

"Fuck, girl, you almost gave me a heart attack! Where the hell did you go?" My elf-goyle asked, but before I could answer, Tyler spoke up.

"Brax, we've got a problem. We think all the underwater portals have been closed somehow. We need to get to the chief and fill him in."

"Pixie titties!" Brax said with alarm written across all of his features. "Becks, get ready, we gotta go!"

WE TELEPORTED to what I assumed was Otto's office since he was sitting at a large desk at the front of the room, head down and shining in the lamplight. The room was giant by any standard with a few tall windows showing off the night sky along the far wall. The bookcases that lined all the other walls only opened up twice for two doors that led in and out of the space.

Each dark mahogany bookcase was filled entirely with new and dated books, tomes, and rolled up parchment. There were plush sitting areas sprinkled around the room for small groups of people to gather together, and I imagined for a second what it would be like to curl up in one of those comfy chairs and get lost in an ancient book. However, those thoughts had to wait since everyone on my team seemed anxious and nervous about what we'd experienced, their worry dripping into my psyche through our shared connection with Brax like a leaky roof in the middle of a hurricane.

"Dragon team?" Otto asked as he finally noticed our presence. "What's brought you here at this hour?" He stood and walked around the large desk and motioned for us to sit in the area closest to him.

"There was a blast in the ocean, and when we went to check it out, the portals were closed," Derrick summed up our findings efficiently. He had sat on the cream-colored sofa with a stiffly straight back, hands clasped together in front of him with a worried expression on his face as he regarded Otto.

"So, the Mer king's finally done it, huh? It's only been a week," Otto said almost to himself as he gazed out the window toward the waves that surrounded Binaria West's hidden island. Hands resting on the armrests of his chair, his lack of any real reaction surprised me.

"Done what, exactly?" Adam asked cautiously.

Otto brought his attention back to Adam and leaned forward, one elbow on his knee while he gestured with his other arm as he spoke. "A while back, a vision came to one of our psychics, showing the Mer king closing all the underwater portals, and instead of handing in her findings like she normally would, she sought me out to tell me in person because of the importance of the vision. It was still fuzzy, but she was also adamant it was going to happen one way or another. You see, Mer King Zale has always preferred the Veil over the Earth, you guys know this, right?"

I had no idea what he was talking about, but the guys and Brax all nodded their agreement, so I went along with it and tried to keep up.

"Well, apparently, Mer Queen Darya was 'kidnapped' about a week ago from Earth," Otto used air quotes and rolled his eyes as he said this, something I was pretty sure he didn't do regularly. "But everyone knows about the mind games he likes to play, especially on his wife, so even though we sent out a team to inquire about Darya, we honestly assumed she'd finally left the king and come back to Earth to be with her family. Her animosity toward her husband is almost legendary," Otto said with a small, sad chuckle. "But, after doing some digging, our team couldn't find her anywhere. They're still out there trying to learn her whereabouts, but so far they've turned up nothing."

"Anyway, as soon as Queen Darya went missing a week ago, King Zale issued a warning to all the merfolk on Earth, saying that unless his queen was found and returned to him, he was going to close off the portals linking the Earth's waters to the Veil's."

"But he's been threatening that since he took the throne a hundred years ago," Derrick said, agitation lacing his tone.

Otto nodded and continued, "Yes, he has, but something about this time was different. Earthbound merfolk started flooding into the Veil after his warning by the hundreds, fearing being cut off from their family and friends permanently. Some who've never even left their native rivers abandoned their homes entirely and fled to the Veil. We've never seen a reaction like this to any of Zale's ramblings before, and we don't know what made everyone take him seriously this time around."

"Why didn't you tell us?" Tyler asked. "Maybe we could've found something."

"You know you guys aren't the only team I have, right, son?" Otto asked Tyler with a smile, and our shapeshifter shrugged.

"We're the *best* team you have," Tyler said with a smirk, leveling his gaze on Otto in challenge, making Otto laugh in response.

Once he stopped chuckling, Otto continued. "Be that as it may, you guys have had your hands full. Speaking of which, what did you learn from the vampire elders?"

Derrick cleared his throat some before he said, "About that, Chief."

"What happened?" Otto asked with a smirk, and I couldn't help but smile at him. He was like a grandfather figure that had so much wisdom it was almost as if he knew everything we were going to say before we said it, having seen so much in his long life that he knew when something hadn't gone exactly to plan. Or maybe, it's that nothing *ever* goes to plan, and he has just learned to not let any new bombshell affect him.

"We were returning the gem to the fairies when Becks got called by some kind of timekeeper flower, pulling Brax and Adam with her, and it took most of our day," Derrick said, and I saw Otto's eyebrows nearly reach his nonexistent hairline.

"A timekeeper flower called to you? I thought they were extinct!" His voice sounded excited, and I smiled at him as he asked, "What'd it show you?"

Before I could answer though, Brax cut in, saying, "That's not important right now. She just saw some of my past from my previous lives. Nothing to worry about in this one." He was dismissive of everything I'd seen, and though I didn't plan on talking about everything right then, I knew I wasn't going to be able to go long without talking with Brax about his past.

"That's fine. But you'll have to tell me later," Otto said with a wink in my direction, and I nodded in response as Brax scoffed.

"There's more, Chief," Adam said, handing over the piece of Absinthe's armor I'd found. "Becks found this in the fairies' forest. We think Absinthe was the one to steal the fairies' gem."

Otto didn't think it over long before he handed the charm to me, saying, "Well, this is news. Put that in your pocket for safekeeping, Rebecca. I'm pretty sure you're the one who was meant to find it."

I was confused but did as he said anyway, tucking the small piece of metal into the front pocket of my jeans.

"We'll have to come back to that later when the portals are opened back up," Otto said dismissively, rubbing a hand down his leg as if it were in pain.

"So, the Mer King actually closed off the portals. That's what we felt tonight?" Adam asked, bringing us back to the matters at hand.

"Yes, I believe so," Otto answered. "However, he must have kept a few open because the world hasn't collapsed in on itself yet."

Another chill ran down my spine, and my eyes went large again. It seemed everything I was facing in this new life was scary in one way or another, and it was a feeling I wasn't happy about reliving constantly, but it didn't seem as if I had a choice.

"True," Tyler said as he brought his hands together in front of him, thumbs rubbing against one another in thought as he stared down at the ground. After a couple beats, he said, "I might be able to feel around for an open portal while I'm teleporting. There's no guarantee, but it's worth a shot."

"Yes, that sounds like it might work. We've got to find a way to open them as soon as possible because the longer they're closed, the more unbalanced the world is going to become, and the sooner the apocalypse is going to start."

'Nothing like a cold dose of reality to give a girl some perspective,' I thought to myself sarcastically.

'I wish he was joking,' Brax thought back at me, and I looked over to where he was sitting beside me, little hands in his lap, wings hanging limply at his back.

"I think the best course of action is to have you guys split up and handle a few things at once," Otto said, drawing my eyes away from my familiar as he stood up and clapped his hands together once. "Derrick, take Brax to the vampire elders and see what you can learn from them about the attack on Rebecca. Tyler, you can take them and drop them off, then I think you should take Adam and see if you can find any open portals to the mer kingdom. If Zale really did shut most of them down, I can almost bet he's keeping one open for his own personal use."

"Yes, Chief," Derrick said as he and the rest of my team stood, ready to execute the plan.

"Rebecca, I want you to stay here with me," Otto answered my question before I could ask it. "We'll have our first lesson tonight."

I was nervous about where my team was going without me, who and what they were going to see, but I was also excited to see what Otto had up his sleeve.

'I'm going to open up our link again when we leave. You don't need to worry about us. We'll be fine,' Brax thought toward me, and I relaxed at his words, knowing I could trust him.

"You guys be careful," I said as I watched them prepare to teleport to their different destinations, unable to stop the empty feeling that spread through me when they disappeared from sight.

"Follow me, I've got some things to show you," Otto said cryptically as he started heading out of his office with me following closely behind him.

CHAPTER 7

BRAX

Tyler teleported us to the center of an old and creepy cemetery I hadn't seen since my last life. Long-established, ornate, sun-bleached tombs sat atop the wet ground all around us, the moon casting weird and ominous shadows off each one. No one spoke as Tyler and Adam started disappearing again, leaving Derrick and me here so they could go portal chasing.

I flew beside Derrick as he chose a random tomb from the masses surrounding us and opened its wrought-iron gate. Once we were inside, he pulled at one of the candlesticks hanging against the wall, causing the stone sarcophagus in front of us to slide back and reveal a hidden set of stone steps.

The crypt was so cold my breath was forming little puffy clouds that dissipated in the shallow breeze flowing through the stone structure, and if my skin could form goosebumps, I had no doubt they'd cover every inch of my exposed skin.

As we descended the stairs, I tried to open up our connection again. It took a few tries because of the distance between us, and with

Tyler and Adam sliding in and out of existence, but pretty soon, I was able to push my thoughts into Becks' mind, knowing all of our team could hear me as well.

'Wanna see and hear something crazy, Becks?' I asked before I sent a mental picture of what I was seeing to her.

'Sure, Otto is just walking me through miles of hallways right now, anyway,' Becks didn't disappoint me with her immediate response. 'Is that the vampire coven's crypt?'

'Yep,' I thought as Derrick and I kept up our pace going down the stairs that we were nowhere near the bottom of yet. 'The vamps of this coven have probably made one of the most significant and intricate engineering projects of all time, and the humans don't even know it exists,' I chuckled some at my observation.

'What do you mean?' Becks asked.

'People can't dig too far into the ground here because as soon as they do, the hole starts to fill with water. It's why they bury their dead on the surface, to keep bodies from floating back up to scare people's tits off.'

I could almost feel her cringe at the mental image she made, and I laughed again.

'But it looks like you're going underground, so how is that possible?'

'This coven made their entire city below New Orleans, where no one thought they could, where no one would think to look. They got help from the witches, of course, but still, it's pretty genius.'

'That's crazy,' Becks thought. 'How big is that vampire coven?'

'I don't know how many vamps are in it now, but I know its members live all over the southeastern United States. This is just their headquarters. The last time I was here was in my previous life when it was brand new. It was huge back then, and even though I don't know that much about it now, I'm sure it's grown and changed a lot since then.'

Seeming unamused by my conversation with Becks, Derrick turned to me when we finally reached the bottom of the stairs. We were in a small concrete room where the only ways to go were back up the way we'd come or into a shiny elevator that appeared remarkably out of place amid everything else in the crypt.

"It has changed a lot in the last few hundred years," Derrick said gruffly.

"I'll say," I said as I glared at the elevator, watching as Derrick pressed the down button.

"Are you ready?" he asked, his face stern and stoic like he was trying to prepare himself for what he might have to face.

I squared my shoulders and balled my fists at my sides, remembering the red-headed vampire sinking his teeth into Becks' neck while Dorian sat there watching him, Becks' blood still wet on his tongue as I came into the room. I wanted revenge, but I knew Derrick and the team needed answers as to how and why the vamps had been attacking Becks. As soon as we got those answers, I had some wicked plans of my own, and I reveled in them as we got in the elevator and the doors closed behind us.

"You can act on your vengeance as much as you want, but only after we get the answers we've come here for," Derrick said with a smile that betrayed him.

"You want blood too," I said as we came to an unspoken agreement through eye contact alone, a gruesome and violent plan forming between our minds as we waited for the elevator doors to open back up.

THE LAST TIME I was here, the bottom of the steps had led into a big open space that was steadily being renovated and upgraded from the dirt walls and floors of packed earth. This time, it couldn't have looked any more different from those humble beginnings.

Marble was everywhere, lining the floors and up the sides of the walls. Even the impossibly tall ceiling was covered in the stuff. Hanging from the beams overhead that stretched from one side of the enormous space to the other were lights strung up on long braided ropes that were giving off an incredible amount of heat, and it didn't take me long to figure out what they were used for.

Spaced methodically, every few feet were giant rectangular planter boxes, made from marble as well, that had plants and trees growing out of them despite their depth below ground. The boxes formed a bunch of different pathways, and I found I was glad Derrick knew his way around down here because I would've been lost otherwise.

I'd been expecting to see at least a few vampires milling about their grand entryway, but instead, the place was deserted without a single vampire around.

"Where are they?" I asked Derrick, fists still balled, thinking the vamps were probably waiting to lure us into one of their traps and spring out at us as soon as an opportunity presented itself.

"I don't know," he said through clenched teeth, obviously thinking along the same lines as I was.

We traversed the space, turning this way and that before we finally came to a set of doors that were taller than most homes. They were made of carved metal depicting some kind of purgatory, but I didn't pay too much attention to them as Derrick busted through.

We entered a room dominated by a bunch of thrones placed in a giant circle formation. Each one was somewhat different from the next, each vampire elder wanting themselves represented as unique to the others if I had to guess. There was no denying this was where the elders lived out their fantasies of ruling the world, although even I could remember a time when they didn't exist. Vampires were still a relatively new species in the grand scheme of things, but that didn't stop the bloodsuckers from pretending like they were a sacred gift to the world.

"There's no one here," Derrick said as we made our way to the center of the room and glanced around us. "Where could they have all gone?"

'Becks, tell the chief the vamps are missing,' I thought toward Becks, showing her all we'd seen and what was going on.

I didn't have to wait too long before I got an answer. *'He said we're going to look into it from this end and for you guys to keep exploring to see if you can find anything there.'*

'Got it,' Derrick finally joined the conversation.

I followed Derrick through the rest of the vampires' coven, but after a long search, we'd come up empty of any clues. Derrick said the last place we had to check was down some stairs and was a place the vamps used for storage. As soon as we opened the doors, a stench crept into my nose that only grew stronger the further we went, and when we finally got to the bottom of the steps, I almost couldn't believe my elf eyes.

There, tossed absentmindedly in giant piles, were human bodies too numerous to count, and the smell was absolutely revolting.

"What the ever titty-loving fuck is this?" I asked as I tried to keep myself from breathing in through my nose, but doing so through my mouth didn't seem to be going over any better either.

Derrick, with a gut like steel, walked over to the closest pile and started examining the bodies closely. He didn't touch them, but he did turn his head sideways a few times, shifting his focus from one body to another before he turned his gaze to me.

"It looks like they've all been bitten," Derrick said, stating the obvious, and I rolled my eyes before he continued. "Problem is, all of their mouths seem like they have blood in them."

His words gave me pause, and I stared at him questioningly.

"Like they were trying to turn these humans into vampires," he said. "That's the only reason they'd have blood in their mouths."

"So, all these people are failed attempts at making new vamps?" I asked him, the shock of the realization sending a wave of nausea through me, amplified by the smell I just couldn't get used to.

"That's what it looks like," Derrick said as he crossed his arms over his chest. "But it doesn't make sense. If a vamp bites a human and then gives them some of their blood, they start the transition instantly. They don't die. They become immortal."

"Well, these fuckers are *nowhere* near immortal."

"Come on, we're not going to learn anything else down here. Let's head back up and wait for Adam and Tyler," Derrick said as we started heading toward the surface, milling over everything we'd seen and the number of new questions we now had to consider.

∽

WE'D ALMOST MADE it out of the cavernous main room to the elevator when something caught Derrick's eye. As he moved cautiously toward it, I followed closely behind him and readied myself for whatever was there behind the large planter.

On the ground, struggling to move, a vampire laid on his back, and the relief that washed over his face was visibly apparent. He released a heavy sigh but met us with an accusatory glare.

"Where have you been?" he asked through panting breaths, and I visually inspected him, but could find no outward signs as to why he seemed like he was dying.

"What do you mean, vamp?" Derrick asked, anger evident in his voice.

"My sire's been trying to reach you for so long," the vampire said wistfully, his gaze losing focus a few times in the few seconds it took him to speak.

Derrick picked him up and propped his back against the planter, squatting down to look the vamp in his unreal bright blue eyes.

"What are you talking about? What's your name? What's going on around here?" Derrick asked, trying to get some kind of information out of him.

"I'm Elliot. My sire, Octavius, has been trying to reach the hunters for help. But all of his requests were denied or ignored," Elliot choked out so slowly it was painful to listen to.

Derrick scoffed. "That doesn't happen. Hunters answer every call, even when nothing is going on to warrant our intervention."

"Lies," Elliot said, and I shared a confused look with Derrick.

"Hey," I shouted, getting the bloodsucker's attention to keep him from passing out, "what did he want help with?"

"Octavius didn't want to die," Elliot said. "But now look at him. Gone, just like the others."

"What others? Where are all the elders?" Derrick asked as he shook Elliot some so he'd reopen his eyes.

Seeming dazed and confused for a second before he remembered what was going on, Elliot replied, "They're either dead, or they've fled. Elders are being targeted and killed off, their entire line dying off with them, as you can see." He made a half-assed gesture to his physical form over a disingenuous laugh.

"Why? Who's targeting them?" I asked.

"We're doomed," Elliot said with an eye roll before he scrunched his face up in pain, a bellowing cough tearing through his whole body.

"Who's targeting the elders?" Derrick asked sternly, his level of frustration reaching a tipping point I could feel.

"A hunter," Elliot said. "A hunter is trying to end our species."

Without another moment passing, Elliot dissolved into a pile of ash right before our eyes. Derrick and I shared a bewildered glance with each other as we tried to comprehend the implications of the vampire's last words.

"Come on, if we missed that fucker, we might've missed others," Derrick said as he turned on his heel, and we started scouring the coven once more with renewed effort, hoping someone down there was alive enough to explain what Elliot had said.

CHAPTER 8

BECKS

My eyes were starting to burn from lack of sleep, but I kept them open as best I could while Otto led me through Binaria West's headquarters. The place was gigantic, and no matter how hard I tried to form a mental map of the lengthy hallways we strode down, my mind just couldn't keep up.

After what felt like forever and a weird mental conversation with Brax about floating dead people, we came to a room with double doors made of pure gold. Glyphs of some kind were etched all over its surface that looked remarkably similar to Derrick's and Adam's tattoos, and even though I had no idea what they meant, I felt a strange pull toward them, almost as if they were begging me to read them.

"What does this say?" I asked Otto as he stood in front of the doors and stared down at me.

"This is the language of the hunters. It's as old as our entire species, and you'll need to learn it over time, but those lessons can wait until things have calmed down some. The writing here is a quote given to the first generation of hunters, and basically translates to: 'With the blessing of life comes the curse of purpose. With our angelic and demonic blood flowing through your veins, you, the hunter, are charged with ensuring balance throughout the five realms, as well as within yourself. For no one can seek to amend the balance of others without first being balanced themselves.

Opposite and equal trials of excellence and failure, calmness and turmoil, and silence and noise are key to fulfilling your purpose. Through pleasure and pain, love and hate, good and evil, a path is forged through your soul. One which you owe your life's very existence to seek out, follow, protect, and maintain. For it is this path, the one made by your soul, and shaped by your past that will ensure your future, and a future for all.'"

I stood dumbfounded for a time as I processed the words Otto spoke, imagining I could actually feel the hefty weight they carried settling somewhere in a spot deep within me that had always existed but never before been explored.

Otto chuckled, probably because my mouth was hanging open like a dumbass as I rubbed at the spot on my chest, where the words felt like they'd physically punctured me. As he pushed the door on the right open, he said, "I always love seeing people's reactions to hearing or reading those doors for the first time. It's always the same. Come through here."

I didn't think I could talk then, so I followed him into the room silently with my eyes on the floor. The darkness of the place confused me as I walked in, and when I looked up, my mouth hung open all over again.

A set of scales as large as a two or three-story building towered in front of me, gleaming in a shimmery blue light it seemed to radiate of its own accord. The scales were made of solid gold, just like the doors to this room, and even though there was nothing on either side to weigh it down, one of the enormous plates was hanging far lower than the other, resting about five feet from the ground. The plate's twin hung high in the air, the bar that it clung to nearly reaching the ceiling with the degree of its tilt.

"Rebecca, let me introduce you to the scales of balance. This is how we know how good of a job we're doing. Or not," Otto said, and for the life of me, I couldn't close my mouth as I took in the enormous structure before me. "As you can see, we've got a problem."

"You don't say?" I said sarcastically as I considered Otto.

He didn't call me on my sarcasm. Instead, he smiled gently and tucked his hands in the pockets of his khakis.

"How do you know which side represents good and which side represents evil?" I asked when I glanced back at the scales seeing no way to differentiate between them. Then glancing around the rest of the room, I asked, "And how the hell did you guys get this thing in here, anyway?"

With a humorous smile, Otto said, "Angels and demons, the makers of our kind, and the first generation of hunters worked together to build Binaria West's headquarters around the scales. They never wanted future generations to question where the balance stood. All you need to do to see what's weighing on the balance is tap into your power, and you'll see what I see."

Bewilderment only delayed me for a second, but soon enough, I reached into myself and grabbed hold of my power, that ball of purple-ish blue that surrounds and protects my soul. Within an instant, I could see things moving over the surface of the plate closest to the ground, things that were no doubt going to give me nightmares if I ever made it back to sleep.

Black and writhing, slimy-looking, and ominous tendrils of something sinister twisted about on the plate, forming one shape before falling into itself and rising again to create another. The first image shown was a man choking the life out of a woman. But that could barely register in my brain before the tendrils were liquefying at the bottom only to rise and solidify in another haunting image, one of fangs and feathers that caused my heart to race and sweat to form on my skin.

"See what I mean?" Otto pulled my gaze back to him, and I was grateful I wasn't seeing the black substance anymore.

"Um, yeah," I said, gulping my fear down.

"The evil side of the scales has dropped significantly since this afternoon, and I'm assuming it has something to do with the closed portals your team found."

Fear of an impending apocalypse spread through me, and I knew it was probably written all over my face. "Why aren't you panicking right now? I mean, how long till the world goes up in flames? Because it doesn't look like we've got that much time!"

"I wouldn't be able to do my job if I panicked every time the scales tipped. There is reason to be alarmed, yes, and reason to act quickly on whatever it is we need to do, but fear will only slow us down. You need to remember that," he said, and a wave of guilt washed over me for my reaction, but I ignored it since Otto kept talking.

"No, the scales have never been this far out of balance before, but I still have hope in everything we're doing, and everything Binaria East is doing as well. They have a scale like this one over in their hemisphere, and lucky for them, I don't think they have a traitor in their midst. Which is probably what's keeping us afloat, so to speak."

"Alright. Okay," I said as I scrubbed a hand down my face then planted my fists on my hips. "What do we need to do?"

Brax busted into my thoughts then talking about missing vampires, and once a plan had been made, Otto led me away from the scales that terrified me without answering the question I'd asked before.

'On to other things, I guess,' I thought as I almost had to run to keep up with Otto as he sped through hallway after hallway with barely a thought given to the people we passed and the weird looks they were giving us. I just hoped none of them attacked me since it could very well seem like I was chasing the chief through headquarters. But I instantly dismissed the idea and laughed at my wayward thoughts because there was no way anyone could think I was capable of causing Otto any harm.

OTTO RUSHED us down into the depths of Binaria West after a few confusing mental conversations that left me with more questions than answers. We were headed to what Otto and Derrick had called the water cells, and as I stepped into the long dark hallway illuminated by blue light shining through twenty or so fish tank looking things, the name made more sense.

There were literal mermaids, one per watery cell staring out at us as we passed, anger and hostility radiating off of them. The mermaids were absolutely gorgeous, breathtakingly beautiful, which for some reason, I kind of expected. However, when I came upon my first merman, I almost wanted to jump backward with the shock of how grotesque he was.

Seeing my reaction and guessing correctly at my thoughts, Otto said, "Yeah, the Mer species has some odd features. Where their females are beautiful, with voices like angels, their males are the complete opposite, with their only musical ability being that of playing underwater instruments. You should hear their symphonies though, mighty powerful those things."

"What does music have to do with anything?" I asked as I looked closer at the fishtails swimming before me, taking in their iridescent sheen and captivating colors.

Otto laughed and said, "Oh, everything if you're a merperson." He chuckled a little as if I was missing something. "You see, merpeople create specific atmospheres wherever they are, simply by using their power of music. And it can make those around them feel whatever the merperson wants them to feel, sadness, happiness, lust, anything. They feed off the energy they create with their music, which in turn allows them to live. They literally can't live without music, or they'll wither away and die. If they were singing right now or playing a conch shell, we wouldn't be able to hear it out here because the glass is too thick, but between the cells is thinner so they can hear and feed off of each other rather than us."

"That's pretty freaking cool," I said as I stared at a particular mermaid, and she stared back at me through the thick glass between us.

"Yeah, it can be when it's used for good, as any power is, I suppose," Otto's thoughts seemed to turn inward for a second before he turned to me, a new idea fresh on his face. "Did you ever hear stories of mermaids luring human men to their deaths as you were growing up?"

"Yes, I read an anthology about merfolk lore in the asylum. It was one of the books that had escaped the psychologists' notice. Why?"

"Well, I don't know how much of what you read was truth or fantasy, but in reality, a long time ago, mermaids did try to lure human men. But not to their deaths at first. You see, human men are much more attractive than mermen, as you can tell."

I nodded my agreement but suddenly felt sorry for the mermen, given their inability to control something so basic as what they looked like.

"Mermaids started trying to strike up relationships with humans, but quite a few were captured in the process, and some terrible fates befell them. Some, for example, were made the headliners of a few circus sideshows where they were kept like caged animals, rather than a human's magic-laced, water-loving counterpart. It was disgusting behavior by the humans, truly."

"Magic-laced, water-loving counterparts?" I asked, wondering what he was talking about.

"Oh, right. You don't know," Otto laughed. "Merfolk are basically just humans with fishtails. They have a touch of magic, but so do most humans. They have souls, so we protect them almost as much as we protect humans. However, since merfolk have a touch more magic than humans, we generally don't have to intervene on their behalf as much."

"Um, okay."

"Anyway, well, a long time ago when all this was happening, word got around through the waters what the humans were doing to their sisters, and all hell broke loose. Mermaids started working together to lure human men, mainly sailors, to their deaths. They'd attract them by song and beauty, and when the men fell head over heels, the mermaids would drown them in retaliation."

"Jeezus," I said, eyes wide as I regarded Otto.

He laughed some at my reaction but continued his lesson anyway. "Yeah, it was getting pretty bad there for a while, so we had to intervene to prevent a full-on war between the humans and the merpeople. Basically, the law states that merfolk must keep their presence from human knowledge, or those found to be in contact with them are sentenced to time here, as you can see," he gestured toward the merfolk around us. "After a few separate offenses, they are sentenced to life here, though not many make that mistake more than once."

It seemed a pretty steep penalty to me for merely interacting with humans, but I was in no position to question the laws the hunters had made, seeing as how I didn't know any of them.

A few minutes later, Brax, Derrick, Adam, and Tyler all came into existence in the hallway with us, Derrick dragging two bodies in each of his hands, and Tyler struggling to keep a slippery merman from getting out of his grasp.

"Put him in this cell here," Otto pointed to an empty water cell off to our left. Tyler vanished, and within a few seconds, the merman was imprisoned, and Tyler was right back where he'd disappeared from.

"That's the Mer king's top guard, and he needs to be interrogated to find out what he knows because he's definitely holding something important back from us," Tyler said with annoyance, and with wide eyes I glanced back at the ugly merman, finally noticing his getup.

He was dressed with golden armor that shimmered like the scales of his tail, and as his eyes landed on me, I felt something twist in my stomach that I couldn't explain, so I swiftly turned back to the group.

The two men Derrick still held had a smell that was starting to reach my nose, and I pulled my shirt up in front of my face to try and stem the stench before it got too bad, and tried to keep myself from freaking out about the fact that no one seemed to be fazed by it.

"This one," Derrick lifted one of the bodies by the shirt he was dragging them by as he said, "was a human and still has blood on his lips. This one," he made the same motion with the other body, "is a vamp I knocked unconscious. He was hiding behind the pile of bodies like the coward he is. I think his name is Mikeal or some such shit.

He's the only elder we found in the whole coven. The rest we think have either been killed or have fled for some reason." Derrick looked down at the vampire in question with disgust, and I tried to keep myself from throwing up.

"Alright, thanks boys," Otto said with a hefty sigh. "Let's take the vamp to his cell and the human to the chemist. Hopefully, he'll be able to tell us what went wrong with the change. Fergus won't be back until tomorrow to examine the body, and I'm sure you guys are beat. So, after we get these two where they need to go, I want you guys to take the rest of the night off. For that matter, come in late tomorrow too. But stay in one of the cabins, so you're not too far away if I need you."

With that being said, everyone moved silently, seeming lost in their own thoughts as we delivered the bodies and jumped to a cabin on Binaria West's grounds.

It wasn't the same one we'd stayed in before, and when I asked about it, Adam said it was because all the other cabins were full right then. This one was just a small one-room building, and though it had everything we'd need as far as a bathroom and a fully stocked kitchen, there was only one big bed in the corner, and soon I started wondering what the sleeping arrangements were going to be. There wasn't but one small loveseat and hardly any floor space to speak of.

Picking up on my thoughts, Brax announced, "Becks and I get the bed. You fuckers can figure out the rest yourselves."

The guys laughed good-naturedly, and I noticed how tired they all looked as well as how tired I felt. It'd been a long ass day, and after I finally relieved myself in the bathroom, I curled up in the bed, called my power with the intention of sleeping so I wouldn't astral project during the night, and fell asleep the instant my head hit the pillow.

CHAPTER 9

DERRICK

"She looks so peaceful," Adam said almost to himself as he laid at the foot of the bed, staring up at Becks' sleeping form. Brax was snoring in front of her, and Tyler laid on the bed behind her back while I sat on the couch going over the day in my mind.

My eyes shifted over to Becks, and a feeling I couldn't name tugged on my heart as it did every time I saw her. She'd had a long day, and I knew the ones ahead of us weren't going to be much better, given everything that was going on, and some part of me simply wanted to shelter her from all of it, despite how much I knew she needed to be there.

I was too tired to argue, so I addressed Tyler as nicely and normally as I could because it had to be done. "Tyler, I know you just got comfortable, but Becks is going to need some fresh clothes and stuff for tomorrow. Can you make a quick trip to the safehouse for what she'll need? We'll all need stuff, but you don't have to worry about ours if you don't want to, just hers."

Tyler looked over at me, and without a word, he disappeared from his spot on the bed. A selfish and territorial part of me wanted to claim his vacated spot behind Becks, but I held myself back. That would, without question, start a fight, and I didn't have the energy for it. With everything that'd happened today, I was willing to do anything to make sure my team rested up well because I knew we'd need stamina tomorrow.

"Do you think we can have her ready for the gauntlet in time? I mean, with everything else we've got going on, we haven't been able to train her hardly at all," Adam said, and I knew the fear that was growing within him. It was growing in me as well.

Adam lived for training and knew full well what was expected of any initiate. Even though Becks was more powerful than any other initiate we'd ever heard of, that alone wasn't going to be enough for her to deal with everything she was going to have to face in the gauntlet.

"I really don't know. I've been trying to think of ways to squeeze in training sessions for us, but so far, it hasn't been possible."

Adam sighed as he laid his head on his arm, still staring at Becks as I saw his eyes getting heavy, worry lines creasing his brow as I knew he was trying to think through our dilemma. "Well, we'd better figure it out soon. I'm not willing to lose her," he said after a few minutes as he reached out a hand and placed it on Becks' foot where it laid outside the covers.

"Me either," I replied, but I was pretty sure he was already asleep by the time I said it.

A few minutes later, Tyler popped into the room with four duffle bags and dropped them without care before he crawled back in the bed with Becks and curled up behind her, wrapping an arm around her middle. Jealousy spread through me for an instant before I checked myself, and instead of remarking on how comfortable he was getting with Becks, I said, "Thank you for getting everyone's things. You didn't have to do that."

"I just would've had to go back in the morning anyway. This saved me a trip. Now shut up and go to sleep," he said, but I could tell there was a smile on his face at my gratitude, and for a second I let myself believe everything was going to work out between us before I fell asleep too.

~

I WOKE the next morning to my phone ringing loudly in my pocket. No one but the chief and my dads ever called this number, so I felt my hand slip my phone out and answer it before I really even thought about it.

"Hello?" I asked, eyes still closed, wanting nothing more than for the call to be over so I could go back to sleep.

"Boy, it's nearly noon, what are you doing still sleeping?" Liam's voice boomed in my ear, and I groaned my response as I made myself get up, knowing this wasn't going to be a short conversation. I'd been avoiding their calls for the past couple days, not knowing how they'd take the news of everything that'd been going on. Though now seemed like as good a time as any to fulfill my obligatory info dump on my dads.

"Don't growl at Liam, it's a good question," Chester said. I was apparently on speaker-phone with all of them like always.

"I am asleep at noon because I was awake for almost twenty-four hours straight yesterday, is that a good enough reason for you guys?" I wasn't trying to sound like an asshole, it's just how I felt right then, being berated as soon as I woke up.

Brock laughed his deep-chested laugh, and despite myself, I started smiling, hearing it as I started making the pot of coffee I was going to need for this conversation. "Oh, you had one of those days," Brock said, and I nodded to no one.

"Yeah, it's been one thing after another, and I honestly didn't think yesterday was going to end." I chuckled as the coffee started pouring into the glass pot.

"I remember one time, Will, your mom, and the rest of us were on missions for nearly three days straight!" Chester said. "When we were finally finished, I think we slept that long afterward, too."

I heard laughter in the background and Liam saying something the rest of my dads thought was funny, but he was too far away from the phone for me to make out what he'd said.

"Alright, tell us about this Becks chick and that familiar of hers. All you told us the other day was that they were coming onto your team. We need details now, boy," Brock came through loud and clear. He had his classic fake-stern tone going on, so even though it might've sounded like he was displeased, I knew better. He was using his stern voice because he was genuinely concerned and really wanted an answer.

"We're in one of the one-room cabins on Binaria West, and they're all still sleeping. I don't want to wake them up. Tell me what's going on with you guys while this coffee brews, and when it's done, I'll go outside to talk to you."

"Well, if it's noon for you, it's noon for them too. Wake their asses up, I wanna talk to them," Liam said as he came back to the phone, a smile evident in his voice, and I rolled my eyes and ignored him as Chester spoke up.

"Nah, I want the lowdown Derrick'll give us when no one's listening. Let the boy get his coffee and talk shit," he said, and I chuckled some more picturing the shortest of my dads putting the others in their place.

"You always were the smartest of us," Brock said as I heard him pat Chester on the back loudly.

"Dammit, Brock," Chester admonished, "how many times do I have to tell you not everyone is half Viking and can handle your big ass love taps? They feel like getting beat with a baseball bat, you ham-handed fuck."

Laughing while finally filling my cup of coffee, I said, "Alright, I'm headed outside now."

"Good, now tell us about this girl and her mutt familiar. The hell does that mean, anyway?" Chester said as I pulled the front door of the cabin closed behind me as softly as I could, the chill in the air making goosebumps rise on my chest and arms. I'd taken my shirt off to sleep last night, and now I wished I had it on but wasn't willing to risk waking everyone so I could go get it. I took a seat on one of the rocking chairs on the porch and settled in, taking some of the first glorious sips of coffee before I answered.

"Alright, what do you guys want to know?" I asked, knowing my question would rile them up.

"Everything."

"What do you mean, what do we want to know? Tell us everything, boy!"

"Boy, if you don't start talking…"

They all started in on me, talking at once, but it just brought a smile to my face as the pain of missing them was eased by hearing their voices.

"Fine, fine, okay. I'll tell you. Calm your tits."

"Calm my what? Boy, who have you been hanging out with?"

CHAPTER 10

BECKS

The smell of coffee woke me up, and even though I wasn't a coffee drinker, for some reason, I wanted nothing more in that moment than a fresh cup of the stuff. I opened my eyes and saw that everyone was still sleeping, except for Derrick, who seemed to be missing.

Tyler was curled around me, hugging me tightly as Brax snored in front of me. Adam was holding onto my calf as if it were his huggy pillow, and the sight made me giggle a little.

Noticing I really had to pee, and wanting to get that cup of coffee, I carefully climbed out of bed, making sure I didn't wake any of the guys as I moved. At the foot of the bed on the floor laid all of our duffels. I hoped I'd find my toothbrush in mine so I could kill two birds with one stone. Sifting through my bag, I smiled when I saw it, grabbed it, and headed to the bathroom.

After handling things as quickly and quietly as I could, I came back out wearing some new clothes, feeling more refreshed than I thought was possible. I heard Derrick's voice outside as I poured myself a cup of coffee. It sounded like he was on the phone, but he was laughing, and something was drawing me toward the sound strongly as if I didn't have a choice in the matter. I pulled the throw blanket off the back of the loveseat and wrapped it around my shoulders before I grabbed my coffee and headed out the door quietly.

When I poked my head out the door, I motioned to Derrick, asking silently if it was okay that I joined him, and he nodded at me with a questioning glare as if I was crazy to even think of asking the question.

As soon as I sat down in the rocking chair next to Derrick, I placed my coffee on the small table between us, pulled my legs up to my chest, and wrapped the blanket around me tighter. The chill of the afternoon was potent, and I shivered some as I watched Derrick pull the phone from his ear and put it on speaker.

"Becks just came outside, guys," Derrick said, and I looked at him like he'd lost his mind. I guess he didn't know I had an aversion to talking to people I didn't know, so I couldn't exactly be mad at him, but I really didn't like being put on the spot without a clue as to who I was talking to.

"Becks, hi!"

"Hey, there!"

"Sup."

I heard three distinct voices. They each sounded way too chipper for how early it felt even though I knew it was afternoon, but I found myself saying, "hi," anyway.

"We're Derrick's dads. I'm sure you've heard of us by now," one voice said, and I looked at Derrick, mouthing the word, 'dads?' and he smiled and nodded at me in response.

"Um, well. No. I haven't heard of you yet," I said, feeling like I might hurt their feelings, but not willing to lie either.

"What? Derrick! Come on!" another voice yelled, and Derrick laughed beside me as a smile curved my lips at the sound.

"Well, you're in for a treat, little one, let me tell you," yet another voice said that had me laughing right along with Derrick.

"Yeah, we're awesome. I was telling Derrick before you came out that we're going to have to meet you and your familiar soon. We don't like not knowing who's in his life, you see," one of the voices said.

Without thinking, I heard myself saying, "I'd love to meet you guys," marveling at the fact that I actually meant it.

"Alright, well, we're throwing a barbeque at our house tomorrow night. You all should come by," someone else said, and Derrick rolled his eyes.

"I already told you we'd come if we have time, Liam," Derrick said, and I heard someone start laughing on the other end of the phone.

"Well, now that someone else knows about it, you might actually show up this time, Derrick. Becks, make sure you come by, okay? We're kicking everything off here at eight sharp, do you understand?"

'So that's where he got it from,' I thought to myself. I'd heard that same thing from Derrick before. The 'do you understand' thing seemed to be ingrained in his vocabulary, and just like when Derrick said it, I didn't sense any malice. It simply seemed as if they were seeking clarification.

"I understand, and I'll do my best to make sure we can make it," I said, fully intending on meeting the men that raised Derrick into the man who sat beside me, staring at me with an expression I couldn't name.

"Okay, well, we'll see you then. Bye snookums!" one of them said, and Derrick's face turned bright red at the name, causing laughter to bubble up out of me as the line went dead, the phone call apparently over.

I was laughing at Derrick's expense, and I didn't mind at all since he was smiling right back at me. We fell into a companionable silence for a while after my giggles died off, and I sipped more of my coffee, listening to the sounds of seagulls screeching in the wind and waves crashing in the distance.

"Would you tell me about them?" I asked quietly, hoping he wouldn't think I was prying. I just really wanted to know who I'd been talking to and who I was going to be meeting tomorrow if I had anything to do with it.

Derrick repositioned himself in his rocker and leaned forward, elbows resting on his knees as he got this faraway look in his eyes and started talking more than I'd ever heard him speak before.

"They're my dads. I had four of them and a mom." I tried not to dwell on the word 'had' as he spoke.

"I'll start this way," he said. "I remember this one day, so clearly as if it were yesterday. I don't know why, because it was just like any other day, but it's stayed with me anyway. I woke up to my alarm clock that morning as usual and started getting ready for school at the academy like I usually would. I was running behind, like always, and as I was running down the stairs, I heard Liam say, 'I thought you'd never get down here.'"

He'd changed his voice to mimic whoever Liam was, and I smiled because I thought he was making an accurate impression of one of the voices I'd heard.

"I was taking the stairs two at a time and nearly fell down as I got to the bottom and then rushed to the kitchen table."

"Brock said, 'Breakfast is at seven a.m., Bud, you're late,' even though I was fully dressed, hair combed, teeth brushed, and shoes shined at six fifty-nine." He laughed some to himself as he reminisced.

"Chester said, 'If you're early, you're on time. If you're on time, you're late.' And I remember he was smirking at me. His glasses were sliding down his nose, and he winked at me over the edge of his newspaper."

"Will came over then and put a plate of food in front of me and joined in with the others. He said something like, 'I hope it's not cold already. You know, if you'd been down here earlier, your sausage and eggs might still be scalding.'"

We both laughed at that before Derrick kept talking.

"My mom busted in then and got onto all of them, one-upping them like the pro she was. She said, uh, something like, 'Guys, leave our boy alone.' She rubbed some hair out of my face and said, 'You can't expect a boy with these gorgeous locks to ever be on time. Primping in front of the mirror is time well spent in my book.' She always laughed at her own jokes, and we'd all just stare at her when she did because she had the prettiest laugh."

I wouldn't dare speak up now and ruin the flow he had going.

"All my dads gave me shit, but I've never doubted their love for me; they're the ones that forged me into the leader I am today. I've still got a lot to learn. I mean, I've got some pretty big shoes to fill, and I'm messing up regularly, but I'm trying, at least.

It wasn't always easy, though. Growing up with a mom and four dads was unusual, even for the hunter community at the time, and I took my fair share of blows from a few closed-minded bullies about it, but I wouldn't have changed it for anything.

As I grew up, I got questioned less and less about my family situation as fewer and fewer hunter females were passing the gauntlet. Now, those same bullies that used to fuck with me are seeing the value in my parents' kind of relationship. Available female hunters are a rarity, so a lot of guys have chosen to share. Of course, there are still those couples that don't want or desire that kind of lifestyle, but the point is that nowadays, that kind of thing is way more common and understood.

Of the four men in my mom's harem, we don't know or care who my biological father is. I never call any of them 'dad' to their face. In reality, I seem to have features and mannerisms from each of them. They are all my dads, and all of them treat me like their son.

I don't think my mom would've been with them otherwise.

She was our rock," Derrick said, and I was utterly lost in the words flowing from his mouth, picturing him as a little kid surrounded by people that loved him. "I watched each of them adore her, and I never fought my own adoration when I started following in their footsteps. When she passed, I think we all died inside some." He paused for a second, his mind lost to memories I found myself wanting to protect him from.

"Will didn't make it six months past her death before he decided to join her. A single shot to the head was his one-way ticket back to her.

When he died too, the rest of us... we just crumbled.

They doubled down on protecting and loving me and each other after that. They're really the closest group of men I've ever met, and when they set their minds on something, they rarely let it go. They're retired from active service with the hunters, and unless they're out with their motorcycle gang or getting fucked up on fairy wine, they are all up in my business. I know it's because they care, but sometimes it can feel a little suffocating.

They're always like, 'What's that hothead Tyler done this time, I could use a laugh. Has Adam had any more visions you need to be concerned about? When are you gonna get some time off to come see your dads? Do we need to talk to the chief for you? Oh, I don't think ol' Otto wants to hear what we have to say. I don't remember ever being as busy as you are all the time. Why back in our day...'

The questions are never-ending, and sometimes they're downright annoying, but I love 'em. And I know I need to spend more time with 'em, I just..." Derrick's voice broke off as he looked up and seemed confused, almost as if he'd forgotten I was sitting there listening to him reminisce.

"Thanks for telling me all that," I said sincerely, reaching out a hand to rest on his shoulder.

"Are your mom and Will not in Heaven or Hell?" I asked, wondering how all this worked since it seemed like there would be no need to feel so heartsick if he could simply pop up to Heaven and see them whenever he wanted.

"Becks, Heaven and Hell aren't like the Earth and the Veil. They're both labyrinths for the newly deceased. And a person's version of Heaven or Hell is unique to the individual person experiencing it. For the first century or so after you die, your soul doesn't even know it's dead. If you've made it to Heaven, you'll relive all the best days of your life over and over again. It's nearly the same thing in Hell. You'll relive the worst days of your life over and over.

Until one day, your soul will eventually realize what's going on, and you'll ascend to live with all the other souls that have ascended from their personal afterlives. It's like communal living with angels and demons at that point, and everybody is weird.

Until then, until that day that your soul realizes it's dead, unless there are some extreme extenuating circumstances, nothing can stop the loop you're living in. I can't even break into my mother's Heaven to tell her she's dead. It's against the rules, even if I could find her. Your parents' souls were one of those extra special circumstances. It'd been cleared with the higher-ups for the hunters to try and find them, but nothing has ever come of it."

Taking a breath, he said, "I'm sorry it's not as cut and dry as you initially thought it would be."

I nodded at him past the lump in my throat, and said, "I'm sorry I asked and made you think through that possibility. I didn't mean to upset you."

Fake laughing to try and brush it off as no big deal, Derrick got up and stretched, saying, "Don't worry about it. I've known how it works my whole life. And for the record, I think my dads will love you. You'll meet them tomorrow, and you'll see what I'm talking about."

He walked inside then, shutting the door behind him, and for a second there, I was anxious that I might have somehow overstepped. I didn't force him to tell me all that, but I hadn't stopped him either. But after a minute or so, he came back out with a fresh cup of coffee and sat down next to me again.

"Enjoy your cup before it gets cold. We don't have long before we have to leave again," he said, and I knew my stern-faced Derrick was fully back in place, ready to face reality.

CHAPTER 11

ADAM

*L*ast night was the most sleep I'd gotten in a while, and I was pretty sure it had everything to do with the fact that Becks was sleeping so close to me. Usually, I had a hard time getting to sleep, and an even harder time staying that way. Nightmares can be a bitch like that. But somehow, I didn't have any problems last night, and the realization that she had that kind of power over me did some weird things to my mind.

When it comes to self-preservation, your body is capable of incredible things, sometimes even terrible things, all just to ensure your survival. I actually had to have a talk with myself for a while after I woke up because my body and mind were irrationally freaking out about how well I'd slept. It'd been so good for me that my animal brain decided we needed to do whatever it took to ensure it happened every night. Like it got a taste of healthy sleep and was unwilling to go back to what I'd dealt with every other night.

An overwhelming part of me, a section of my brain large enough to cause real concern, made it its whole mission in life to figure out and plan a set of actions that would lead to Becks sleeping next to me from now on. But I thought if I put any kind of action behind my thoughts, I would be acting selfishly somehow.

However, I still felt almost panicky at the thought of trying to sleep without her again. Last night was an unusual circumstance, and I couldn't very well go around demanding sleeping arrangements first thing in the morning. I'd sound like a nutjob. Not to mention the fact that when Becks finally invited me into her bed for real, I wouldn't let it be for a reason as stupid as keeping my nightmares away.

So, despite how much my monkey brain kept going back to how to preserve future sleep-filled nights, I ignored it as much as possible as we met the chief again in his office.

"Hey, Dragon team," he said, standing from his desk as we appeared, and I noticed he looked like he still hadn't slept at all.

Brax flew right over to him, noticing the same thing I had and pulled at his cheeks, surprising our chief for a moment while Becks giggled at his antics beside me.

"Chief, you need sleep. Want me to knock you out?" Brax asked as he backed up some but still hovered in front of the chief with his hands on his hips, big gray wings flapping thoughtlessly behind him so little bursts of air were lifting and moving some of the papers on the chief's desk.

Chief smiled and patted Brax on the shoulder. "As soon as I'm done talking to you guys, I'm going straight to that couch over there for a few hours. No need to knock me out, Brax, but thanks anyway."

He walked over to us then and said, "Your prisoners are still waiting to be interrogated, and Fergus is already knee-deep in the human's autopsy. He also took a blood sample from your vamp for some reason?" He asked that part like a question he thought we'd know the answer to, but seeing as how none of us spoke up, he continued undeterred.

"Who knows with that one," he said under his breath, but then looked at Becks. "My deputy chief is finally going to make a speech to the oldest initiates at the academy today. I've been pressuring her to do it for a while now, and I thought it'd be a good opportunity for you, Rebecca, since you guys are here anyway. I thought Tyler could take you to watch it while the rest of these guys go handle the prisoners. What do you think?"

Becks glanced around at each of us, and I, for one, nodded to her that I thought it was a good plan. Anything that prevented her from having to deal with more depressing shit was okay by me. The girl had been through too much already, and when it was possible, I wanted to ease her transition into this new life as best I could.

"Okay, we can do that," she made her decision, and I could practically feel Tyler preening off to the side. Sometimes being our team's only teleporter was a hassle for him. There were also times like right now, where I would've given anything to sit next to Becks in a darkened auditorium instead of dealing with prisoners.

"Oh, good," Chief said as he walked past us to lay on the couch by one of the windows. "I think the two of you will really hit it off nicely. Tina doesn't know much about you, but she's definitely curious to meet you since I told her I'd added somebody to Dragon team."

"Uh, okay," Becks said as we all watched the chief pull his jacket off and ball it up to use as a pillow before he laid his head down and closed his eyes.

We all just kind of stood there for a second before the chief cracked an eye open and said, "It starts in five minutes, you guys better get a move on."

His words triggered us all to move out of his office and into the hallway outside his door, a few chuckles escaping Brax as he said something I didn't quite hear to the chief. I listened to the chief's laughter in response as the door closed behind Brax, and when we all came back together, Derrick was right there ready and willing to dish out orders as usual.

"Tyler, go ahead and take Becks to the auditorium at the academy, we'll catch up with you guys later."

I watched as Becks slid her hand into Tyler's and faded from view before I turned my gaze back to Brax and Derrick.

"Alright, it'd probably be best if we split up too," Derrick said.

Without waiting to take a breath, Brax said, "I've got dibs on the vamp," causing Derrick and me to laugh softly.

"Okay, that'll work," Derrick said as he turned to me, and Brax disappeared, "which do you want? The Mer guard or dealing with Fergus and the dead human?"

Fergus was one of Binaria West's chemists/biologists. Basically, he was our eccentric live-in scientist, and not many of my teammates knew how to deal with his specific breed of weird. Especially Derrick, so I already knew I'd be handling Fergus so Derrick wouldn't have to.

"I'll take the dead guy," I said, and Derrick nodded at me, noticeably relieved, and we each headed off in different directions.

~

As I was getting closer to Fergus' lab, I could already hear him yelling about something.

"Well, this is just terrible! Who would do this? Why? No, no, no…" I heard him say as I entered the lab and saw him staring into his microscope, moving from foot to foot, clenching and unclenching his fists in front of him as he danced about.

"Anything I can help you with?" I cut off his soliloquy, startling him. He jumped at the sound of my voice and fell into his microscope, making it shake with the impact.

"Well, you could start by knocking! Geez, man." He straightened himself and pushed his glasses further up his nose. I knew for a fact he didn't need them. He just liked the way the glasses made him look. Those, coupled with his signature plaid button-downs and white lab coat, complete with a pocket protector, he was every bit the scientist he wanted the world to see him as.

"Actually, you should have been here hours ago. What took you so long?" Fergus made his way around the large table and over to the drawers beside the windows, not giving me the chance to answer before he started talking again.

"Nevermind, it doesn't matter. You're here now. Where's the rest of your team?"

Again, I knew better than to answer, he'd cut me off anyway, which is essentially why the other guys on my team hated dealing with Fergus in the first place. However, I knew if I let him rant and ramble, I could pick up what he was putting down, so to speak, without losing my temper.

"Off finding nymphs or something, like every other hunter, I presume. Whatever, let them get the tree sap for all I care. I've told every hunter not to proliferate with those randy spirits, but of course, no one listens to me. And you see, this is what happens!"

He hastily shoved a petri dish at me, and I took it to see what in the world he was talking about. There was clearly something staining the dish's surface, but it just looked like a blob of some kind to me, rather than anything meaningful. I glanced up at Fergus with a questioning glare, making him roll his eyes and sigh at me in return.

"Oh, come now. You must recognize this!"

I shrugged and offered him an apologetic smile, the best I could do given the circumstances.

"Fine, come with me," he said as he led me to the other side of the long room and pointed at the large television screen taking up residence along the far wall. "Watch the tv like a good little hunter, and I'll show you what you need to know." His chastisement didn't bother me at all because I knew he was getting to the good part now.

A few seconds later, an image showed on the screen that looked like healthy human blood cells. I might not've been a wiz at much, scientifically speaking, but I knew a red blood cell when I saw one.

"Okay, this, Hunter Adam of Dragon team, is an example of a few healthy human red blood cells. You see how they're all shaped like circles and slightly beveled?" he asked, and I didn't even bother nodding because he wasn't paying me any attention whatsoever.

Fergus was staring down at his microscope, talking through whatever his point was, and I really don't think it would've mattered if I was in the room or not. He'd be talking like this anyway. I just hoped he would stay on track with why I'd come to visit him in the first place.

Hastily removing one slide and putting in another, the image on the screen changed dramatically. I thought he was still showing me some kind of cells, but they most definitely were not human.

"These are the cells we had in storage from a healthy vampire," he said, and I heard myself making a 'huh' noise as I recorded the info in my mind.

The vampire cells were purple, jagged in shape and appearance, and were actually moving under the microscope. When I thought about it, it kind of made sense since vampires are immortal and what-not, but it was still surprising.

"Now, here's a blood sample from your dead human," Fergus said as he changed out the slide again, and my mouth dropped open as I listened to him. "As you can see, the human started the change, but somewhere in the process, all of his blood cells ruptured. That's why it looks like a red and purple massacre instead of cute little round balls of life."

"What does this mean, Fergus?" I asked, hoping I didn't throw him off too much by speaking.

He scoffed at me like I was missing something and said, "It means, Adam, that for some reason, none of those bodies in the covens' basement were able to change into vampires! Meaning, not only did the elders not drain them for food purposes, which I could at least understand because it keeps them healthy, but they also caused these humans to suffer through agony for weeks, if not a full month before the humans eventually died."

I turned to him then, the implications of what he was telling me worrying me and making me furious at the same time.

"There were a ton of bodies down there from what Derrick said. You think all of those humans died the same way?"

"Well, I tested the human's clothing as well and found several other samples to examine. Apparently, cells rub together when you pile bodies up," he said sarcastically. "Each of those samples had a different DNA profile, and every one of them resisted the change in this manner."

I turned back to the screen and found it hard to believe the elders had tried so many times when they had to have known, after a while at least, that their venom wasn't working anymore, that it was killing these humans instead of changing them. The thoughts made my stomach turn, so I asked the only logical question I could think of.

"Why couldn't they change? Can you tell that from what you've gathered from the victim?"

"Well, no. I couldn't figure out what was going wrong from the dead human. But I got to thinking that we had an elder in our cells, so being as wise as I am, I gathered a sample from him."

"What'd you find?"

Getting excited, which surprised me, given our circumstances, he said, "Look at what I found."

The next image on the screen showed jagged black cells, so dark I couldn't see through them at all like I could with the others.

"This is the elder's blood. It's been infected by some kind of virus. Look here," he said as he enhanced the image I was seeing. As the picture zoomed in, I saw dots of purple being wrapped up and swallowed by black spider looking things.

"What is that?" I asked.

Scoffing again, Fergus said, "That's a virus, like I said. Please pay attention. When I take one of these black *things* and put it on some healthy vampire tissue, watch what happens."

Purple cells started turning black right before my eyes at an alarming speed.

"Now, watch what happens when I place some of the infected vampire blood on some healthy human tissue." The bright red tissue started to change to purple, but almost instantly after that, I began to see black seeping in as well.

"Alright, so what does this mean?" I asked as I turned to face Fergus.

He took his glasses off his face, rubbing them clean with the bottom of his white lab coat as he answered me. "This means the end of the vampire species completely."

Shocked, I took a step toward him. "The scales are already too far out of balance to handle an entire species dying off. What do you mean, completely?"

Seeming more serious than I'd ever seen him, he gazed at me with big brown eyes. "Yes, completely. This virus is not only killing the humans the vampires are trying to change. Eventually, it kills off its host too. And we all know what happens when an elder dies..."

I finished his sentence for him, "His entire line, every vampire he's created, and every vampire they've created, dies with him."

"That's not the worst part though, Adam. The worst part is that the virus? It was made in a lab."

"Made in a lab?" I asked dumbfounded.

"Yes, it's some kind of synthetic compound. It's as if someone, and I mean someone even smarter than me, created this virus on purpose."

CHAPTER 12

BRAX

*B*inaria's prison cells were many, divided up along different hallways and corridors labeled with their species name, each spelled with one magical cocktail or another, explicitly tailored for the creatures it was built to contain.

The tiniest cells were the funniest to me, the ones for creatures like rogue ass pixies or flower nymphs or whatever because their tiny cell doors reminded me of something I could probably find in Alice in Wonderland. What made it even funnier was when the creatures inside started glowing because they were pissed off for whatever reason. I didn't even try to hide my gurgly chuckle as I passed by a few of them to get where I was going, knowing it would piss them off even more, which would only make them glow even brighter.

The cells for vampires were a few corridors down, brightly lit and designed to keep them fed, while also ensuring the vamps couldn't escape. Even their increased strength wouldn't allow them to bend or break the bars or tear apart the stone walls that held them in.

As far as feeding went, hunters were never going to supply their captive vamps with fresh humans to sate their thirst, it would go against everything they stood for. They also couldn't let the vamps slowly rot away, not dying, but feeling every second of starvation because they couldn't feed. That too would've gone against the values they held most dear.

So instead, they set up a feeding system: large vats of stored blood, donated and stolen from blood banks around the world in small enough quantities that they were never missed, and then kept cool until it was feeding time.

Every day, five liters of the artificially warmed liquid would descend down tubes on the wall and collect into a basin in each of the vamps' cells. Every imprisoned vamp was given a canteen they could then use to collect drinkable amounts of the blood by just the touch of a button on the basin.

It was actually a very sophisticated system, inhumane though it may have seemed to some. However, it got the job done without endangering more humans. Ultimately, the hunters were fulfilling their end of the bargain and then some.

They didn't have to let vampires, or any other creature for that matter, serve out sentences for lesser crimes if they didn't want to. They could technically just kill whoever and whatever got in their way if they saw fit. But most hunters were good enough to realize that killing everyone who fucked up some was too evil to maintain balance, and so they offered sympathy and lesser punishments when it was possible.

It didn't take me long to find the elder I was seeking, seeing as how he was one of only a handful of other vamps incarcerated at the time. He was also the newest prisoner if what I was reading over the cell doors was any indication. There were screens above each cell listing out all the pertinent information a guard might need to know.

Apparently, the four other vamps on the block had been locked up since the eighteen hundreds for the collective crime of trying to cross into the Veil without permission multiple times. But as interesting as that might've been, all thoughts of the other prisoners fled from my mind as I saw the vamp I was searching for.

Above his cell, his screen said his name was Mikeal, that he was an elder, and that he was being held for questioning regarding an attack on a hunter and other crimes against humans.

"Are you who they've sent to question me? You'd think since I'm an elder, I would at least warrant an actual hunter's interrogation, not one of their familiars poking around in places he doesn't belong," Mikeal said like he was bored as I looked through the bars at him. He was leaning back against the far wall of the cell with his arms crossed loosely over his chest, his black hair slicked back as if he didn't know how to blend in with the current time's society like the moron he certainly was.

"Nah, you're not that special," I said as I hovered outside his door, being careful not to let my wings hit the wall on the other side of the hallway I was flying in. "You got me instead, make it count, fucker." I crossed my arms and leveled the creature with a menacing smile meant to antagonize him.

He was quick to answer since I'd called his importance into question and rose to take the bait just like most vampires would've done. It was almost as if a sense of entitlement came right along with being a vampire. I couldn't stand that trait in anyone, much less someone who was hiding out in a darkened corner like a fucking coward where he thought no one would be able to find him.

Using his increased speed, he ran over to the bars, clutching them in his hands as he stuck his face as far through them as he was physically able, spitting out at me, "If I'm not special, then what do you want?" I guess he thought his motions would scare me or at least startle me. But I had a fairly good inclination about what kind of a person he was on the inside, and his actions proved me right since I expected him to do something along those lines, being the egotistical ass he was.

Without shifting at all from where I flew, I said, "I'm here to question you." I wasn't going to spell out how badly I needed answers from him. I had to hide my cards and only reveal them cautiously when the time was right. If he got the feeling he held all the information we were likely to get, he'd hold out and not tell me what I needed to know, and I couldn't have that. Not when Becks had already been attacked once and still had a price on her head.

"About what? How your precious hunters ignore the creatures they've sworn their lives to protect? How I had to hide because no hunter was going to come and save us? Because I could give you an earful on those subjects," he said as he pulled his face out of the bars but kept his hands clinging to them, knuckles white with the effort.

"Sure. We can start there. Go ahead. Give me an earful."

Mikeal chuckled without humor at that, his bright blue eyes narrowing in on me as if he'd been waiting for an excuse to let his thoughts loose, and I'd given him the go-ahead as if I didn't know and wouldn't be able to handle what he was about to throw at me. He couldn't have been more wrong. I knew full well that if I let him think he had the upper hand, he'd lay it all out for me, and just as before, he took the bait.

"Yes, let's start there," he said with a cocky smile as he dropped his hands from the bars and started pacing slowly through his cell. "The beginning seems fitting."

I fought against rolling my eyes at him for being so dramatic, but an impatient sigh did escape me, though he didn't seem to notice.

"We'd heard rumors of elders in other covens not being able to change humans anymore, and honestly, we laughed at the absurdity of such a notion. Elders' venom not working? It wasn't even a remote possibility. Ours was the most potent venom out there. However, after a while, a few elders in my coven began acting differently, not showing up to our gatherings, avoiding meeting our eyes, that kind of thing.

We unfortunately, still brushed those early warning signs off too, though. Giving our brothers and sisters time to handle whatever it was they were going through. But then came the day that changed everything.

It was a day of feasting four years ago. All the coven was gathered together as we celebrated the return of Ambrogio, the oldest vampire in existence. I'm sure you've heard of him," Mikeal said but didn't even look up to see if I acknowledged what he'd said or not, lost in his own retelling as he was.

"He was coming over from Transylvania to visit his children, as he did every year, and we'd had everything prepared for his visit. We'd even had a fresh supply of young black-haired women brought in exclusively for him, all tranced and ready to make sacrifices of themselves to our oldest leader because we knew they were his preferred meal.

Everything was going superbly. Music was playing, candles were lit, blood was flowing, clothing was coming off. Ambrogio had even taken a liking to me that night and asked me to sit next to him, even let me partake in some of the women we'd procured for him. Something he'd rarely done since I'd met him. It was becoming a magical night, indeed.

They brought up a fresh young thing to Ambrogio, but she had a smart mouth and was fighting through her trance as if she were more than just human. Well, this seemed to pique Ambrogio's interest keenly. He sat her down right between us, made her lay down with her head in his lap, her legs in mine.

She was arguing as best she could with Ambrogio, which made him like her more, I think, and Ambrogio said he was going to make her his child of the night. The girl didn't understand what he'd meant, but that didn't matter to him. He bit down on her wrist and pulled some of her blood into his mouth before he let her arm fall and bit his own. He opened her mouth and put his wrist up to it. You see, normally, the venom is already working its way through a human's body at that point, and she clung to his wrist and sucked greedily, just as usual. However, when he pulled himself away from her clutches, she started retching.

I'd never seen anything like it in all my years. And neither had Ambrogio, I could tell. He started getting angry, wondering what was going on. For a second there, he'd actually accused *me* of bringing him a *broken* human. But the elders of my coven who'd been acting strangely before came to my defense, thankfully.

They admitted they were sick, and told Ambrogio they thought he was sick too. As you can probably imagine, he didn't take this news very well. Not well at all, actually."

"What kind of sickness did they have, and what does this have to do with the hunters?" I asked, interrupting his long-ass monologue.

Shooting daggers at me with his gaze, he said, "The sickness prevents our venom from creating new children! It's one of the few things we treasure, being able to make them from those we deem worthy. It's what makes this immortal life tolerable! That girl died a month later, writhing in pain, never completing the change, never even getting a chance to see her fangs grow!

Ambrogio stayed with us while we tried to figure out what was going on, and all the while, he was ordering us to keep trying. To keep finding different humans, convinced that it wasn't us vampires that were the problem, and instead, blamed it on something going on in the humans themselves.

We sent word to the hunters multiple times. Eventually, we even begged for their help, but none ever came and did a thing! A few times, we were even outright *denied* the help we needed!"

"That's not possible," I said, remembering the oaths of the hunters and Derrick's words from the day before. Hunters never ignored a request for their help. They always checked it out, whether it turned out to be something worth their time or not.

"Believe what you want, familiar. That's what happened. It's not as if we're allowed to come find the hunters in an emergency, even though they can have access to us whenever it suits them," he said with a hefty dose of sarcasm. "We have to rely on the teams that watch and check in on us, and the teams in charge of us were nowhere to be found most of the time. And when they were around, they didn't believe us and wouldn't lift a finger to help because it might endanger their precious humans. They didn't even care when we showed them the massive pile of bodies we stacked together to get their attention. So, we eventually gave up any hope of the hunters ever coming to fix anything and tried to figure it out ourselves."

"All those bodies, those were your attempts to figure it out your-selves?" I asked as disgust wormed its way through me.

Not seeming remorseful in the slightest, Mikeal said, "Of course! We had to see what could be done; if it was every vampire that was infected or just a select few. And before he died, along with his entire line of successors, Ambrogio went on a killing spree, saying that if he eliminated all the infected vampires, he could stop the progression of it spreading to others. However, I didn't stay around long enough for them to find out if I was sick or not. I'm smarter than that. I fled like most of our children already had, once it was apparent there was no getting rid of this sickness."

"If he was the oldest of your lot and all of his line died with him, how are there any of you left?" I asked.

"He didn't sire all of us. Do you not know our history, familiar?"

"Apparently not, enlighten me."

Running a long-fingernailed hand over his smooth hair, he said, "Elders are those that don't know who sired them, and we have strict laws in place to prevent sires from abandoning their children, so our fate doesn't become someone else's.

I'm an elder. I, and the others like me, just woke up like this one day with no guidance whatsoever as to what was going on. I didn't have memories from my human life, and before I found a group of others like me, I'd never even heard of vampires. They took pity on me, like they'd done for each other, and took me under their wing. We formed our society as you know it now. We called ourselves elders and made laws for all of us to follow."

"So then, why was Ambrogio so special? Just because he'd been a vampire for longer than anyone else?" I asked.

"Precisely. He'd been alive longer than any of us, and basically became a father figure to everyone."

"Where did you wake up as a vampire?" I knew I was getting off-topic, but for some reason, something told me I needed to ask.

He looked thoughtful for a second before he spoke. "I'm not really sure. Most of us assumed we were made somewhere around what is now Transylvania, but the early days of a new vamp's life are foggy at best. And recalling locations when you can travel so far, so fast, seems like a waste."

"Anytitty," I said, trying to get us back on track, "so, *what's-his-face* went on a killing spree. I imagine you weren't the only one that fled, am I right?"

"Oh no, most of our children deserted us long before Ambrogio ever started killing those around him. Most of them broke off ties with the coven completely, choosing to take their chances and go their own way. I only know of a few that stayed in contact with their sires, but even those relationships began to fall off after a while. Some tried to stay together with their brothers and sisters, but most went off alone and stayed away."

I ran through the implications of a bunch of rogue vampires running amuck without a coven, and the impact of what that could mean made me nervous. "But don't you guys need to be around others of your kind? I thought your species needed that whole hierarchical shit to stay sane."

"We usually do," he said, a contemplative expression on his face. "That's just how bad things became."

"Well, in all of your hiding, did you happen to hear anyone talking about a female initiate in any way?"

I could tell my question had piqued his interest, and I wasn't sure right then whether it was going to work in my favor or not. His head tilted slightly, and he started moving closer to the bars.

"Her name wouldn't happen to be Rebecca by chance, would it?"

Rapidly, my anger resurfaced more than it already had, but I kept it under wraps well, knowing if I blew it now, I'd never get the information I was seeking.

"Yes, that was her name," I said, making sure I put emphasis on the 'was' part of my statement. Hopefully, no one knew Becks had survived her attack if they knew about it happening in the first place, and I didn't want to give it away if he didn't already know.

"About a week or so ago, a couple of my children had come to visit and check on me. They'd said they'd met someone who could cure us all. All they had to do was kill an initiate before she went to the gauntlet. I'd told them it was probably just a ploy to get them to do someone else's bidding, but they were adamant this girl was the answer we'd all been seeking. However, that was the last time I saw them before you guys picked me up and brought me here."

"Who was this someone who said they had a cure?"

Mikeal shook his head with a legitimate look of sadness. "I don't know. My children wouldn't tell me." His expression then turned hopeful. "Have you talked to my children Dorian and Robert? Were they right? Have they found a cure? Fergus said I only have about a month left before this sickness kills me for good."

I realized then that this was a dead end. Dorian never spoke a whisper of who'd hired him, and the red-headed vamp Tyler killed never got a chance. The fact that even Mikeal didn't know who'd led Dorian and Robert to pursue the hit on Becks shredded that last bit of remaining hope I still held on finding out who knew about Becks, and in the process, made me act colder than I usually would.

"Your children are dead, and you should probably prepare yourself to join them," I said before I flew away from him, not even the glows coming from the tiny cages able to bring a smile back to my face.

How was I supposed to protect Becks when I didn't even know who was trying to kill her, and my last lead turned out to be useless? Her name was already flowing through the ranks of the hunters. Nothing to be done there. That was going to happen regardless of what I did, given how different and out of the ordinary her upbringing had been. Not to mention the fact that if she was the next hunter queen, like the guys all seemed to suspect, everyone would know her name soon anyway, and my job would only become that much harder.

At least I now knew why they were trying to kill her: to get a cure for the vamps.

'Well, fuck that,' I thought. I'd let the entire species die off before I let them take Becks from me.

CHAPTER 13

DERRICK

There are times when I really hate my job, like when we're under attack or I feel like I'm missing something. Interrogating assholes though, I tended to enjoy, especially if it was someone like Reginald. He was the Mer king's closest and most highly trusted guard whom I'd had run-ins with before. Every time I'd ever had any kind of interaction with him, the experience had left me with a bad taste in my mouth. I knew if a little bit of my sadistic side were to come out, it was best if it happened with someone like him who was all kinds of creepy.

As soon as I stepped in front of the glass that kept us apart, his beady eyes landed on me from the other side. The water cells for merpeople were only half-filled with water, and each of them had areas for them to perch on the edge of a concrete slab as they would on a rock if they weren't imprisoned. Reggie, as he was also known, according to the screen above his cell, was perched upon his shelf, tail shifting and swaying in the water as he leaned back on his hands, almost as if he were sunbathing in the UV lights that lit his cell.

I pressed the button beside his cell that would allow us to speak and hear one another, and almost as soon as the mic was on, I heard, "Come to gloat and see me caged like a common criminal did you, Derrick?" His grotesque features and odd bone structure made all of his 'ck' sounds come out with annoying clicks around them, forcing me to pay closer attention to what it was he was actually saying.

Mermen were a wrathful and resentful bunch, and really, who could blame them with the way they looked compared to their female counterparts? This one, in particular, was a perfect example of the disparity between the two.

His face had a lot of loose and discolored skin in different places, almost as if he'd been very heavyset at some point in the past and then lost a bunch of weight, but the skin that grew to cover it had stayed behind. Though I knew that probably wasn't the case since it was a common feature among mermen. I could even see where things were growing in between the folds on his face as if he'd never bothered cleaning between the skin there. I could just imagine the kinds of marine life that fed on his face as he was swimming around, and the image the idea conjured up made me want to gag.

His body wasn't any better, I realized as I noticed he'd shed his armor and dropped it to the bottom of the cell's pool. In fact, I thought more things were growing on his chest and stomach folds than there were on his face, and that was saying something.

Shaking myself mentally to get my head back in the game, I ignored the creature's looks and set my mind to the task ahead of me.

"Not gloating at all, Reggie. I just need to know why the king closed the portals and where we can find him," I kept my voice clear and steady, doing everything I could to sound like Brock used to when I'd done something wrong as a child. He'd always been considered the disciplinarian of my household, and I'd admired how he played the part.

Reggie scoffed and lied blatantly, "He closed them to keep the fish happy, and you can find him up your hunter ass."

Quickly, I called my power and said the spell that would make him feel like his every muscle was cramping. His whole body tightened up for a split second, and he slid into the pool, looking like a log floating downriver. Eventually, he resurfaced and leveled me with a glare.

"Lie to me again, and the pain will last longer next time. The choice is up to you. Now, where is the king, and why did he close the portals?"

"Eat a jellyfish, you bipedal sponge dick, I'm not telling you anything."

"Alright," I said as I hit him with another muscle spasm, making it last a few seconds longer than the last one.

He was obviously in pain and shaken from my spell, but again, he kept refusing to talk. After a few instances of this back and forth, I'd had enough, not even finding a tiny bit of joy in the torture anymore, which pissed me off even more.

'He's probably not the king's most favored guard for nothing,' I reasoned and knew I was going to have to resort to extreme measures if I wanted to get the information I'd come for. However, I did give him one final chance to tell me what I needed to know.

"Look, Reggie, I could invade and examine your mind and memories for myself, but I promise you it will be one of the most excruciating things you've ever felt. I don't use that particular power unless I have to. But, again, the choice is yours."

"Bring it on, my mind is as closed off as this ce..." His words were cut off from reaching my ears as I pressed the button that turned off the mics and speakers, watching him closely as I started the spell. His enraged words were still spewing from his mouth until he started grabbing his head in pain and fear, and I saw his mouth fly open in an inaudible scream that would've no doubt ruptured my eardrums had I been able to hear it.

The spell was a long one to say and was not something I wanted to do or took any pleasure in. It forced me to see the world through my target's eyes, hear their thoughts as if they were my own. I'd never done this to someone with pure thoughts, so every time was a test of my willpower and the strength of my mind. And there was no question about whether this fool's memories would be any different.

A few seconds later, I was in his mind, sifting through his memories...

"Why does this weak piece of shit need so much fucking luggage, huh? What's she carrying in this thing anyway?" I asked Tobias, the queen's main guard, as I loaded up her belongings for the royal voyage to see the Earth-bound merfolk.

It wasn't even my job to be doing, yet somehow, the bitch had roped me into the detail anyway, saying that she didn't have enough guards to help since the king killed them.

I was supposed to be protecting him while he got his rocks off with the hired help, and maybe even catching a peep or two of my own while he was at it. But no, instead, I was loading huge ass clamshells full of random shit into the back of a carriage with some dumb fuck that was too loyal to the queen to even answer my questions.

"Fine, don't answer me, it's not as if I couldn't have the king kill you too," I said, eyeing Tobias with a sinister smile. Sure as seafoam on a wave, the fishtail-whipped bitch blanched and faced me as he should have from the second I'd started talking.

"I do not know what the queen has packed, nor do I know why she needs all of it," he answered tightly, knowing better than to anger me.

I couldn't listen to that part anymore, so I fast-forwarded through his thoughts until I found another memory that might be useful...

I had just sat down next to the king and across from the queen in the carriage as the dolphins started their slow trek across the ocean to the portal we'd use to get to Earth. Why we couldn't use the king's personal portal was beyond me. I knew he wanted that portal to be kept a secret, but in all the time I'd known and worked for the king, I'd never seen a time where it could've been used to harm anything.

King Zale was telling Queen Darya that she was to stay by the riverbank during the celebration. He didn't want her embarrassing him like she had the previous year. She just sat quietly as she usually did and said the appropriate responses when necessary. Queen Darya was an incredibly dull merperson like that.

However, when Zale started telling her that their daughter, Princess

Margo, was to be courted on this trip, that riled up more life in the queen than I'd ever seen from her before.

"Margo is only twenty-five!" Darya yelled at the king, though I had no idea why she was getting so upset. Yes, it was still considered young by Mer terms, but she was no child by any means either.

The king handled that little outburst promptly enough though. A swift slap to the queen's face shut her right up, and I had to put my hand in front of my face to contain my laughter. It was for naught though because the king elbowed me with a smile of his own as he pointed out the glum look on the queen's face. She'd turned red, and there was a handprint starting to form on the pale skin of her cheek. It reminded me of the time I'd watched through the cracks of their chamber door to see the king make those same kinds of marks on other parts of her body, and within seconds, I was reliving those images fondly.

I utterly despised this merman and everything he stood for, but I had to keep searching his mind and memories.

Though I now had proof of the Mer king's personal portal, I knew I'd feel better if I were to get something more substantial. However, if I was going to find more information I could use against the Mer king, I needed to do it quickly.

Time was not our friend in this line of work. I had a feeling the assembly would be over soon, and Becks would be seeking out the rest of us. I had no intention of letting her see me using this particular power.

So as hurriedly as I could, I skimmed through Reggie's thoughts, pausing only long enough to get an idea of what was going on until I got to the part where the queen had stayed back with her guard by the riverbank. The king had taken a helpless young mermaid from the celebration to a secluded part of the Earthbound nobleman's lodgings. I knew I was getting close to when the portals closed in Reggie's memories.

That's where Reggie had started being a creep again, unfortunately, watching through closed doors as King Zale fucked and almost beat the life out of the poor creature he'd taken a liking to.

However, what the king did next, even in Reggie's memory, was out of the norm. He didn't seem sated and content as he usually would after episodes like that, and started making his way back to the queen.

I'd guessed he still had some demons to let loose, and I did not want to miss whatever he had planned for the queen when he met back up with her. However, as he was nearing where we left her, the moonlight growing brighter in the night sky, the king suddenly stopped, and I had to stop myself quickly as well, lest he find out I was following him.

Zale was just floating there, his face barely above the water's surface as he looked to the riverbank. It took me a second to see what he was watching, but once my eyes lit on the queen's form wrapped in a walking man's embrace, lips locked together passionately, I knew what my king was seeing, and fear of what he might do and who he might lash out at started to make my heart race.

But the king didn't move from his spot. I glanced back to the queen and watched her literally grow legs and walk out of the water with the man whose hand she was holding. When he turned to face her, I caught a glimpse of what he was, and I couldn't understand what the queen could see in an incubus at all. His telltale tiny black horns gave him away. One glance to my king proved he knew what the man was as well.

After a slow and passionate kiss on the river's edge, the incubus led our queen into the woods, and Zale started moving toward where she'd left all of her belongings on the bank of the river.

I followed closely behind him, but not so close that he would know I was there and watched as he took in the sights around him.

"Reginald," *the king called, jerking me from my spot in alarm.*

"Yes, your majesty?" *my voice came out strong despite how embarrassed I was to have been caught.*

"Check these guards and tell me if they're alive or not."

He wasn't going to kill me for following him? Wasn't going to go after the queen? I couldn't believe it. Hurrying along, I checked each and every guard that floated limply by on the surface of the water and reassured the king that they were all simply passed out and unconscious, breathing a sigh of relief for them since it would offer them an alibi.

However, the king surprised me when he said, "Kill them where they float *and come find me through my portal when you're done. It's time we cut this place off for good, and I don't want any witnesses."*

He then proceeded to take the dolphin-led carriage away, driving it himself, leaving me to dispose of the bodies in the human world, which was no easy task.

'At least he didn't kill me,' I thought as I watched him disappear downriver before I set about what I had to do.

I could hardly believe what I'd seen transpire through Reggie's thoughts, but I had to keep going anyway despite how sickening it was to watch him murder all those defenseless guards.

Once I finally made it back to the king through his portal, he had his trident out and was already preparing the spell that would close every underwater portal but his.

"You know the hunters will be barging in here the second that spell is cast, right?" I asked King Zale cautiously to ensure he knew the ramifications of his actions.

"Let them come. I'll be needing their services soon enough. Tell the entire kingdom that the queen has been kidnapped by someone on Earth and that in one week's time, I will be closing all the portals, so no one else in our kingdom meets her same fate. Make sure they think it's for their own good, Reginald."

"But, sire. She wasn't kidnapped, she left willingly," I said, but immediately regretted my words as the king rushed toward me and held me by my throat, cutting off my ability to breathe the air out of the water around me.

"You are the only other witness; do I need to kill you too?"

"No, no, no, your highness! I'm sorry. I shouldn't have questioned you!" I could barely get the words out of my mouth.

"Do what I've told you to do, and don't make me question your loyalty again."

I pulled the power back into myself from Reggie's mind and scowled at the dumbass where he was huddled in a ball shape on the ledge, squirming around in pain as his mind probably felt like it was being ripped apart. It was a consequence I usually felt bad about inflicting on another living soul. Still, as I remembered what it felt like to be inside his head, thinking his thoughts and considering his actions, I had only a tiny sliver of sympathy left for the creature. And that sympathy was the only thing that saved his life. If I hadn't had that, I'd have killed him right then and there, but something about it made me pause. Instead of helping to heal him or kill him, I turned and walked away, leaving him to writhe for a few weeks while his mind recovered from my spell.

'There it is again,' I thought as I went in search of my team, 'that bad taste in my mouth.'

CHAPTER 14

TYLER

*W*hen we landed in the back of the auditorium, the assembly was starting, and everyone had already found their seats. Still holding Becks' hand from when we'd teleported, I led her to a couple of empty seats in the back row, and we sat down at what was basically the equivalent of a graduation speech being spewed from Professor Hawk. If I wasn't mistaken, he was using the same tired rhetoric he'd used before I'd entered the gauntlet.

"That's Professor Hawk," I whispered in Becks' ear. "He's the dean."

Becks nodded at me but seemed to be enthralled by the speech, as well as by the other initiates that surrounded us. Every now and then, I caught her sneaking glances at them, probably comparing herself to them before she looked back at the stage.

After his speech was over, he introduced Deputy Chief Withers, and even I perked up in my seat. "Tina Withers," I whispered to Becks again. "She's got the highest rank under the chief and is basically the official go-between for Binaria East and West."

"Why is everyone sitting up straighter for her?" Becks whispered back as Tina made her way to the podium.

I opened my mouth to answer her simple question but closed it again because I realized I didn't have a simple answer. Before Tina made it to the podium, I got out, "I'm sure you'll pick up on it when you hear her speech," however, that just made Becks crinkle up her eyebrows at me.

Quickly, I leaned in and kissed her cheek, making her blush as I squeezed her hand, and we both focused on the stage.

"Good afternoon, initiates," Tina spoke, quieting all the whispers and stopping all the movements from the crowd. "I don't usually come to your ceremonies, as you know. But as you also may know, there's no denying the chief, so here I am." She lifted her arms in a *what-could-I-do* motion that caused a few giggles from the crowd, and Tina smiled at them before she continued.

"I remember sitting where you are now, worrying about whether I'd make it through the gauntlet or not, and I'm here to tell you, your training at this academy has prepared you well. You've got what it takes to see that part of your journey through without much issue. However, I want to talk to you about life after the gauntlet, after you've received the rest of your powers."

Becks sat forward in her seat some, listening carefully to Tina as her hand subconsciously squeezed mine tighter.

"When you're a true hunter, and your new powers have been revealed, you'll be placed on a team that will be your lifeline in this realm and all the others. They are who you will spend the majority of your life with, so it's imperative you work well together, and that you trust the other hunters on your team. They're the ones who will always have your back, even at the worst of times. I know without my team, I would've been lost after what I went through."

I didn't think the auditorium could get much quieter, but somehow it did as Tina began talking about her past.

"The chief thinks I should tell you guys everything that happened, though I don't see how that could really be beneficial to you. What I believe you do need to know is this: I lost my family in a horrific turn of events simply because I am a hunter. It was only because of the rest of my team that I was able to pull through the aftermath.

You see, as a hunter, a lot of the people and creatures you are going to help will not see you as helpful at all. In fact, they might outright hate you for being what you are, and for the power you can wield over their lives.

You will have to deal with their hostility daily. Sometimes the anger and resentment they hold for you will be so intense they'll be willing to do some despicable things to end you. You'll need to stay forever vigilant to keep yourselves, your teammates, and your families safe.

My advice to you is this: Follow the missions the chief gives you to the letter. Listen to your gut when it tells you something isn't right. Bond with your new teammates as best you can. But I am confident you will all do great things. I know each and every one of you personally, and I, for one, am grateful for what you will be adding to our organization because you each show promise. I promise to do whatever I can to keep you all safe, personally. You matter more to me than you know."

She didn't talk about everything I thought she was going to. However, her exit from the auditorium was still met with resounding cheers from the initiates as they applauded much more than just her speech, a few whistles being thrown in for good measure.

I didn't want to miss an opportunity for Becks to meet Tina, so I warned Becks quickly that I was going to teleport us, and after she nodded, I jumped us backstage.

Tina was making her way behind the curtain when her eyes lighted on where we stood in the hallway that led to the stage's back entrance. A big, friendly smile spread across her mouth as she saw us, and she reached out a hand immediately to Becks.

"Hello, I'm assuming you're Dragon team's new team member. Becks, right?"

Becks shook Tina's hand with a smile of her own and responded, "Yep, that's me."

"It's good to meet you, Becks. Tell me, is that Brax character your familiar?"

Becks laughed at that and said, "Yep, he's mine. How do you know him?"

"Oh, he's been coming here for years. I swear, the mouth on that beast. It gets me every time," Tina said with a laugh, making both Becks and me laugh as well as we pictured the elf-goyle.

"He is pretty awesome," Becks said as she looked to the floor in thought.

"You can say that again," Tina said, "He came in one day and started yelling at everyone about pixie titties or some such nonsense, and my teammates and I were too busy laughing to really even hear what he was saying."

"That's not hard to imagine, actually," Becks said, both of them giggling.

"I love your shirt, by the way," Tina said, gesturing to Becks where she stood. Her shirt said, 'fuck mornings' and stretched across her ample chest in ways that affected me a little more than I wanted it to.

"Oh, thanks! It was like a dollar at the second-hand store," Becks gushed, and Tina laughed.

"I'd love to hang out and get to know you more, but I need to head back to the chief. He just messaged me about something having to do with vampire emails. I have no idea what that means, though," Tina said as she eyed the phone in her hand like it didn't make sense to her.

"I can jump you back there, we've got to meet the rest of our team there anyway," I said, and within a few short seconds we were all laughing and hanging out outside the chief's office while he finished up a meeting with some other team. Tina and Becks got along relatively well, confirming even more that the chief just knew things.

A short while later, Brax, Adam, and Derrick all showed up with grim expressions and tight mouths, none wanting to talk about what had happened while we were separated, effectively stopping the banter the girls had been volleying back and forth.

Eventually, the chief was done with his meeting. When the other team left, he motioned for us to enter, anger evident on his face.

"Maybe you can explain this confounded contraption, Tina," the chief said as we sat around his desk, and Tina followed behind him to his computer.

"Look," the chief said as he tried to do something on the machine, "I'm denied access!"

"But you have the highest clearance of all of us," Tina said as she leaned over the chief and started clicking the mouse, confusion and frustration marring her features.

"I know. This dab-blasted thing…" the chief started, then noticing we were in the room as well, got his anger under control. "Sorry, Dragon team, I was checking into the vampires' issues from my end, but there's a block that won't allow me to see the files. I swear this computer hates me. So, tell me, what did you guys find out?"

CHAPTER 15

BECKS

A little over an hour and a half and a lot of talking later, I ruminated over everything I'd just learned from all of my guys as some random guy worked on Otto's computer. The rest of us stayed quiet while he worked, not wanting to continue our conversations while he was in the room, waiting for him to finish before we started talking again. I'd learned an insane amount of information before the guy got there, and my brain already felt like I'd tried to cram too much stuff into it at once.

The fact that somebody was deliberately trying to kill off all the vampires at a time like this was downright disturbing, especially considering the observation Adam had made while he explained what Fergus told him.

"We've got to do something soon. Whoever's done all this knew exactly what they were doing. It's like they're attacking the vamps on two fronts: one, where they're infecting the elders with this virus that will kill them all eventually, and two, where they're targeting and killing elders specifically, so the whole line dies off."

As if infecting them with the virus wasn't offing them fast enough for their liking, so they started pitting them against one another, and that's why they've all gone into hiding. They're afraid of getting infected if they aren't already, and they're afraid of each other because they each blame one another."

Upping the stakes, even more, was the fact that Fergus also told Adam that the only way he saw a solution to any of this was if we could somehow find an elder who hadn't yet been infected and then used their untainted blood to heal the rest of the species.

The complications came in with the fact that no one, not even the elder in the cells, knew if there were any uninfected elders left, much less where we'd have to go to find one, as Brax stated clearly. Apparently, Mikeal had made it sound as if there were none left.

That got Derrick to ask about who the first vampire was, speculating that if we could find that vamp, he might not be infected.

The problem with that was, though, that no one knew how the vampire species originated. Otto said that as far as he knew, vampires began showing up sometime during the medieval period, and as far as the records claimed, the hunters of the time just assumed a new species had been created, and they started managing them like they did everything else.

They kept a record of all the elders they knew about, but what classified them as elders in the first place was the fact that they didn't know who'd sired them.

"I'm in," the greasy-haired guy who'd been working on Otto's computer said before he sniffed loudly and rubbed at his nose with the back of his hand. "Don't know how anybody was able to block your access, Chief, but it didn't stay that way for long on my watch. You call me if you need me again."

"Thank you, Samuel," Otto said as he took a seat in the chair behind his desk, Samuel slinking out the door without looking at us at all.

"Alright, let's see here." Otto's eyebrows drew down as he skimmed through whatever he was staring at, and my mind kept sifting through everything I'd learned while I waited for him to finish.

There was all the information Derrick had gained from the Mer guard to consider, too. The way he told it, the whole situation sounded like a daytime soap opera.

Otto, Brax, and the guys agreed that something had to be done to find the Mer king and bring him to justice. The crimes he'd committed, like abandoning all the Earthbound merfolk that didn't make it across to the Veil before the portals closed, abusing the queen and others, ordering his own defenseless guards to be murdered, and the fact that he actually closed the portals, were all enough reason for hunters to step in and dish out punishment.

But his whereabouts were still unknown.

Otto made a good point though, when he said our best bet was to find the queen and try to enlist her help in taking down the Mer king. "If you can get her to rally her people against the king, it may result in a battle, but I'm pretty sure all the merfolk will follow their queen. They love her, and the king's reputation has never been good, especially with those that live right there in his kingdom. I bet they'd take up arms if it meant they wouldn't have to deal with him anymore."

Tyler had spoken up then, asking about where the queen could've possibly gone with an incubus, and it was Tina that laughed before she answered him.

"Remi's an incubus that is always setting up shop right next to the ocean, and for a long time, we've heard rumors that it's because he's having a secret love affair with a mermaid. If it's Remi that she's gone off with, I know exactly where they'll be. Well, at least I have a general idea."

Apparently, this incubus, Remi, ran a black-market club of sorts for all the 'magical dirty deals' as Tina put it. "We don't want to shut it down because it's a sure-fire place to find intel sometimes. Plus, he moves it around every few nights like a speakeasy. We always know where it is, but he doesn't need to know that," Tina explained for me, which I was grateful for.

I liked her. She reminded me of Ava, and I missed Ava something serious already. Tina had short blonde hair that was brown at the roots, soft green eyes, and smile lines. She looked to be in her forties, but I really had no idea how old she was given the life expectancies for hunters. When we'd been talking before, something about us clicked, and that didn't often happen for me. I grew up and lived almost my whole life without a single friend until Ava came around and wouldn't leave me alone. She grew on me right away, and after experiencing Ava, I had high hopes that I'd be able to add Tina to my extremely short list of friends.

"Well, Mikeal and Elliot weren't lying," Otto said, jerking me out of my thoughts. "There are a ton of requests for help from the vampires here, but they were all hidden away."

"I'm sorry, Chief," Tina said from where she sat across from me in the leather chair. "Is there anything in there that could help us?"

Otto sighed and turned to face all of us. "No, I don't think so. At least, nothing new."

We all sat there for a minute in silence, lost in our own thoughts until Otto spoke again, resolution back in his voice, a decision made whether he liked it or not because it had to be done.

"Here's your checklist Dragon team: One: Find the Mer queen and see if you can get her to stand against her husband. Two: Look through records, go searching around, whatever you need to do, but find an uninfected elder so we can stop this before it goes farther than it already has. Three: Go back to where Becks was born and see if there's any way to follow up on that note her friend gave her. And four: Find the pixie's sacred seed. I hate to think about all those souls going to the Void just because their seed was stolen.

Take a few hours to pack everything you think you'll need and prepare yourselves. If the Mer queen is with Remi, your best bet at finding them would be to go to his club tonight. And even if he's not the incubus she's gone off with, you still might be able to get an idea of who it actually was."

"Yes, Chief," Derrick said as we all stood and made our way toward Tyler.

Before we faded, though, I heard Otto say, "Make sure you warn Rebecca about that lair, too!"

~

A FEW HOURS LATER, after we'd gone back to the beach safe house to change and grab a few things we needed, we were standing outside of what looked like an abandoned warehouse on the waterfront of some industrial part of New Jersey. It smelled. I didn't like it. Plus, the guys had insisted we dress up for wherever we were going, and the five-inch heels I'd bought the other night and the sexy dress I was wearing did not fit where we were at all.

I wasn't pouting, but I was close to it as I hobbled on wet and puddled cement in loud ass heels I'd hated from the moment I started walking in them, despite how awesome they made my calves look.

The guys and Brax all laughed at me as I followed them down a dirty alley, and Tyler chuckled, "Babe, you're really gonna fall if you keep death glaring your heels instead of watching where you're going."

"Nah, keep your death glare, then you might not even need to fight anyone. Everyone's gonna tremble at your feet, just from the look on your face," Brax added with his gravelly voice, making me roll my eyes.

"We're fighting? Who said anything about fighting?" I asked everyone, my anger spiking up a few notches as I almost twisted my ankle as I walked, frustrating me even more. "You guys haven't taught me that much about fighting, and how the fuck am I supposed to beat somebody's ass dressed like this, anyway?"

They all succumbed to laughter, and I groaned as we rounded a corner in the maze of deserted buildings surrounding us.

"Alright, seriously, Becks," Derrick said as he fought so hard not to laugh at my expense that I could tell his cheeks were pink even in the dim light offered by the moon overhead. "You're about to go into an incubus lair. Yes, it's a club and bar and whatnot as well, but I need to warn you about what it'll be like in there."

"Let me guess. The baddest of the bad, the burliest of the burly, something along those lines?" I asked as I pulled the bottom of my skirt down so it wouldn't show my ass.

"Yes, but you've also got to be prepared for the atmosphere."

"What about it?" I asked, wondering what in the hell he was talking about.

Brax giggled and said, "I'll be doing a perimeter check while you're inside, keeping watch from out here." Then looking at each of the guys, he said, "Good luck with her. Oh, and I'll kill all of you if she gets hurt." Even though he was smiling as he said it, I knew he meant every word. Before I could say anything to him, he disappeared and left me with the guys.

"Why isn't he coming with us?" I asked, my anger reaching a critical tipping point because I was just not in the mood for any of their shit right then.

"He's not allowed inside because familiars tend to get too territorial in places like this, but I'm sure nothing will stop him from going in if we let him know we need him," Adam said from beside me. His arm was brushing up against mine, steadying me as I'd walked, though I don't think he knew how much a help his presence had actually been for my unstable ass feet.

Derrick smoothed a hand through his hair as he finally answered my question. "An incubus is basically a sexual demon, and many of them make their living on Earth by running places like this. The atmosphere is charged by his presence alone, which makes everyone that enters and breathes in the air around them much more in touch with their desires than they normally are. The longer someone's in there, the more susceptible they are to the atmosphere he's created."

I had no clue what he meant by that, and said, "What now?"

"It means that what you truly desire, at your core, is brought closer to the surface every minute you're inside a place like this," Tyler clarified hastily.

He'd lost his smile, and instead, was wearing a worried expression on his face as he tucked his hands in the pockets of his nice jeans, his forearm muscles stretching out the rolled-up cuffs of his white button-up shirt, the caricatures of his tattoos accentuated by the cuff he wore on one wrist. He had a vest on over his shirt, and I found I couldn't keep looking at him because the sight was too distracting for me to handle while I was still trying to figure all this out.

'Is he worried my desires will become an issue?' I wondered, self-consciously.

'I don't think he's worried about your *desires, Becks,'* Brax thought to me from wherever he was.

"So, what am I supposed to do here, then?" I got myself back on track as I leveled a glare at Derrick. He was wearing a suit, complete with tie and all, tightly fitted to his body, and though I found him distracting as well, at least he had his coat on, hiding most of his body from my sight.

'What the hell, libido? Chill out already,' I chastised myself for barely being able to focus on the words Derrick was saying.

"Just follow our lead. Hopefully, we won't even be in there long enough for it to affect us," Derrick said.

"Speak for yourself, the atmosphere is so thick I can feel it out here already," Adam said as his eyes traveled appreciatively down my body slowly. I felt my eyes get large, and my belly flip as I watched him.

Without thinking, I perused his form as well, taking in his dark brown leather jacket, zipped up halfway and hiding his weapons, but also showing off the white t-shirt he wore underneath. His jeans were loose but fit perfectly over his round backside. As soon as I realized what was going through my head, I snapped my eyes back up to Derrick quickly.

I ignored their chuckles at the embarrassment that was probably written all over my face and got my mind back under control.

"Desires... got it," I said as I tried not to blush as they all stared at me.

"Just..." Derrick said, "don't be alarmed by what some people's desires make them do."

"Okay?" I said as Adam took hold of my hand, and we walked to a carefully hidden door. Derrick knocked a distinctive rhythm that had the door opening by a girl clad in only a bikini and a smile.

"Welcome to Remi's lair, hunters," she said in a low and sultry voice, her eyes trained on me, not on the guys as I'd assumed they would be. "May all your drinks be full, and all your desires fulfilled."

Her bright green eyes were locked on mine, holding me captive as the guys led me through the door. Adam even had to pull me a little to make me keep walking.

'I just want to talk to her for a minute,' I thought. I almost pouted as we turned a corner, and I couldn't see the woman anymore. But then reason won out, reminding me that I had to ignore what I wanted while I was in here to get the job done and stay on mission to find the Mer queen.

When I looked around and took in everything going on in the large warehouse, it was as if we'd entered another world entirely.

Everything was designed in orange and red tones with purple, blue, and gold accents, making the whole place seem more vibrant than I'd ever imagined a place could be. Sheer curtains hung delicately from the ceiling to act as makeshift but see-through walls, large colorful pillows were thrown about everywhere, tassels hung from round lamps that illuminated the space like candlelight, pathways between the cushions showed a carpeted floor designed with a mosaic pattern, and music was playing, but I couldn't for the life of me tell what kind it was, or even what language it was in.

There were people and creatures everywhere, doing *all kinds of things* I was *so* not expecting to see them doing. I had to force my eyes to Derrick's back, so I wouldn't gawk as we walked through the space.

We'd barely made it halfway through the building before I heard someone yell out above the sound of the music, "Mandy!"

My teammates all stopped and turned around, looking behind me at whatever the ruckus was, and I followed suit, dropping Adam's hand as I turned around.

Three men I'd only seen in pictures ran up to me like they couldn't get to me fast enough. As soon as they reached me, they all towered over me and stared down into my face, their expressions wide-eyed and panicky. Well, at least they *were* until realization dawned on their features. Then, instead of seeming happy or relieved, my parents' old teammates appeared absolutely murderous.

CHAPTER 16

BECKS

"*W*ho are you, and why are you wearing her body, you filthy creature?" the one with long dark hair and tanned skin like mine asked angrily.

All three of them, Brandt Rivers, Logan Howell, and Benjamin Razner, all stood around in front of me, caging me in between them and my guys, though I didn't know which face to place with which name. Their stances were aggressive, their eyes cutting as if they were trying to see right through me, and the whole situation caught me off guard.

"What?" I asked a little weakly.

As soon as the word escaped my lips, a few things happened all at once:

The Viking looking guy in the middle reached out to me with both of his big hands, but Derrick reached up and grabbed him by the throat before he could touch me. Adam pulled me back behind him, and a ferocious growl escaped Tyler as he stepped toward the man aggressively, his skin starting to shake as he battled his beast.

But as intense as all that may have been, what really surprised me was the reaction I felt slip from me without thought.

A flash went through my mind of Rick when he'd grabbed me, and right away, my power answered my fear and panic without my permission.

My power lashed out instantly, knocking all of them away from me at once. The force of which made their bodies pull a few curtains down and had them knocking into a couple of unsuspecting people and creatures as they flew backward and landed a few feet away in a heap of pillows and limbs.

"Oh!" I heard myself say as I watched all of them try to get their wits about them.

Derrick, Adam, and Tyler were fast, apparently not as fazed as the other men were by what I'd done, and they came back over to me in haste. They each took up positions around me, but something seemed to have shifted at that moment. None of my guys appeared to see a need to stand in front of me anymore, but rather, stood firmly *beside* me, and I had to fight against my thoughts, so they didn't get all *I'm-a-real-part-of-this-team-now*.

The other guys, however, stood slowly, eyes never leaving mine as they began pulling weapons from where they'd had them hidden in their clothes before.

I knew then that this was a misunderstanding, and that I really didn't want it to escalate any further. I knew that if I wanted to prevent a full-blown war between all of these men, I would have to step in somehow. And with the boost of confidence my power and my guys' subtle behavior had given me, I strode confidently toward my parents' old teammates, a calmness settling through me as I moved.

"I'm not Mandy," I said to the men, "nor am I some kind of shapeshifting doppelganger or whatever." The men stood up straight, anger and hostility still radiating off of them. "I'm Malcolm and Amanda's daughter."

The men all froze in what could only be described as shock, and it took them a bit of silence to start putting their weapons away. I saw the thoughts they were thinking move across their faces, shifting through stages like anger, confusion, hopefulness, and finally settling on a mournfulness I could feel in my bones.

"We didn't even know she was pregnant," the dark-skinned man said as he came over, looking closer at me as if he were trying to see the truth of my words in my face.

The other two men came over as well, but it was the long-haired tanned guy that spoke, "What's your name?"

"Becks," I said, full of relief since all the tension finally seemed to have fled the space between us.

"Short for Rebecca, right?" The Viking-looking one asked as he shared a weighted glance with his comrades.

The dark-skinned man smiled lovingly and said, "That's what Mandy always said she'd name a girl if she ever had one: Rebecca."

I didn't know what to say to that. Some part of me wanted very strongly to smile and ask them about everything they knew, but an even more significant part of me became self-conscious at that point, and I ended up staring at the floor for a few seconds instead of saying anything.

"You look so much like her," one of them said, but I couldn't even bring my head up to see who'd said it. An overwhelming need to cry was settling inside me, and I was having to work really hard at keeping the tears at bay as thoughts of my parents' souls being ripped apart worked their way through my mind and my heart simultaneously.

"Hey," the long-haired man said as he pulled at my chin gently to make my eyes meet his.

For some reason, my power and my anxiety were both silent at his physical touch, and I was thankful I didn't have to worry about them while I was feeling all kinds of sadness otherwise.

"Why are you upset?" he asked, and despite myself, a little pained sob escaped my throat as my eyes started filling with unshed tears.

"I never even knew her. I never got to know either of them."

My parents' team looked at each other and then back to me. "Let's go have a seat," he said, and soon both of our teams were all moving to sit around in a circle on the pretty pillows that littered the floor beautifully, and introductions were quickly made. The Viking was Brandt, Ben was the dark-skinned guy, and Logan was the long-haired man, and as I stared at each of them, I cemented their names and faces to memory.

My tears seemed to have fled with the movement and the talking, and I tried to remember what my team had warned me about this place we were in, about how my desires would be more out and on the surface, the knowledge reassuring me that I wasn't this sad little wuss simply because my real parents had been brought up in the conversation. It was just the atmosphere affecting me.

As we settled in and I uncomfortably tried to keep my dress from sliding up at such an inopportune time, Brandt asked, "How old are you?"

"I'm eighteen," I said, finally finding that crossing my legs and holding a big pillow over my lap to cover myself was the best and most comfortable option I had available.

"Oh, so you must have gone through the gauntlet early like your mother then. Tell me, what were your scores?" Ben asked, and I knew my eyes got big with worry at his words.

Luckily though, my guys didn't seem too mussed about telling my parents' team that I hadn't gone through yet since Derrick said as much before he asked a question of his own. "Are you guys still working as hunters? I thought you'd all left a long time ago."

"Hold on, what do you mean she hasn't gone to the gauntlet yet? You guys are on a mission right now, right?" Logan asked, hands raised in puzzlement.

Again, I knew I needed to step in and clarify. "Yes, we're on a mission, but my parents died when I was two, and I was put up for adoption and raised by humans." I thought about adding the part where I was institutionalized, but I didn't want to cry again, so I avoided it as best I could.

"Why weren't you raised by hunters? That's insane. Humans would have no idea how to care for a hunter child!" Brandt said, getting visibly angrier as he spoke.

"Well, that's a bit complicated," I started. For some reason, I really didn't want to disappoint these men, but I felt like I was already. "My familiar would probably do a better job explaining it since he was there."

"You have a familiar too?" Logan asked, his eyes going wide, sweat starting to form on his brow.

I didn't know what about that fact would cause that kind of reaction, but I dismissed it as the atmosphere fucking with him. "Yes, is that a problem?"

"When did you say you were born, again?" Logan asked as he pinched the bridge of his nose, his eyes shut tightly with the motion.

"I didn't, but I don't mind telling you. I was born on February 2nd, 2002.

"And are you right-handed or left?" Logan asked almost timidly.

"Left, but what does that have to do with anything?"

Logan looked at his teammates, and they looked at him, their expressions going from being as confused as I was, to ones of visible curiosity as their eyes all shifted back and forth between Logan and me.

"What?" I asked, glancing between all of them.

"I..." Logan started but didn't finish as he rubbed his hands down his pants a few times and started breathing faster, looking all around at everything but me.

Adam leaned against me then, his shoulder sliding behind mine some as he spoke. "I think Logan is your biological father, not Malcolm."

I whipped my head around at Adam, planning to yell or something, but the words got stuck in my throat. Slowly, I turned back and scrutinized Logan. His eyes were wide with... 'What is that? Sorrow? Sadness? Fear?'

My mouth dropped open at the implications of my parents' life, and I started getting angry for who I'd thought my father was. "My mom cheated on Malcolm with you, and that's where I came from?"

They all looked shocked and taken aback by what I'd said, but I needed answers. I needed to know what kind of a person my mother was because foolishly, I'd already put her up on a pedestal in my mind, and the thoughts that were churning through me right then threatened to knock her right off.

"No, Becks," Brandt said in a soothing tone. "It wasn't like that." He shared a quick glance with his teammates before he continued. "We were all with her. And we were all okay with the situation."

I was taken back by his words. "But she was married to Malcolm," I found myself arguing, though I didn't want to.

Logan seemed to pull himself together as if he'd accepted the changes in his life and was now ready to handle it head-on. He leveled me with a calm gaze and said, "She married Malcolm while we were all on Earth because we needed the paperwork for the mission we were on. It had nothing to do with him being more important to her than any of the rest of us were. Your mother loved all of us, and we all loved her. We still do." His voice broke some on that last part, and I felt heartbroken for him. For all of them.

I was still finding it hard to reconcile though, and it took me a minute to figure out why. But luckily, we were in the perfect place to have my feelings about something float up to my consciousness quickly instead of leaving me to wonder.

I'd been struggling to sort out my feelings for Derrick, Adam, and Tyler from the moment I was placed on Dragon team. I'd wanted them all but was unwilling to choose between them. I'd decided within the short time we'd been together already that I wouldn't be with any of them since my heart wouldn't let me pick just one, though the prospect of that broke my heart completely.

I'd been feeling terrible about how incredibly selfish it was for me to want not just one, but three men at the same time when other people on this planet were lucky to only find one.

Not to mention the fact that I wasn't even sure I could have a normal relationship in the first place, given everything I'd been through, and specifically because of all the damage Rick had done to me. I was scared of even the *idea* of sex or letting anyone in at all.

The idea of any kind of relationship seemed too far outside my scope of capabilities. Still, at the same time, I found my mind thinking about those kinds of things almost constantly, my body reacting to my guys despite my brain yelling at me for it.

I'd been feeling guilty about the kisses I'd shared with Derrick and Tyler, hoping against hope that they wouldn't hate me for kissing someone else, while at the same time, I felt slightly dejected that I hadn't experienced any kind of intimacy like that with Adam yet.

It was a crazy set of ideas and feelings that I couldn't ignore despite how hard I tried.

Hearing about my mother's relationship with her team brought all of those feelings to the forefront of my mind, and I knew my initial, misguided anger at her wasn't really anger at all. It was jealousy.

I was jealous of the fact that she'd been with all of her teammates, and I couldn't do that with mine.

Even if Derrick, Adam, and Tyler all wanted to be with me in that way, which I still wasn't positive that they did, there was the simple and insurmountable problem of Derrick and Tyler's relationship that would also prevent it from happening.

I scrubbed my hand down my face as I tried to get my mind to think about something other than my own fucked up desires, and looked back to the men before me.

Then, with the weight of a Brax-sized statue, an emotional weight landed on my chest as my eyes fell on Logan. My biological father. I found myself staring at him in wonder, unable to speak, or even form a coherent thought.

"You're my father," I heard myself say a few seconds later, and with the words spoken, something solidified in my mind and heart. He was right there, close enough to reach out and touch, living and breathing and everything, staring right back at me with an expression that mirrored my own.

"Seems so," he said.

"I don't care about biology, we're all your fathers now, Becks," Brandt said with a deep-chested chuckle.

Logan nodded at Brandt's words, and then a smile started to curl his lips as he said, "I can't wait to get to know you."

Immediately, tears filled my eyes and fell down my face as a sob tore from my throat, my emotions inescapable and unrelenting as I put my face into the pillow in my lap, and I cried as the tears of a thousand unrealized dreams met up with a thousand more hopeful possibilities.

"Why didn't you guys go on the run with Malcolm and Mandy? What made you stay behind?" Derrick asked the remaining members of Essence team while I sipped the drink Tyler had given me so I could calm down.

They'd been trying to keep the conversation light and factual since I'd had my emotional breakdown, and I was grateful to all of them for it. Once I'd finally gotten my tears to chill out, they'd all made jokes to make me laugh and turned their focus to other things that needed to be discussed.

"It was a hard decision, Malcolm being the only one to go with her. None of us liked the idea, but we all knew two people would be harder to track than five. Since they were the ones who'd met with the leaders of Binaria West and were already legally married in the United States, it would make things easier for them if it was Malcolm who went with her. We kept in contact with them for a while after they fled. We even helped them get set up with everything they'd need while they were on the run," Ben explained.

"But soon, we realized that by keeping in touch with them, we were putting them in danger," Brandt said.

Tucking his black hair behind his ears, Logan added, "We thought that if we stayed away from them, we'd be keeping them safe. And that last night we were together, we all made the decision. We knew it was the last time we were going to be able to see them for a while, and we'd tried to make it as special as possible..." he paused for a second, "and I'm guessing that's when you were conceived."

"Gotcha," I said before I sipped some more of my lemon-flavored drink. "Do you guys know what they found out?"

Ben sighed, his brown eyes turning sad as he regarded me. "They found evidence proving there was a traitor in Binaria West, pointing out how missions were being switched around, given to the wrong teams, things like that."

"Oh, yeah, I knew that part," I clarified. "What I meant was, do you know what they found out that had them making a deal with Absinthe?"

"Absinthe?" Logan all but stood up as he heard the name. "What does that fucker have to do with anything?"

Adam sighed and asked, "You guys don't know?"

"Obviously, boy. What are you talking about? What don't we know?" Brandt asked hostilely.

Derrick cleared his throat and said, "That's how they were killed..."

A retelling of my life ensued, all the key points noted and accounted for, and I wasn't happy about it, but I did feel like they deserved to know what had happened.

They'd been under the impression, as had most everyone else in the hunter community, that apparently my parents had died by the hands of other hunters, the ones that were ordered to bring them in. However, from what Essence team was telling me, they could never find that team and deal out their own form of justice given the fact that not too long after they left Malcolm and Mandy, they were ordered to take up operations for Binaria East, not West.

The only reason they were back here now was that the mission they were on (something about a rogue Pegasus or something) had them over in this hemisphere. And the reason they were in the incubus lair right then was that they always made an effort to visit their old stomping grounds whenever they got a chance.

Once they knew as much as we did about everything surrounding Malcolm and Mandy's lives and deaths, they were visibly upset and seemed to be having trouble handling their emotions.

"Becks, I'm sorry, but we've got to be heading out," Logan said sincerely as he and the rest of his team stood up. "We've been here too long already, and this... this is a lot to take in."

"I get it," I said as I stood up as well.

"Can we trade phone numbers so we can stay in contact with you?" Ben asked sweetly, and not a sliver of me wanted to deny them the simple but incredibly impactful request.

After they left, Derrick, Tyler, Adam, and I all sat back down and just breathed for a few minutes. They each had their own drinks, and as we sat there going over everything that'd transpired, we each sipped slowly, letting ourselves have the time to acclimate.

Eventually, the silence was broken by a sweet and passionate female melody being sung from somewhere in the back of the ware-house. It was calming and reassuring, and as I listened to it, I felt myself stand and start to sway along to it.

"Becks," Adam said as he put his drink down on the floor and stood in front of me. "Are you feeling okay?"

A small giggle fled my mouth at the worry in his voice, and I reached out to pull him closer, leading his hands to rest on my hips as I said, "I feel great. I've got a bunch of dads like Derrick, there's awesome music playing, and I've got you guys with me. So, can you stop worrying and just dance with me?"

His concerned face faltered instantly, being replaced by his sweet smile as he started moving with me slowly to the music that filled the space all around us. I'd kicked off my heels when I sat down earlier, so I wasn't uncomfortable in the slightest as I wrapped my arms around Adam's neck and let his body guide my movements.

That self-deprecating voice started to pipe up about how I wasn't that great of a dancer. Still, with the atmosphere's help, that voice was silenced in a flash, another voice whispering of living life to the fullest, ultimately winning out in the battle over my emotions.

Adam had lost his brown leather jacket, and the sight of his white t-shirt was doing crazy things to my body. I found my eyes raking over him hungrily, my hands squeezing his strong biceps as I ran them down his arms. When I glanced up into his sapphire eyes, I almost melted at the emotion I saw in them.

So slowly it was almost painful, Adam took a hand from my hip and pressed it lightly to my cheek, his eyes never leaving mine as he asked, "Can I kiss you, Becks?"

A gulp of air quickly filled my chest as my lips parted of their own accord, and I nodded my head 'yes.' Adam licked his lips and brought them to mine in a kiss, so light and soft, my heart stuttered in my chest.

Everything was right in the world. Maybe not everywhere, and maybe not for long, but at that moment, it was for me.

I couldn't think about anything other than his tongue dancing with mine, the way his hand felt on my face, or how incredible and alive my body felt right then. Until Derrick tapped Adam on the shoulder, effectively ending our slow makeout session, so he could ask me to dance. Adam looked to me for an answer, and when I couldn't give him one because again, I couldn't choose between them, Adam smiled sweetly at me, kissed my lips one more time, and then walked away, the heat of his body leaving rapidly, only to be replaced just as fast by Derrick's solid form.

He wrapped me up in his arms, squeezing me with the perfect amount of strength, turning our slow dance into more of a moving hug session than a dance, my heart racing with happy emotions because of it. Derrick's mouth moved near my ear as he whispered, "Can you show me how you're feeling again?" then, added, "Please?" in an almost pained sounding whisper.

Knowing that at that moment, I'd do anything these guys asked of me, I reached into my soul and slightly brushed against my power with the intention of showing him how I felt, and his response was immediate. He sent his lips to mine with a heated and passionate kiss I found myself accepting, meeting, and reciprocating just as fervently.

However, I realized a little too late that I'd sent out how I felt not just to Derrick, but to Adam and Tyler as well.

Each of them stepped up on either side of me, placing their hands on my belly, my lower back, my shoulder. And with all three of them touching me at the same time, something in me broke away, something that'd been holding me back from experiencing these men fled my soul, and I knew I was in some deep shit.

If this didn't work out for whatever reason, I knew I would never be able to heal from it. I wanted each of them so much I could hardly stand it, and as they passed me back and forth, one kissing me here, another planting soft kisses on the back of my shoulder there, someone running his hands through my hair, I knew I'd never get enough of this feeling. I'd never felt anything like it, and I never ever wanted it to stop.

My brain was lost, and I was no longer able to analyze who was doing what, when, or why. Reason had entirely left my body, and good riddance. Who needed to overthink anything anyway?

Someone pulled the curtains closed around us, someone else laid out and fluffed the pillows on the floor, and the entire time, someone was always distracting me with roaming hands and heated skin.

When next I took a breath, my dress was coming off over my head, and I had a moment of clarity where I knew exactly what was going on, precisely what we were about to do, and rather than feeling fear of what it might be like because of my past, I was actually looking forward to how good it *could* be. How *not* scary it was with these three.

Tyler leaned over me as he gently set me down on cushions that felt as soft as clouds. His eyes met mine as he fell to his knees before me, and I knew his beast was right there as well, directly beneath the surface since his eyes were glowing the same way they had when I'd walked in on him playing guitar the other night. His lips met mine again, and his fingertips traced down the front of my shoulder, around the outside of my bra, and down my side, where they slid in the waistband of my underwear, skimming over the sensitive skin across the lowest parts of my belly.

Adam was off to one side of me, kissing up the side of my neck and down over my shoulder, his hand rubbing my back gently. Derrick was doing the same thing from my other side, and somehow, even with all the emotions that were flooding through me, I was able to pick up on the subtle way each of them let the others have their space, but fully took up their own as well.

The backflips my stomach usually did were nothing compared to what it was doing now. A longing like I'd never felt before took over every part of me, and before I even knew what I was doing, I pushed back on Tyler's chest, forcing him to lay on his back as I climbed on top of him with a self-confidence I didn't know I had. Immediately, I felt the proof of his arousal between my thighs, and the feeling only spurred me on even more.

Adam and Derrick followed me, my movements not giving them any pause in continuing their slow and deadly assaults on my senses.

Tyler's eyes were going back and forth between glowing and not glowing that deep green color they always showed, and as I leaned down to kiss his neck, I felt the shiver that tore through his body from my actions.

Slowly, I started unbuttoning his vest, then his shirt, finally exposing that chest of his to my eyes, and I gazed at him greedily, my senses almost becoming overwhelmed with how intensely I wanted him.

Derrick slid behind me then as I realized both he and Adam had left my side for a second. When I looked back at Derrick questioningly, I saw his shirt was off, the swirling lines and designs of his tattoos distracting me for a moment before Adam caught my attention and pulled my lips to his.

He'd settled beside me again, sans shirt as well, and as I rubbed a hand over Tyler's smooth chest in front of me, my other hand found purchase on Adam's chest. My whole body quivered, a moan escaping me without thought as Derrick started kissing the other side of my neck, down over the front of my shoulder, inching his way toward my breasts as his fingers spread through my hair and pulled lightly.

Tyler reached up and wrapped his arms behind me to unclasp my bra, quickly grabbing the straps before they fell off my shoulders. I broke my kiss with Adam as I stared down at Tyler in confusion, but as he started slowly pulling my bra down and off my shoulders, I knew he was dragging out the anticipation on purpose.

The looks on his and Derrick's faces where they stared at me were absolutely ravenous, and the sight of their reactions to seeing me sent uncontrollable shivers through my body and pebbled my skin instantly.

When the cups of the bra finally uncovered my nipples, they were already as hard as rocks, and the way the guys were nearly salivating at the sight of them had me close to falling apart right then and there.

Once the bra was entirely off me, Tyler glanced up and asked with breathy worry, "Is this okay?"

I could hardly stand the wait and couldn't nod my head fast enough to get my point across that what was happening was absolutely okay with me in every sense of the word. Urgently, his mouth captured my nipple, and my hands grabbed onto him tightly, one fisting in his hair as another dug my fingernails into his shoulder. I couldn't help it, his tongue just felt so good.

Adam reached over and grabbed my other breast while his other hand slid down my lower back in tiny soothing, circular motions, and I almost fell apart again.

Surprising me, Derrick lifted me off of Tyler and made me look in his eyes as I stood before him. I really wanted to pout again, but the way he was staring at me gave me pause. Tyler and Adam stood up too, and Derrick made a point of meeting everyone's eyes before he spoke, a silent message to listen the fuck up loud and clear on his features.

"We don't know if you are the next queen yet. But if you are and we do this, we could be binding ourselves to you, Becks, and you could be binding yourself to us. Now, and forever. We might not be able to go back and change it. I need you to be sure. All of you need to be sure that this is what you want, just in case," he said, and my breath caught in my throat.

'Is he seriously asking if I'm okay with this? I've wanted them from the moment I met them.'

"Of course, I want each of you," I said.

But then I remembered he wasn't talking to me alone. He was talking to Adam and Tyler as well, and suddenly a fear I'd never known in my life spread through me like wildfire. Somehow, I was able to peer over at Adam, where he was standing beside me with a hand still planted on my back.

"I will always want to be with you, Becks," Adam answered Derrick by speaking directly to me, and some relief washed through me, a smile and a joyous feeling replacing it altogether.

Then I turned to Tyler, and my fear shot through the roof. He and Derrick were just staring at each other, eyebrows drawn down as they weighed their options.

I'd never felt so panicky in all my life up until that moment, wanting them to agree to be with me more than I'd ever wanted anything. I wanted them more than I'd wanted to get out of the asylum, more than I'd wished I didn't have abusive adoptive parents, more even than I'd wanted to see the supernatural world again. I wanted all of them more than I could've ever imagined, and waiting for their answers was enough to drive me crazy.

Derrick said, "I'm all in. And I am willing to share Becks with you if you'll allow it."

He was letting Tyler make the decision, shocking me as he abdicated his control of the situation. My eyes were big as I scanned Derrick's and Tyler's expressions, but Tyler wouldn't look at me.

He was staring at Derrick, and it was in that moment, that very instant, I knew he didn't want this as badly as I'd thought he had. I knew he wasn't going to say yes, but for some reason, my dumb ass just stood there half-naked and exposed, waiting for him to say it out loud as my heart started to crack.

Finally, Tyler's eyes met mine, and they were no longer glowing. His face was hard, the lines of his chiseled chin set as his deep-set eyes bored into mine.

"I can't," he said as my entire world crashed in on itself and a pain like I'd never felt in my life stabbed through me with pinpoint accuracy. The breath I'd been holding squeaked out of my throat as I stared at him, praying I didn't hear what I thought I had.

"I can't live my life without you, Becks. So, if that means I have to live with sharing you with them, I will," Tyler finished, and immediately, I slapped the fuck out of his shoulder as tears fell down my face yet again.

"What the fuck is wrong with you?" I screamed at him, unable to get a hold of my emotions. "Making me feel like that? What the fuck, Tyler!"

His expression changed from affronted to worried really fast as I felt myself starting to glow again, but I didn't care at all, and I followed him as I pushed him back. "I can't live without you either, asshole. Not without any of you guys! Why the fuck would you make me question how you feel about me?" I asked right before he grabbed me by the back of my head and pulled my mouth to his in a crushing kiss I felt all the way down in my toes.

My words died off, and my anger subsided with them as Tyler's tongue swayed against mine. Once my body calmed from the absence of my anger, I stopped glowing, and Tyler's grip on me relaxed, his kiss becoming softer and more leisurely as he took his sweet ass time exploring my mouth with his while Adam and Derrick descended on my body with kisses of their own.

As if they were working as a team, Adam and Derrick sank to their knees beside me, and each of them slipped a finger into the waistband of my underwear. They slid them down the length of my legs, each of them grabbing hold of my hands, helping me to gingerly step out of the garment, and as much as I wanted to look down at their faces, Tyler held me captive so I couldn't.

My stomach was swirling in the best way possible, heat growing inside me as my breath came faster and faster. Hands started sliding up and down my legs from my ankles to my inner thighs and back, stopping just short of touching the most sensitive part of me, torturing me in a sweet synchronicity I couldn't comprehend.

Tyler pulled away and looked in my eyes as his hand slid up to cup my jaw tight enough for my eyes to jerk up to his. "Lay down," he commanded, his voice thick and husky as his eyes began to glow, and every part of me wanted to obey him as my stomach sailed away with the flight of a million butterflies.

I was barely even settled on the carpeted floor between the pillows before Adam crawled on top of me, drowning me in sweet kisses that started on my mouth but slowly and steadily traveled south until his tongue drifted around one of my nipples, sending a wave of pleasure through me with every new flick of his tongue.

Derrick and Tyler were out of my line of sight until Adam's kisses trailed even further down, slowing around my belly button before they kept going and landed at the top of the inside of one thigh, never touching the place I wanted him to before he switched sides and started kissing and licking my other thigh, torturing me even more.

When I thought I couldn't take any more of the wait and was holding myself back from pushing Adam's face where I wanted it, Tyler's mouth landed on one breast at the same time as Adam's mouth landed on my core, tearing an audible gasp through my throat, pulling air into my lungs as my body jerked at the intensity of the feelings.

Unconsciously, I turned my head to the side, riding the wave of pleasure out, and when I looked up, Derrick was there, long, thick cock in hand as he pumped away watching me unravel before him. The sight of him watching me was so erotic, I could hardly stand it. His eyes met mine, and without thinking, I reached out and took over for him, grabbing hold of his erection, lightly at first as I got used to the feel of him, and then tighter as I saw how my motions affected him.

Adam's tongue was working miracles around my clit as his finger traced circles around my entrance, and slowly, his fingers slid inside me as his tongue left my core, and his eyes went in search of mine.

Still working Derrick while Tyler palmed and nibbled at my breasts, I met Adam's heated gaze, the intensity of his stare alone nearly enough to send me over the edge. He pumped his fingers in me, slowly at first, and then in rhythm with my racing heart, and before long I was coming undone over his hand as his tongue attempted to lap up every trace of my pleasure.

When I was done reeling, Adam withdrew his fingers and stood up while Derrick moved in between my legs smoothly, and Tyler moved to where Derrick had been like they were playing a game of magical, musical hunters.

However, when I tried to watch Adam and Tyler remove the rest of their clothes, Derrick pulled my gaze to his sternly, his hand turning my face to look at him as I felt the tip of his cock right outside my entrance waiting on me to give him the go-ahead.

"You can't get pregnant unless we all desire that you do in our souls, and there's no such thing as diseases for hunters, given our bodies' abilities to heal themselves," he said, clearing up answers to questions I hadn't even thought to ask yet. For a second there, I almost felt foolish about not thinking of them myself before my vagina took over my emotions, but in short order, I let my reservations go since I didn't need to worry about any of it now.

"I'm going to ask you one more time, and then you're mine. Do you want to be bound to me, Becks, now and forever?" His voice was strained as he asked me for my permission again, as if he was barely able to get the words out with how intense everything we'd already been doing was.

With no reservations at all, I leaned up, grabbed his hips with my hands, and pulled him into me, sheathing him deep within me, and despite how my body shook at his incredible length, I was able to say, "Yes, Derrick, now and forever."

His lips descended on mine as he started rocking into me slowly, each thrust met with a dash of his tongue across my lips. He filled me up completely and took up all the space above me as he hugged me to him, his forehead falling against mine for a second before he lifted himself, and his pace quickened.

A growl reached my ears as Derrick built me up toward another orgasm, and I turned an angry glare on Tyler, where he sat naked on his knees next to me. His eyes met mine territorially, and I leveled him with a frown of my own as I grabbed his cock from his hand and squeezed, shutting up his growl in a flash.

He looked like he didn't know what to do, so I started pumping my hand on him, and his gaze softened, his shoulders relaxing. After a few beats, his hands threaded into his hair as he watched my hand moving on him like he couldn't believe what he was seeing.

I felt so empowered in that moment, reining in both Tyler and his beast while Derrick pounded into me, and after a few more thrusts, I came around Derrick so hard I thought I might actually be exploding.

Derrick's release didn't come too long after mine, pulling himself out just in time to spill himself on my belly. The sight of his seed on me made a new heat begin to rise through me all over again. As he wiped me clean with a towel he'd procured from somewhere, with the softest touch imaginable, I kept up my pace on Tyler while Adam slid up to Derrick's vacated spot.

Awaiting entrance as Derrick had, Adam's sapphire eyes met my own as he leaned down, his face mere inches from mine.

"What do you say, Becks? Now and forever?" His sweet, velvety voice slid over me like a tidal wave. Instantly, I knew I wasn't going to have to wait much longer before he'd have me reaching yet another emotional release. That man probably could've talked me into an orgasm with his voice alone. I loved the sound so much it had everything in me screaming for him to fill me.

"Yes, Adam. Now and forever," I said before he pushed himself inside me and I nearly came within the first few seconds he was there.

Seeming to pick up on how high I was already flying, he stayed there without moving for a second while my body relaxed around him, and he smiled down at me. My hand was still working Tyler, though I had let my rhythm slip up a couple of times while Adam distracted me. But once Adam picked up the pace, I found it even harder to concentrate on what else I thought I should be doing, and at some point, I unintentionally let Tyler go.

He didn't seem to mind though. When I released my hold on Tyler, Adam sat back, nearly on his heels as he slid me closer toward him, raising my hips off the ground, and started pumping into me at a different angle that almost had me coming apart at the seams. As Adam began his torturous pace, Tyler slid his mouth smoothly over my nipple while his hand palmed my other breast, and the combination of what they were doing to me had me coming in no time flat. Adam's release followed closely behind my own, spilling onto the top of my thigh as my head spun.

Derrick was laying beside us, watching us like a predator would stalk his prey as his hand worked his cock, but I barely even had time to let that register in my mind before I was cleaned off, and Tyler settled between my thighs.

Emotions were going haywire inside me from all the pleasure. I almost felt like crying with how good I felt, but I was able to hold the tears back somehow as Tyler began whispering in my ear.

"We can stop now if it's too much for you to handle," he said, and immediately a little surge of anger spread through me despite my emotional craziness. There was no way I wasn't going to have all of them right then. Not a fucking chance.

"I can handle anything you guys throw at me," I said with a healthy dose of false confidence I didn't quite know if I could live up to, but Tyler smiled at me in return like he was proud of me, so I knew I'd said the right words.

Looking me in my eyes with his glowing, Tyler said, "You'll never get rid of me if we do this, I hope you know that."

His words had me giggling, and when I pulled his ear to my lips, I said, "I'll never want to. I want to be with you now and forever, Tyler."

He sighed in my ear as he slid himself inside me, his mouth resting on my neck as my eyes closed in ecstasy. He rocked into me as his hands slipped around to cup and squeeze my ass, the weight of his body resting on my chest, my fingernails unintentionally digging into his back as I just tried to hold on.

As the intensity was reaching its inevitable peak, Tyler shocked the hell out of me by sinking his teeth into the part of my neck where it met my shoulder, and the most intense orgasm I'd felt yet ripped through me, making me cry out as both Tyler and I came at the same time.

He spilled himself deep inside me, and at that point, tears really did start to form in my eyes. I might not have known what that bite meant on an intellectual level, but on a primal one, I knew exactly what it meant. He'd claimed me as his, and the thrill of that realization rocked me, tears sliding from my eyes as my emotions made me crack.

"Oh, God! Did I hurt you?" Tyler asked, his eyes huge and worried as I gazed up at him, confused for a second about what in the world he was talking about.

Once I figured it out, I said, "No, I've just never been this happy in my whole life," as a few more tears slipped out before I could stop them.

Within seconds, I was wrapped in a four-person hug that left me speechless, and later on, after we'd all talked like old friends to calm my emotions, I fell asleep like that too.

CHAPTER 17

DERRICK

"*E*xcuse me," a sweet-sounding female voice woke me the next morning. I was lying on the floor, blocking anyone who may have tried to enter through the curtains' makeshift door while my team slept behind me.

I sat up and glanced back at my team, noticing that both Adam and Tyler had their arms wrapped tightly around Becks as she lay between them, their legs a tangled mess. The sight made me smile, but also didn't help my morning biology, and self-consciously, I pulled a pillow into my lap to cover myself.

"Excuse me, but it's time for your team to go," the voice said again, making me jerk my head around. Somehow, I'd already forgotten what'd woken me up to start with.

The woman was wearing a blue, flowing, sheer dress that left nothing to the imagination, and her eyes were a pale blue that matched it perfectly. As soon as I saw her eyes, I knew what she was, who she was, and right away, I was on my feet, the mission back at the forefront of my mind.

"Mer Queen Darya," I said before I cleared my throat.

"Please don't call me that here," she whispered angrily before her voice rose back to its normal pitch. "Your team needs to go. Now."

"You're who we've come to talk to," I said, hearing my team shift around behind me, probably getting dressed hastily if I had to guess.

The Mer queen crossed her arms over her chest and met my face with a scowl I could almost feel. "I am not going back to him, and I don't care what the hunters think about it. You can't tell me who to be with. That's outside the laws, even for you hunters."

"Oh, we're not here to tell you to go back to that asshole," Becks said as she walked up beside me, readjusting the dress she'd just put back on. "We're here to help you."

"Help me?" Darya scoffed. "I don't know what you all are up to, but you need to leave now. You've all reached your atmosphere exposure limit, and I will not have a bunch of crazed hunters running around disturbing our other guests."

Adam and Tyler walked up to stand with us then. In true Tyler fashion, he said, "We've got things to say and questions to ask, and we're not leaving until you've heard all of it. Whether we're crazed or not when you hear it is your choice, though." He finished buttoning up his vest and looked back up at Darya, where she seemed to still be thinking over her options.

Finally, she sighed in acceptance and said, "Fine. Finish getting dressed and meet me outside."

Once we were all dressed, we grabbed our things and headed out into the alleyway, the buildings around us effectively blocking the too bright, early morning sunlight.

"Let's get a little further away to have this conversation, whatever it's about," Darya said as she led us through the buildings and back out to the waterfront. Once we were a safe distance away, she turned to face us, crossing her arms over her chest, waiting not so patiently for us to speak.

"Okay, Queen Darya, here's the deal: Your husband has caused all kinds of chaos, and from what we know, we're assuming he's out there looking for you right now," Adam said with genuine concern in his voice.

"I don't care what he does. I left him, and I'm not going back!" She was adamant.

"You don't care that he closed the portals, and now families have been ripped apart because they can't get through to each other?" Becks asked with more insight than I'd thought she'd gleaned so far. It was a question that visibly went right to the queen's chest.

Her irritated facade cracked, eyes going wide and melancholic as she asked, "He actually closed them," while worry seeped into her voice.

"Yes," I said plainly.

Now was not the time for subtlety or tiptoeing around her feelings. She needed to know what her people were going through, and what her options were as soon as possible, no matter if it hurt her feelings or scared her in the process. "All the underwater portals have been closed except for his. However, we believe that if you were to rally the merpeople behind you, we could help you take the king off his throne, and we could dole out the punishment he deserves for his crimes."

"Oh, now you want to step in?" she asked with a humorless and bitter chuckle. "Where've you been up until now, huh? His crimes? They didn't just start when he closed the portals, you know."

Tyler wiped a hand down his face in agitation before he said, "Well, we haven't had proof until now. But now that we do, we want to move forward with this. We can do it with or without your help, but your people need a leader, and we know they'd happily accept you. Maybe even you and your incubus lover. Who knows? But we need an answer."

Becks walked up to Darya then, reaching out a soothing hand to rest on the Mer queen's shoulder with an expression of understanding on her soft features. "Do you think your merpeople will help you take the kingdom from him? Is that what you want to have happen?"

Darya looked worried and thoughtful for a minute, but eventually said with resolve, "I'd love to run my kingdom the way I think it should be run, and yes, I think they will follow me. But my husband's army will fight for him. I'd be asking regular merpeople to take up arms against trained guards. It's not an easy decision."

I understood what she was saying. Going to war was never a decision to take lightly. However, from what I knew of the merpeople, the only reason they'd tolerated the king was out of fear. If she gave them hope, someone to stand behind, I knew they'd fight with all they had. Hope is more powerful than fear.

"I don't think the king's guard will follow him as closely as you might think," Adam said. "One of my abilities is being able to see the future sometimes, and I've had a vision of you sitting on the throne. Your incubus was sitting beside you too, fishtail and all. It could change, but that is entirely dependent on the choices you make right now."

Queen Darya sighed and said, "Okay, I'll take your word for it. But what do you think the best course of action would be at this point? I mean, I can't even get through the portals to talk to my people."

She was finally on board, and I was instantly relieved about it.

"Here's what I'm thinking," Tyler started, his logistical mind taking over, and I readied myself to interject when his plan took its inevitable wrong turn. "Over the next few days, you rally all the merpeople on Earth. Get them to follow you. While you're doing that, we'll find the king and lead him back to the castle in the Veil. Then, when you've gotten enough of them to agree to stand with you, we'll make our move.

We'll go through his personal portal and force him to open the rest of them back up before we take him to Binaria West. When they open, you'll need to be ready. We'll have probably caused a big enough scene by then that we'll need your help to make it out of there with the king in custody."

I stared at Tyler for a second. He'd actually come up with a better plan than I had, and it took me a bit to wrap my mind around it. Deciding not to second guess him, I turned back to the queen. "How long will it take you to get your Earthbound merfolk ready?"

Tyler didn't miss it when I went along with his plan, given the fact that he looked at me like I'd sprouted horns, but I ignored him as I waited for Darya's answer.

"I'll need a week. I can get to all of them in that time," she said resolutely, standing taller than she'd been standing before, cold determination setting across her features.

I nodded, acknowledging each of my teammates before I said, "Alright, that means we have one week to find the king and make sure he's back at the castle to open the portals." Then glancing back at the queen, I said, "We'll meet you here one week from today."

"One week," she repeated as she shook each of our hands and turned to leave, walking back to the club with haste, probably excited to share the news with her incubus.

"Where's Brax?" Adam asked. "He needed to hear that."

"I'm right here," I heard Brax say from behind me where he was perched on one of the wooden pillars that jutted up from the water and prevented any boats from hitting the concrete barrier we were standing next to. He'd blended in with the stony gray buildings, pavement, and water so well, I hadn't even noticed him sitting there when we'd come out.

"Sounds like a good plan to me. But you guys seriously need to shower. I can smell all the sex from here," he said, and I felt my face get hot. I couldn't tell what he was thinking, or how he felt about what'd transpired last night, which he certainly knew about already, but I could guess he wasn't too upset since he wasn't trying to stone us to death.

Apparently, he read my thoughts because he said, "I knew what I was getting into when I accepted you guys for Becks' team. Sex is a necessary part of being hunters. Anytitty, with the number of times I've had to hear you guys think about Becks sexually and vice versa, I'm surprised you've all held out this long. Now hurry up and teleport us, Tyler. I might be okay with what you guys did, but that doesn't mean I want to smell it all day."

A SHORT TIME LATER, we were all clean and dressed in our typical attire and having lunch in the safe house as we went over our plan for everything we had to do.

"How are we going to find an uninfected vampire elder?" Tyler asked as he shoveled spaghetti into his mouth like a heathen.

I rolled my eyes at him as Adam said, "Well, they said Transylvania is where they thought they were made, right? Why don't we just start there?"

Brax huffed around his mouthful of food but didn't say anything.

"What?" Becks asked him, knowing her familiar wasn't saying something he was thinking.

Brax put down his fork and glowered at the ceiling with a heavy sigh. "That's where my first charge, Phillipa, died. I haven't been back there since, and I was hoping I'd never have to."

Becks looked upset and empathetic as she said, "I didn't see the part where she died. Did you stay with her till the end? That must have been terrible for you."

Brax leveled an expression on Becks that I hadn't seen him wear before, and couldn't really define. He crossed his arms and huffed again, but answered anyway.

"Might as well get it over with and tell you guys what happened." He swallowed and laced his hands in his lap before he started talking.

"I did stay with her, even though at first, she couldn't see me. I knew she was cold, so I started a fire in the cave and kept it going to help as much as I could.

It was about two days later, and she was this close to dying when her eyes started following me everywhere I moved around her, and I knew she could see me. I didn't understand it, and it wasn't like I could go back to the angel tribunal and ask them what I was supposed to do with a human charge that could see me. I had to figure it out like every other gargoyle.

Anytitty, I kept the fire going and tried to keep her happy as best I could by like, dancing around or shaking her rattle for her, but I knew she wasn't going to last much longer. She'd have bouts where she wouldn't stop crying, then she'd use up all her energy and just lay there. It was absolute torture watching her suffer like that.

But then I got the bright idea that I might be able to steal some goats' milk from some of the farms nearby and give it to her. So that's what I did. I kept her going for a long time like that, just giving her goat's milk and trying to keep her as safe as possible, given all of her issues.

Which was almost impossible, by the way. I had to block her in that cave so she wouldn't get burned by the sun, I had to block the back of the cave too so she wouldn't fall into the stream that ran through it, and eventually, I even had to move the fire up higher so Philippa wouldn't burn herself when she started being able to crawl around. The only things she had in the cave were her blankets and her rattle. If I left anything else in there, even the metal cup I used to use to pour milk into her mouth, she'd somehow figure out a way to hurt herself with it."

I think we were all blown away by what he was saying, but Becks asked with happy bewilderment, "You kept her alive? For how long?"

"For a while," Brax said as he looked down at the table, "I was living off the bats that lived in the cave. There were a million of them that flew out every night and back in before the sun came up every morning.

I'd say she was about a year and a half old when goat's milk wasn't enough for her anymore. One night I jumped up and caught a bat as they were flying out like I always did, and she surprised me when she did the same thing and snagged one for herself. She ate it like a champ as if she'd been eating them her whole life." His sad smile got more prominent as he reminisced.

"After a while of that, I knew she was going to need more than bats to get by, so I started hunting in the woods outside the cave. One rabbit would feed her for days, though, so I didn't need to do it often. And I started to get hopeful then. But right when I thought everything was going to be okay, that she was going to turn out alright, she started getting sick."

Brax paused and took a deep breath, his eyes filling up with tears as he talked. "I just didn't know what to do. I tried to keep her as happy as I always had, making her laugh, playing with her, all that. But she was getting weaker and weaker by the day it seemed, no matter how much food or water or milk I gave her, or how often I cleaned her in the stream. Eventually, I knew there was nothing else I could do. She wasn't going to make it.

I was holding her, rocking her back and forth, pleading with the angels to not let this be the end of my charge's life, but she died in my arms anyway, and as soon as her heart stopped beating, I was jerked out of Earth and put in front of the angel tribunal to await my judgment."

"I'm so sorry, Brax," Becks said sincerely.

He just wiped his eyes and shrugged. "It was a long, long time ago, no need to worry about it now."

"What's the angel tribunal?" Becks asked.

Brax sighed again and said, "Well, it's basically three angels with sticks so far up their asses they barely even move when they speak. They're the ones who decide if a gargoyle has done a good enough job protecting their charges and determine how that goyle will spend the rest of eternity.

The highest honor a gargoyle can achieve is to earn fertility by doing a good job during their lives. The lowest is to be sentenced to an eternity of watching bad things happen and never being able to do anything about it. Those goyles that fail are forced into living an existence of stone, never able to help anyone, though they can watch everything that's happening around them. Which goes against everything that makes them a gargoyle in the first place."

"What did they say to you after Philippa died? And why'd they give you a human charge, to begin with?" Adam asked, seeming utterly perplexed as if he were just as confused about Brax's past as I was.

"Well, I still have no idea why they charged me with protecting a human child that was going to be abandoned so shortly after she was born. The angels hardly ever explain their reasons for why they do the things they do. But I think it had to do with the fact that my mother, once she won her fertility, went to the elf prince she'd been in love with for centuries to mate with, while every other gargoyle just mated with other gargoyles. I'm different because of who my father is, and I think that's why they thought I should be charged with something different.

But when I was jerked up there after Philippa died, they said they needed time to think over my case because they didn't have enough evidence to choose my fate, one way or the other. Which really just meant that I spent an ungodly amount of time waiting in blackness for them to make up their minds."

"Waiting in blackness?" Becks asked.

Brax ran a hand through his blonde hair before answering her. "Yeah. It was like I couldn't move and I couldn't see. I could hardly even think. I was surrounded by it, and time didn't seem to exist. But eventually, they pulled me out and told me they'd come to a decision. They were going to assign me to a different case, as unprecedented as something like that was. The angels said I was going to be charged with protecting a hunter this time around, and that it was probably my half-elf side that had skewed my previous life.

They didn't even give me time to ask a single question, the cuntsuckers. They threw me right into the Veil with some dumbass psychic hunters who'd become pregnant. Roland was born about nine months later."

"Hold on," Tyler said. "You were Roland's familiar? Roland, like the Roland that was a fucking celebrity in the eighteen hundreds for doing so well until he lost his damn mind and almost single-handedly brought on the apocalypse?"

"Look, I didn't say I was perfect, okay? I've got a past, just like you, shapeshifter. And Roland was going to end up losing his mind whether I was his familiar or not! I tried my fucking hardest with that fool, but nothing I did ever mattered to him. I don't want to talk about this anymore. It's not important right now, anyway," Brax said, folding his arms across his chest, his wings twitching behind him as he talked.

"How many charges have you had?" Becks asked.

"You're my third. And my last chance at winning fertility and seeing my mother again, if you must know. The angels said explicitly after Roland died that they weren't going to let me squeeze by with a life of mediocrity again. That if I didn't do a good enough job with my next charge, you, Becks, that I would be sentenced to stone. They said I better make it obvious in this life that I deserve to earn fertility."

Becks spoke aloud what I was already thinking. "That's an insane amount of pressure. And then when all that stuff went down with Absinthe and the asylum, you must have already felt like you'd failed."

Brax looked at Becks with his emotions painted clearly on his face. "Becks, you are by far the best charge I've ever had. And I would want you to live the best life possible whether the rest of my eternity rested on it or not."

Words didn't pass between them, but I was positive thoughts were flowing through their connection for the next few minutes, a silent conversation meant only for Becks and Brax since he'd shut the rest of us out for it.

I glanced at Adam and Tyler, giving Brax and Becks more space, and they each met my eyes doing the same thing for our newest teammates.

I didn't know what all this meant, or why the timekeeper had even brought Brax's past up to begin with, but I was starting to get the feeling that Brax had just as much to do with this whole situation as Becks did.

It was an unsettling thought.

It was bad enough when the entire world's existence rested on our shoulders. But now, Brax's eternity sat there as well. And though he'd only been my familiar by proxy for a short time, there was no way I was going to let him live the rest of his forever out as a solid piece of stone, locked in eternal sadness for failing. He was too good for that.

CHAPTER 18

BECKS

"What you need is closure," I said to Brax as our mental argument turned audible.

"No, what I need is for you to drop it, and let all this go already! Pixie titties! I know the timekeeper fucked with your memories and emotions and all that, but fuck, I really don't need to go back to Philippa's cave!" Brax yelled.

We'd both risen from our spots at the table during our mental disagreement. I was standing there trying to convince Brax of how I just knew he needed to go back to that cave because something inside me would not let the idea go. He was floating around in front of me, all huffy and wing twitchy, shooting down everything I thought or said.

"What's all this about going back to Philippa's cave?" Adam asked as he and the rest of the guys stood up as well.

I sighed and dropped my arms to my sides before I said, "I don't know why, really, but something is telling me that we need to go back, that it'll make Brax feel better if we do. Like, we need to go right now, that's how strongly I feel about this."

"There's a gazillion other things we *need* to do too, girl! Much more than I need closure or whatever," Brax said mockingly, and I started to get angry at how stubborn he was being.

I felt it in my chest, the same kind of feeling I'd had in the pixies' forest when I'd found the piece of Absinthe's armor. Except I wasn't even asking my power for guidance, it was just coming out of me anyway, without me asking it to.

"Becks, are you sure? Because if you're wrong, we might end up hurting Brax more than we'll end up helping him," Derrick said, his words giving me pause.

But the more I thought about it, the more I knew I was right, that Brax had to go back. The words, *'it's the only way,'* kept floating through my mind, though I had no idea what my mind was talking about.

"I'm positive," I said after a few beats of consideration, and Brax deflated in front of me, his wings dropping his form to the floor with a thud. It made my heart hurt to see him upset, but there was no denying the pull on my chest, the call my intuition was making clear.

Derrick rubbed a hand through his hair and said, "Alright, that decides it then. We're going back to this cave. Brax, Tyler can teleport us to the general area, but you're going to have to lead us to its specific location."

Brax was standing there, his eyes wide with sadness, tears starting to form on the rims of his eyes. Though my heart broke for him and his pain, I just couldn't let it go. Finally, Brax sniffed and rubbed his eyes as he said, "Fine. Let's get this over with and be done with it."

In the next few minutes, we were standing in a thick and mountainous forest, and I knew right away we weren't far from the place I'd seen in Brax's memories.

"Just keep up," Brax said before he took off, flying straight like he could find the cave with his eyes closed, not waiting at all to see if we were, in fact, all keeping up.

I'd had to tap into my power to run through the forest, and I'd had to stop a few times as we passed by a few roads and houses that had obviously popped up since the last time Brax had been here. But eventually, Brax began to slow, and the subtle shift in the terrain started to look familiar to what I'd seen in his memories.

When we could see the cave over the next hilly rise, Brax stopped completely, and though I couldn't read his thoughts because he'd closed them off to me or wasn't thinking loud enough for me to hear them, I knew he was going to need some encouragement to get him to go any further.

As softly and sweetly as I could, I reached out and grabbed his hand, where it floated in the air and squeezed lightly. Brax looked at me with all kinds of emotions running across his face, and without thinking, I pulled him into a hug he reciprocated without hesitation.

Our bond strengthened as it always did when we made physical contact, and I knew it was offering him the encouragement he needed to keep going.

When he pulled away, and he started flying closer and closer to the cave, the guys and I all followed silently behind him, letting him take his time as he worked through whatever emotions he was feeling.

I had a fleeting thought about how the cave was still intact and hadn't been overrun with people in the time that had passed since Brax was here before, but dismissed it quickly since most of what was going on in my life didn't make much sense, either.

"See? There's nothing here but painful ass memories," Brax said solemnly.

"I didn't think there would be. But I did hope it'd give you some kind of closure to be able to say goodbye, at least," I said as I walked up to the cave entrance and stood behind Brax.

He turned around and faced all of us then, the anger radiating out of his short form unmistakable.

"Closure? I don't get closure, Becks! I'm not supposed to! My job has been to protect others since the day I turned twelve when my mom had to leave me, and I got my first charge. Only if I'm lucky will I get to make a tiny bit of a difference. Once my time is up this time, that's it! I'm done. And whether I get fertility and an afterlife in

Heaven with my mom or not, or I become a statue for eternity, none of that will give me any kind of closure from what happened here."

His impassioned words turned to gasps between tears, and I wanted nothing more than to reach out and touch him, but as I went to do just that, movement from the cave caught my eye and made me stop.

"She was so tiny! And I did everything I could possibly think of to save her! That girl was my life! Just like you are now, Becks. I can't," his words left his throat as something jumped out of the cave and tackled him to the ground.

My team and I went into attack mode instantaneously, but within a split second of seeing his attacker, I was too busy being stunned to do anything other than gape at the sight before me.

"What the ever titty loving fuck?" Brax screamed as he wrestled on the ground, trying to see what was going on. "Get the fuck off me, what-" his words died on his lips as his eyes finally met his attacker's.

She had crawled off him and was sitting there smiling a two-year-old, fang-filled, toothy grin at him, looking like she was the happiest she'd ever been in that moment.

Brax took to the air on his wings as he stared at her in shock, saying, "Philippa?" in a voice filled with emotion. Then it seemed like he didn't know what to say or do next other than stare at her like we all were. It was as if we were all frozen, none of us willing to move as we watched the little girl eye us.

She seemed to take a keen interest in Derrick then, tilting her head sideways as she surveyed him. Philippa stood up and walked smoothly over to Derrick for a child her size, and as she neared him, his shocked face started to change as he smiled down at her. Once she reached him, he said, "Hey, Philippa. It's nice to me-"

His words were abruptly cut off as Philippa jumped up onto him and sunk her tiny fangs in the side of his neck, her tiny fingernails sharp as she attempted to dig them into his skin so he wouldn't get away.

It all reminded me of a cat video I'd seen where a lady had been messing with this cat, thinking it was funny until that cat started attacking her, and the lady couldn't get the cat off. That's how Derrick looked with a small two-year-old vampire going to town on his neck as he tried futilely to get her off of him.

However, that seemed to spark Brax into moving since he hurriedly flew over and pulled Philippa off of Derrick, admonishing her as he went. "No, Philippa, we don't bite hunters," he barked, pointing his little finger at her after she'd released Derrick and was sitting on the ground with her legs crossed beneath her.

Derrick seemed like he couldn't believe what was happening, Adam was trying and failing to contain his laughter, and Tyler was probably about to pee himself with how hard he was laughing as he watched everything play out in front of him.

Immediately, Philippa's eyes got big as she peered up at Brax, the hurt from his admonishment written all over her beautiful, dirty little face. She stared at him for a second before she put her head on the ground and covered her head with her hands.

"Aww, Brax. You hurt her feelings," I said as I walked over to Philippa, trying my hardest to ignore Adam and Tyler as they continued to find the entire situation funnier than they could handle, and carefully placed a hand on her back.

She looked up at me then, and the sight of her dirt-smeared cheeks, pink with her emotions, and her tangled mass of long blonde hair made me smile. For a second, I thought she was going to try and eat me too, but after a bit, her face relaxed, and she climbed right into my lap and wrapped me up in a tight hug.

Something passed between us, some burst of energy of some kind, and I hugged the little monster tighter to me in response.

"What does this mean?" Brax started thinking out loud. "Does this mean I have two charges? How am I supposed to protect both of you? How has she stayed here this entire time? How has no one found her yet? Oh, Philippa," he finally floated back down to us and got her to look at him again. "I'm so sorry. I didn't know you were here."

A sob tore from his throat as he plopped to the ground, his legs splayed out before him as he put his head in his hands and cried.

Philippa released me and ran over to him swiftly, climbing onto his lap to hug him. She was almost as big as he was, and the two of them together was an adorable and heartwarming sight. He cried on her shoulder, and as everyone came to their senses around us, Brax held onto her as he took to the air to hover beside me.

"You know what this means, right, Brax?" Derrick asked, the wound on his neck already mostly healed in the time that had passed since Philippa had attacked him.

Brax huffed as he plainly read Derrick's thoughts and said, "We won't know anything for sure until Fergus tests her blood, so don't even speak about it yet."

Taking that as the best answer he was going to get under the circumstances, Derrick nodded at all of us, and we each put a hand on Tyler so he could teleport us back to Binaria West, Philippa in tow, finally leaving the only home she'd ever known.

"YOU FOUND HER WHERE?" Otto had asked once everything had calmed down a bit.

Philippa had tried to attack him when she met him too, but one growl from Brax had her rooted to her spot. She froze where she clung to Otto, her eyes going wide as she looked at Brax, but once she realized he'd only been warning her, she'd relaxed in Otto's arms and started poking at his face, pulling on his shirt, thoroughly checking him out as best she could.

Otto hadn't seemed to mind though. Even when she started pulling at his ring of white hair, climbing up him hastily so she could literally sniff the stuff, he'd chuckled happily. At the same time, Brax explained who she was, and eventually, we all made our way down to the labs to talk to this Fergus person.

The scientist in question was bent over a microscope when we all walked in, but one glimpse of Philippa had his eyes practically bulging out of his head.

I didn't like the way he looked at her, but there was nothing I could do about it since Otto and the rest of my team seemed so adamant about having Fergus check her blood to see if she'd been infected or not. I could understand their reasoning but still didn't like it for some reason.

She was clinging to Otto and eyeing up Fergus like he was the juiciest snack she'd ever seen when it dawned on me that she was probably hungry. It would explain why she'd wanted to eat nearly every new person she met as soon as she saw them.

"Don't you guys think we should feed her before Fergus goes stabbing her with needles?" I asked everyone around me at once.

Brax sighed and said, "Yeah, that's probably the best option. Keep an eye on her, and I'll go get some blood from down in the cells really quick," before he disappeared.

As soon as Brax wasn't there anymore, Philippa slunk down Otto's body, leaving him altogether as her eyes stayed plastered to the spot Brax had disappeared from. She walked up to the spot and started jumping and flapping her small arms in the air above her head in what I think we all assumed was a terribly sad attempt to get him back or go with him.

No one said anything as we all watched her do this, and I couldn't let her stay that way, let her live in that pain without even trying to ease it or reassure her in some way. So, I stepped toward her and said, "Hey, Philippa."

I caught her attention, but she still kept jumping and swatting at the air. Only now, it seemed as if she was trying to communicate with me, trying to inform me that Brax had left. Her beautiful little face should've had tears running down it with all the emotions I saw in her eyes, but none formed, and I had a fleeting thought wondering about whether vampires could cry or not, but I dismissed it quickly.

"He's coming back," I said softly as I sat on the floor in front of her so she wouldn't see me as a threat. "He's gone to get you something to drink."

Hearing my words, Philippa stopped jumping and brought her tiny hands to her mouth as she stared at me.

"Yes," I said, smiling. "Brax is going to feed you."

The change in her emotions happened so fast it could've given me whiplash as she smiled and came over to stand behind me. She started playing with my hair where it hung down my back, humming the same song I'd heard her father singing to her the night he'd left her. It was eerie, and I started wondering how she could've possibly remembered the tune, but I ignored the chill that ran down my spine as her manipulations continued to knot up my hair.

Otto, Derrick, Adam, Tyler, and Fergus, all seemed to be locked in a trance-like state where they couldn't take their eyes off the little monster behind me. It was kind of annoying, actually. Here I was, thinking they'd be plotting or planning our next move or something, yet they were just standing there staring instead.

"So, after she's eaten, what exactly are you going to do, Fergus?" I asked, and my question had its desired effect since it snapped them out of their Philippa stare-fest.

Fergus ran his hands down his lab coat a few times as he looked around, probably trying to get his bearings about him again, but recovered soon enough. "Well, Initiate Becks, I'm going to draw some of her blood and see if she's been infected by the same synthetic virus that plagues the elder vampires. If she is infected, then you guys will have to go searching for someone else, but if she isn't, I'm going to see if her blood can save the infected ones. I'm not certain yet, but I have a feeling she might be the first vampire to ever live, and if that's the case, she will need to be protected more than any other, because if she dies, it would most certainly kill off the entire species."

He began moving things around, preparing for what he had to do, I assumed, but something about what he'd said pricked my senses as wrong, though I couldn't quite place what it was exactly. I tried thinking through what I thought was off, but was interrupted by Brax's reappearance in the room.

"Okay, ya fiend, here ya go," Brax said as he handed an unopened blood bag to Philippa.

She took it from his outstretched hand, but then stared up at him in clear befuddlement.

"You drink it," he said as he made motions with his hands to indicate what she needed to do, but still, she looked at him like she didn't understand.

"Oh, just hand it here," Brax said as he gently took the bag from her hands and bit into it before hastily shoving it at Philippa's lips so none would spill, encouraging her to drink it.

She realized then what he'd meant, and once the blood hit her tongue, she sat down and started drinking from the bag greedily while Brax wiped at his tongue with his hand to get the blood off.

'At least she's not a picky eater,' I thought.

Brax stopped wiping his mouth and smiled down at Philippa as he projected his thoughts to me. *'She never has been.'* The expression on his face was sweet and loving, and I was so happy seeing it, I barely even noticed Fergus sneaking up behind Philippa with his needle.

As he pricked her arm, she barely flinched, but I found myself getting angry for her.

"What are you doing? You could've waited until she was done," I said, standing as my anger shot up a bit.

Fergus barely let the words get out of my mouth before he was cutting me off. "It's best to do it while she's occupied. Everyone should already know this. I swear, sometimes, you snowflake initiates are the dumbest I have the displeasure of working with."

"Excuse me?" I asked, taken aback by his blatant hostility, my hands balling into fists unintentionally.

"What? Are you deaf as well as dumb?" Fergus asked calmly as he pushed his glasses further up the bridge of his nose with one finger, leveling me with an unapologetic stare.

"Look, motherfucker," I said, but was cut off promptly by Adam breaking in between us.

"Becks," he said, drawing my eyes to his, "Fergus has no filter." He turned a glare on the scientist, but Fergus didn't notice since he'd already turned around and was putting Philippa's blood on a slide for his microscope.

"I can see that," I said as I crossed my arms where I stood, fuming already from the guy's insults. "Maybe he should work on that."

"I won't," he said, and I had to work really hard at not lashing out at him.

We needed him to see if Philippa was sick, and from what I knew, he was the only one who knew how to discover that vital piece of information. So, despite the growing contempt I felt for the man, I bit my tongue and didn't say anything else as he did what I needed him to do.

However, I had a strong feeling that he was doing it for selfish reasons, not for the good of the vampire species, and I suddenly understood what that inkling was I'd had before.

Fergus had been looking at Philippa the exact same way as he was looking in his microscope now. He didn't see the child. He only saw the experiment. And that didn't sit right with me. Not at fucking all. But I knew I had to get over it if I wanted the results from the tests he was running.

"Well, well, well, little missy," Fergus said a few minutes later as he took a step back from his microscope, planting his hands on his waist, staring right at Philippa where Brax held her in his lap and sat on the floor next to me. "You're exactly what we need."

Otto had been leaning against an unoccupied counter to my right as he'd waited, but at Fergus' words, he perked up and asked, "What do you mean, exactly?"

Fergus looked like he wanted to smart off again but apparently thought better of it, given who he was talking to. "This girl is the oldest known living vampire, and she has not been infected. Her blood can cure the virus and stop it from spreading."

"How do you know?" Otto asked.

Fergus smiled, and I guessed it was because he was going to be able to show off in front of Otto. "If you look at the screen, I'll show you," he said as he slid his glasses up his nose and leaned over his microscope again.

I turned around to see the screen he was talking about, and as it turned on, Fergus' running commentary steadily drove up my sense of worry with every word he said.

"Okay, so these are a few human red blood cells. They're all healthy and normal. Now, when I add some of the girl's blood, you'll see how quickly it changes the human's. The speed with which a vampire's blood changes a human's has always been an indicator as to whether a vamp was an elder or not, but I've never seen a case where it worked this rapidly. This means she's definitely the oldest we've ever encountered. Probably the oldest in existence."

Fergus barely even stopped for a breath, much less paused to see if everyone understood what he was saying with how lost he was in his own demonstration.

"Now, this is an infected vampire's blood cells. You see the hints of purple beneath all that black? Well, it would all be purple if the vamp wasn't infected, but the virus is steadily eating away at these purple cells."

I thought I knew where he was going at that point, but I still couldn't bring myself to take my eyes off the screen as he kept explaining.

"Now, when I add some of that girl's blood to the infected vampire's cells," he said as he placed some of Philippa's blood on the slide, "it heals the vampire's cells completely, turning them all purple. And watch how fast it does it. It's remarkable, I tell you. This virus is synthetic, but because she's basically the mother of all vampires, none of that matters. Her blood cures it all!"

I'd stopped watching the screen as I turned to stare at the scientist, his enthusiasm making all the red flags in my brain shoot up.

"So, what do you propose we do?" Otto asked as everyone else focused on Fergus again.

The scientist didn't hesitate or sound remorseful in the slightest as he said, "We need to take blood from the girl regularly. It's the only way. Really, we need to take it as soon as she makes it to ensure maximum potency. The best way to do that would be to just have the sick vamps drink directly from her. But we do have to keep her healthy so she can make more," he said this almost as an afterthought. "So, I'd say, every two days we should be able to cure about..." he paused to do the math in his head, and I found my fists balling at my sides again, anger searing through me at the image his words portrayed.

"What the fuck do you mean, her blood is the only way? Does that mean all the vampires that haven't died yet have to *feed* off of her? How many vampires are there in the world?" My voice was calm and low even though I was near rage on the inside.

"Were you not listening? Yes, her blood is the only way to save their species. Please pay attention, I hate repeating myself," Fergus said as he turned his nose up at me.

"Well, you can fuck right off with that," I said as I picked Philippa up out of Brax's lap and slung her around, so she clung to my back as if I were giving her a piggyback ride. She giggled in my ear as she wrapped her arms around my neck to hold on, the motion strengthening my resolve and reaffirming my stance.

"Rebecca, he's right. If her blood is the only way, we have to figure something out," Otto said.

Running a hand through his short dark hair, Derrick said, "There's no need to get upset, Becks. We're just talking right now."

It was as if they had no idea why I was so upset like they couldn't see what I saw.

'What the fuck do they expect me to do? Just sit by and watch as they offer Philippa up as the vampires' token blood bag? Well, they have another thing coming. No way am I going to allow that, and I don't care if they don't think I have a say in the matter. I have one because I damn well say I do!' I thought.

Philippa had already been through too much, was *currently* going through too much to be able to handle what they were proposing. She'd just left what was basically her centuries-old prison! The girl needed time to acclimate, to see the world.

I mean, I knew she wasn't going to be able to grow up, and that part really fucking bothered me, but other than killing her, I had no idea how to fix that particular problem. So, the next best thing would be to find a way to make her happy while keeping her safe until we could figure something else out.

'Maybe witches can help?' I wondered even though I had no idea

whether that kind of thing was even possible. However, I knew I couldn't sit around and let Philippa remain a two-year-old vampire girl forever. Nor was I going to allow anyone to use her as bait to lure out and cure all the sick vampires. And I certainly wasn't going to let them dehumanize and belittle everything she was and boil her entire essence down to only being worth what her blood could provide.

'There has to be another way.'

"Becks, babe..." Tyler said as he inched closer to me, arms outstretched before him, "I need you to calm down."

I knew I'd begun to glow again as my power seeped into every part of me, but it didn't seem like the bad thing they were making it out to be.

As Adam and Derrick started moving toward me with the same hesitation in their step, all I could think about was that my power use felt right. Like I was supposed to be doing what I was doing.

"I am calm," I said truthfully. Yes, I was pissed off, but I wasn't losing my rational capabilities at all. If anything, my brain and my power were working together in unison, even though I hadn't necessarily asked them to.

"What you guys are proposing isn't going to happen, and I'm preparing myself for whatever it'll take to prevent it. Philippa is not going to be food for the rest of the vampires. I won't allow it. She's not going to live out her days, having others drink her blood as soon as her tiny body makes more of the cure. I refuse to let that happen. Come what may," I said.

Brax flew over to me and placed his hand on my shoulder, the three of us standing as a united front against whatever the rest of my team, Otto, and Fergus decided to do next. I didn't even need to hear his thoughts to know he had my back, and Philippa's.

Fergus looked at the three of us, mainly me, with the most contempt I think I'd ever seen on a person's face in real life, and said, "And what makes you think you have a choice in this matter, *initiate?*"

A growl escaped Tyler's throat as he whipped around to face Fergus, stalking toward him while Adam and Derrick came over to stand in front of me before turning and glaring at Otto.

They'd all moved at the same time, not a word spoken between them, and some part of me found that fact incredibly flattering as their actions bolstered my self-confidence.

Tyler grabbed Fergus by the lapel of his white coat and dragged him out of the lab, forcefully pushing him out of the room as he said, "Get the fuck out before I kill your dumbass on purpose." Then he closed the door in Fergus' face and came over to stand beside the rest of his team and me.

Otto's eyes were big, his bushy eyebrows nearly reaching his nonexistent hairline. "Becks," he said with hesitation evident in his voice, "I would never allow what Fergus was saying to actually happen." He kind of smiled then, and I felt my power starting to subside some. "I was going to say as much, but you beat me to it."

"Then what do you plan to do?" I asked, ready to defend Philippa even against Otto if need be.

"I think the best thing to do would be to simply take Philippa's blood, maybe once a week. It'll be like she was giving blood. No feeding necessary. We'll cure as many vampires as we can that week, and whichever ones die, die," he said with a shrug that made me smile.

My glowing stopped at his words, and I felt my body beginning to relax as I said, "That sounds like a far better plan than what Fergus suggested. But if giving blood that often becomes an issue for her, I want to renegotiate." I was still smiling but was one hundred percent serious.

"Of course," Otto said as Philippa climbed off my back and ran over to Otto, climbing up him as if he were a tree instead of a person. "Well, aren't you just the cutest thing," he said, and the rest of the tension that'd filled the room seemed to leave without a trace.

"Well, not to spoil the moment or any progress we've made here, but there's the issue of what we're going to do with her," Adam said, bringing up a subject I hadn't even thought about yet. "She's not going to live in that cave anymore, but we can't take her with us everywhere we're going to need to go."

Otto laughed as Philippa put both of her hands on his face and mushed his lips together. "I'll keep her with me while you guys aren't here. Do you want to stay with me, little lady? Sure, you do," he said sweetly, and though the idea of her staying with him relieved some of my worries, I also felt the immediate sadness of knowing I would have to leave her.

I hadn't known her for long, but already, that tiny baby had stolen my heart.

My mind had been working the entire time, trying to find an alternative solution to even the one Otto had said, and suddenly a new one popped in my head, and I heard myself yelping out, "What about a duplication spell or something like that?"

Everyone turned to look at me like I'd lost my mind, so I knew I needed to clarify. "Like if witches or spellworkers could take just one vial of Philippa's blood and then duplicate it with some kind of magic. Could that work?"

Otto seemed contemplative as he thought about it while Philippa laid her head down on his shoulder, her eyes getting heavy. "You know? It might," he said. "I'll have a chat with some of our other spellworkers and see what they can make happen. As long as the duplicate blood has the same potency and still cures them, we could definitely use it."

"You're way smarter than you know, Becks," Derrick said then, a look on his face like he couldn't figure me out. Then turning his attention back to Otto, he said, "For that matter, if the virus is synthetic, then maybe Fergus could use what he has of Philippa's blood already to make a synthetic cure that wouldn't require getting more blood from her."

"Those are some great alternatives," Otto said, bouncing Philippa lightly as she slept on his shoulders.

'Vampires sleep?' I wondered as I stared at her.

'Apparently, this one does,' Brax thought back at me.

"Well, if you're sure you don't mind watching her, we do have other things to handle today," Derrick said.

Otto smiled and used his hand in a shooing motion as he said, "Of course, I'm sure. Go on, handle saving the world and whatnot. She'll be here when you get back." And as an afterthought, he got my attention, "Becks, don't worry. I won't let anyone mess with her while you're gone. No one will make a move until we've cleared it with you first."

"Thank you, Otto," I said as I looked at him like he was crazy. "But why? I mean, you're the chief, after all, it should be your decision, right? Not mine?"

"Well," Otto said, "it might normally be my call, yes. But I personally don't feel like I've got a dog in this fight at all. However, you most certainly do. Philippa might as well be your long-lost sister with how you both share a connection with Brax. And I've never been one to step in between family if I could help it. Plus, I can't ignore how adamant you've been about defending her, and how your power seeks to protect her. Especially before you've gone to the gauntlet."

I was trying to wrap my mind around what he was saying, but it took him explaining a little more for me to get it.

"Since you haven't been yet, we have to assume that all of your powers, whatever they are, are rudimentary at best compared to what they'll be when you go through the gauntlet. We can all guess at what you might be, or what your powers will be, but no one will really know until you get the rest of them, and we can actually classify you. What if you turned out to be a psychic like Adam here, and I'd ignored what your instincts were telling you? I could very well be put in an even worse situation by ignoring how strongly you've felt about her."

His words finally began making sense, and I breathed a sigh of relief and worry as I tried to take it all in. I knew I was different, and somehow that difference had saved Philippa today, so I had to be thankful at least for that aspect. However, the pressure on my shoulders for getting through the gauntlet seemed to keep increasing with everything we did or every encounter we faced, and I wasn't too happy about it. What if I failed? What if I didn't even make it through the gauntlet in the first place?

If that happened, then I would've just been this girl they all knew one time that died with so much potential. Or even worse, if I made it through and didn't turn out to be what they all expected me to be, I'd end up as a big ol' disappointment.

"You guys go on now, I've got Philippa," Otto said, snapping me out of my thoughts.

"I don't know when we'll be back, but we'll check in as much as we can," Derrick told Otto as we filed out the door, passing by a fuming Fergus as we left.

I ignored him as we traveled a short distance away, and I looked back to see Brax softly kissing Philippa on her head before he flew over to us. There were tears in his eyes as he joined back up with us, but his thoughts were closed off to me, and I knew better than to poke at him right then. He needed to feel what all had happened, and it seemed like my team agreed with me as we all silently made our way through Binaria West's headquarters.

CHAPTER 19

BRAX

*E*veryone had been pretty quiet after all the revelations with Philippa, being careful about what they said or thought around me, but their efforts didn't block out their worries completely; I still heard their concerns and questions. Becks, especially, wanted to see if I was okay, wanted to know what I thought about everything that'd transpired, but didn't voice anything because she didn't want to upset me. However, none of them needed to worry at all; I was actually feeling better than I had in a while.

Though it had come as a complete shock that Philippa was still alive, and I felt a tremendous amount of guilt for not knowing she'd been there all along, a lot of things clicked into place and began to make sense where they hadn't before I knew about her.

Things like why the angels hadn't been able to decide my fate for so long finally made sense to me, now that I knew what they must have seen once her human heart stopped beating. They'd seen that she hadn't actually died, and therefore, they didn't know what to do with me. I imagined they sat around for a long time, debating whether they should send me back to watch over her or just give me another charge and be done with it. Eventually, they chose the latter, but I found I wasn't nearly as angry at them as I'd been before I knew about Philippa.

But even with concerns lacing their thoughts, soon enough, it was back to business as usual. The team decided fairly quickly that the best thing to do next would be to investigate the cave where Becks was born before we all had to get ready for the barbeque at Derrick's dads' house.

"I don't know the cave, so I can't teleport us there directly," Tyler said as they were hashing out the plan.

"Don't worry about that," I said, "I'll teleport there and then pull all of you to me. It feels weirder than when Tyler teleports, but it's the best way, given the circumstances."

Adam spoke up then, asking, "What do we need to know about this place before we go?"

I hadn't seen much about Adam's past in his thoughts during the time I'd known him because he always closed that part of himself off, even from his own thoughts. But it was becoming apparent to me that he never liked going into a situation without knowing the lay of the land first.

"Well, nothing should be jumping out of the walls or anything, if that's what you're asking," I said. "It's just a remote cave on the Pacific coast that Malcolm and Mandy found by chance when they were trying to get away from the hunters that were following them. She was super pregnant and about to pop, so once they found the cave, they stayed there until after Becks was born, and they were both well enough to travel somewhere else."

"How long did they stay there?" Becks asked, no doubt wanting to piece together any bits of information she could get about her and her parents' pasts.

I ran a hand through my hair as I tried to remember accurately. "I think they stayed for about two weeks total. But I was mainly focused on you, and whether you were going to be okay, so my count could be off."

Becks nodded to herself, and Derrick said, "Okay, then, let's go ahead and go."

Within the next instant, I was hovering in the mouth of the cave, giving it a good once over before I started pulling the rest of the team to me. As they steadily appeared next to me, I glanced around the cave, noticing it didn't seem like it'd changed at all since the last time I'd been here.

It didn't sport a lot of square footage, but what was there had been perfect for what Malcolm and Mandy had needed at the time. They'd built a fire ring in the center of the cavernous space, and the circle of rocks Malcolm had used to contain the fire still laid where he'd left them years ago. Even the ceiling above the fire ring was still black from the continuous fire they'd had.

Over on the right side was a natural rock formation they'd used as a bed because of the way it was shaped. It was close enough to the fire for warmth, but it also kept them off the ground that could sometimes be soaked from the spray that fell in from the crashing waves outside. On the left side was an area that had acted as their makeshift table where they ate and butchered the meat Malcolm had hunted while they were here. The whole space was basically oval-shaped, and as the team materialized, they began exploring.

"What is it with you and caves, Brax?" Tyler asked me with a pointed glare and a smile as he walked toward the fire ring.

I chuckled and said, "I have no idea," as I flew in behind him.

Standing over by the wall with the butchering table, Derrick called everyone's attention to something he'd found. "Check this out," he said as I looked at the picture carved into the surface of the rock. "Is that supposed to be the five realms?" he asked with confusion as everyone walked over to see what he was pointing at.

"This looks like the picture we're shown in the academy depicting the five realms. You see how it kind of resembles the Olympic symbol just without any of the rings touching?" Adam asked.

Tyler ran a hand over the carved surface, saying, "I think so, but these lines shouldn't be here."

Each of the five rings were supposed to be completely separate from one another. However, there were lines carved into each one, connecting them all to one ring in particular, the ring off to the side, which normally represented the Void in every other picture I'd seen of this drawing.

"I don't know what it means. Let's keep searching," Derrick said, and everyone walked away to keep looking.

"Um, guys?" Becks said a few minutes later, making all of us look to where she'd walked to the very back of the cave.

"What?" Derrick asked as we all started moving toward her.

Becks' back was turned to us, but as we neared, she turned around, both hands upturned with something in each. "Is this the pixies' sacred seed?" she asked, lifting her right hand, which indeed held the precious artifact.

Becks handed it to Derrick so he could take a closer look, and he said, "Yeah, this is it," before he pocketed the seed. "What's that say?"

Becks unfolded the paper that was in her other hand, and another piece of Absinthe's armor fell out, clanking across the stone floor toward Adam.

"You're so close now, Becks! I knew you would find this. Soon, you'll need me, and I cannot wait until that day. Just speak my name four times on those beautiful lips, and our journey can really begin," Becks read the note, and my anger began to consume me as I thought about that jinn talking to her that way. "What the hell does this mean?" she asked, but I couldn't answer because I had no clue. But as I was about to say as much, Adam reached down to pick up the piece of Absinthe's armor and fell to his knees as a vision took hold of his mind.

"Let me see that," Derrick demanded, hand outstretched to take the note from Becks.

She handed it over willingly, all thoughts of the note forgotten from her thoughts as she stared at Adam, where he'd frozen on the floor. "Is he in pain?" she asked.

Tyler came up beside her and wrapped an arm around her waist as he looked at Adam as well. "Some visions are worse for him than others. It's just part of the package with Adam, watching him deal with the things he sees. Our best bet is always to let him tell us about it when he's ready," Tyler said softly to Becks, and I was wondering why he wasn't losing his temper like I was over the note Absinthe had left for Becks since typically, his anger outpaced even my own.

Angrily stuffing the note in his pocket, Derrick said, "Well, we're not going to wait around this time. I don't care if it's cloudy, we need all the information we can get at this point." He waited for a few beats then switched subjects quickly as he asked, "And what does Absinthe mean by 'soon, you'll need me'?"

No one answered as Adam came out of his vision with a start that made Becks jump, leaning forward on his hands and knees as he tried to get his breathing under control.

"Are you okay?" Becks asked as she placed a hand on Adam's shoulder, but he brushed her off by standing up and turning away from everyone. He didn't notice the pain that crossed Becks' face when he did it, but I felt it race through my heart as if the pain she felt was my own.

"I'm fine," he said as he laced his hands behind his head, slowed his breaths, and stared out of the cave mouth as if it offered the peace his soul was seeking.

"I know you probably don't want to talk about it, but we need to know what's going on, Adam," Derrick said as he stepped up beside Adam, arms crossed over his chest as he pressured him into talking.

Adam shook his head and lowered his hands to his sides, "You don't need to know this. It probably won't even happen anyway."

"Adam, don't make me force you to tell me," Derrick warned, and I think everyone was as surprised as I was. In all the time they'd worked together, I don't think Derrick had ever threatened Adam with an alpha order, much less actually given him one, but with the stern set of his jaw and Absinthe's words to Becks floating through his mind, I had no doubt that the circumstances we were in today could change all that.

Adam turned an exasperated glare on Derrick as he thought through his options. I read what I could of his thoughts, but they were still garbled from experiencing the vision, and it was difficult to latch onto one idea before another started streaming in. I did pick up, however, that Adam knew he could take Derrick in any physical fight, but that if Derrick did give him an alpha order, he'd have no choice but to tell us everything.

Instead of talking to Derrick, Adam turned to Becks, where she was watching everything with anxious wide eyes and worry. "Have you been thinking a lot about Absinthe?" he asked.

Becks shook her head some before she said, "No, not really. Why?"

Speaking more sternly than I'd heard him talk since the night Becks killed Rick, Adam said, "Well, don't."

"What did you see?" Derrick's voice had gotten even sterner than before as he asked Adam again, but Adam was having none of it.

He turned and got up really close to Derrick, so his mouth was near Derrick's ear as he said, "You can give me an alpha order if you want, but it'll be the last thing you do."

"What the fuck, man?" Derrick asked as he backed away from Adam, looking at him like he'd lost his mind completely, knowing just as well as I did that if it came to blows, he wouldn't stand a chance.

Tyler walked away from Becks then, playing a role I never thought I'd see him play. "Adam, take a walk. Hell, *everyone* take a walk. Derrick, back off and let him calm down. Becks, stop worrying, and Brax, stay with Becks. I'm going to stay here. Everybody has ten minutes to get their heads right before I'm going to jump all of us to the pixies to return their seed, and if you're not here when we leave, you're not going."

CHAPTER 20

DERRICK

"Sorry I pushed you, Adam. I knew better, I'm just worried about all this Absinthe shit," I said as we all formed back up at the cave mouth.

He didn't say anything, but he nodded, and that was good enough for me.

"Okay then, Tyler, we need to check in with the chief before we head out to the pixies. He needs to know what we've found here."

"Alright, let's go," Tyler said as we all placed a hand on him somewhere, and he teleported us to the chief's office.

The chief was sitting on the floor with Tina and Philippa, where they all played with some dolls someone had found somewhere. When we popped into the room, Philippa jumped up and ran over to Brax, arms stretched out, hands making grabby motions like she wanted him to pick her up. He didn't refuse her, and as we all started talking, he occupied her off to the side so we could tell the chief what he needed to know.

"She seems pretty happy. Has she been any trouble?" Becks asked as if the burden of Philippa's behavior somehow belonged on her shoulders as we all sat around the chief and Tina.

"Not at all," the chief said as he stood up from the floor and took a seat in a chair next to me. "She's brightened up this place more than I think anyone ever has." He laughed as he looked over at her, but after a few beats, he turned back to us and asked, "So what'd you find?"

We explained everything we'd found in the cave over the next few minutes, but not even Tina and the chief could get Adam to talk about the vision he'd had. That man was as stubborn as they came when he set his mind to something, and his visions had always been a touchy subject for him.

Eventually, everyone gave up trying, but I wasn't too upset because I had to trust that at some point, if I needed to know something he'd seen, Adam would tell me the essential parts. Becks didn't have that kind of confidence though, and I could tell she wasn't dealing with Adam being upset very well, but there was nothing anyone could do until Adam came around and opened up.

"So now you guys are headed to the fairies and pixies?" Tina asked when we were done explaining everything.

"Yeah, you guys should get a move on with that. The pixies have already gone too long without their seed for my liking," the chief said as he stood up, and we all followed suit.

"I agree. We're headed there as soon as we leave here," I confirmed, and Tina sighed next to me.

"I'm going to head out too," Tina said, making the chief look at her.

"So soon? You just got here, and we haven't gone over everything yet," the chief said. Then second-guessing himself, he added, "Well, I guess we did spend a bit too much time playing with that baby over there. Check in with me later after you've handled whatever it is you're doing these days." He laughed some as Brax came over with Philippa.

Tina smiled at Philippa as she answered the chief, "Will do, and I call dibs on babysitting this one next time." She sighed again, picked up her tote of files, and walked out of the office with a wave at everyone as the chief took Philippa from Brax's arms.

"You guys go, me and Philippa are just going to keep playing until you all get back. Does that sound good, little lady?" He continued to talk to Philippa, descending further and further into goo-goo-gagas as we all said our goodbyes and put a hand on Tyler.

Within the next few minutes, we were standing in the fairies' and pixies' forest, and without thinking, I took hold of Becks' hand. Probably so she wouldn't go sniffing more magical flowers or something, and I reveled in the fact that she didn't pull away from me. I didn't know why she would, but self-doubt kept creeping through me anyway, even without any evidence to the contrary.

"Hunters, you're back," Queen Agatha said happily as she flew over with King Preston.

"Yes. King Preston, we've found your sacred seed," I said as I pulled the seed out of my pocket and held it out for him to take.

The pixie king smiled and called over another pixie to take it wherever it was meant to stay.

"Have you found anything about our missing children?" Queen Agatha asked, and I felt like shit that we didn't even have a lead to follow with their missing heirs.

I ran a hand through my hair before answering her, but Becks released my hand and walked toward them, answering the queen as she moved. "No, we haven't found anything yet. Have you guys heard or seen anything since we were here last?"

The king and queen both shook their heads, but it was Preston that spoke. "No, you guys know as much as we do about how or why they were taken."

"Okay, well, we'll keep looking, and I'm sorry we haven't brought you any better news," Becks said in a sincere placating tone. "But how's the alliance working out? I mean, you all seem to be getting along pretty..."

A shot rang out through the forest then, and within the next second, Becks was peering down at her side, a hand placed gently to a spot that was already starting to bleed profusely between her fingers.

Brax urgently flew to her side to put pressure on the wound as Tyler shifted without warning. He took off in the direction the shot had come from, but he didn't make it far before we all realized we were surrounded.

There were hunter teams I knew, as well as a bunch that I didn't, and all kinds of different creatures forming a circle around us, caging us in with the flyer monarchs.

Adam already had his twin daggers out and at the ready as I pulled mine out as well. Without any words needing to be spoken, Adam and I turned our backs on each other, facing different directions as Tyler's wolf backed up to us again.

The three of us formed a kind of triangle shape around Becks where she was lying on the ground with Brax at her side, the fairy queen and pixie king helping to staunch the blood that kept coming out of Becks' side. She hadn't cried out or said anything, and I didn't know whether to be worried about that, or to see it as Becks just being tougher than I'd ever given her credit for.

The group that surrounded us started moving in, getting closer by the second as my adrenaline shot through the roof, all of my senses working together at the peak of their abilities.

"Did I get her?" a woman's voice rang out above the sound of the blood pumping through my ears, and the chaos of screaming fairies and pixies as some of them fled while they could.

Looking around to see where the voice had come from, I saw Tina step out from the ring of traitors, and my mouth dropped open, anger surging through me.

"Nope," Becks yelled as she stood unsteadily from the ground, noticeably in pain, but as stubborn as a mule. "I'm still here, Tina. You wanna tell me what all this is about?"

She stood beside me, and I quickly noticed her shirt had been ripped off at the bottom, forming a kind of crop top that showed off where the rest of her shirt had gone. Brax had apparently used it to wrap up her wound, and from what I could tell, he'd done a damn good job of the task since I couldn't see any blood seeping through the wrappings yet.

"Don't engage with her, Becks," I whispered to her, but I knew in my heart nothing I said would prevent Becks from doing what she thought she was supposed to do.

She eyed me, giving me a look that said, 'I've got this,' and instead of following my advice, she stepped away from our group and closer to Tina.

"It's nothing personal, Becks. With what you could become, I just can't have you getting in my way," Tina yelled as she walked even closer to us, but was still out of range as she stopped about fifty yards away.

"Tyler, can you shift into something else and take her out?" I whispered back behind me to the beast, where he growled and snarled at everyone who was standing against us.

"Go," Tina screamed, and everyone and everything that had formed up around us started rushing toward us, weapons drawn, teeth bared, claws out, and fangs dripping.

"Brax, get Becks back," I got out before I started running toward the group headed my way. I couldn't look back to see if he'd listened since by the next beat of my heart, I was battling against four hunters I didn't know.

Being in a fight to the death is a crazy headspace to be in. Every enemy you kill means nothing to you at that moment because their faces won't haunt you until later. Everything blurs in your periphery, but sharpens and focuses more than usual on what's in front of you. You can't think about what you're doing because it causes too much distraction. Instead, it's almost as if your brain clears your mind of anything else that could possibly matter, even going so far as to shut off your emotions completely. At least that's what happens when I fight for my life and the lives of my teammates.

The people and the creatures I fought meant nothing to me. I didn't feel the loss of their lives from this world as anything other than a tally to be knocked down, a box to be checked off. Their faces would show up in my dreams, but that didn't stop me. I tore through those I faced without hesitation despite the blows I knew they were landing, though I didn't have the capacity to feel them yet.

The snarls and screams I heard in the background faded from

importance since they weren't coming from the people I cared about. However, when I heard Becks cry out over the mayhem surrounding me, my brain didn't work like normal. All my focus shifted to her survival, distracting me from the hunter who had his blade sliding up my chest.

The pain was instant and burning, searing its way through me, but I ignored it as I slid my dagger into his heart, and turned to run back to Becks.

Brax was flying and fighting a group of goblins off to the right, unintentionally leaving Becks unprotected as he fought. As I made it over to her, I realized she wasn't being attacked, so it took me a second to figure out what was going on. She was writhing on the ground, holding her side as black tendrils started to snake their way up her veins throughout her body like track marks on a heroin addict.

She gritted her teeth and growled with her face into the ground as she clutched at her side, curling herself up into a ball of pain.

In the next instant, I was knocked over by something hitting me over the back of the head with the force of a freight train, and I knew a few minutes had passed before I came back around.

When I came to, I couldn't see anyone but Becks where she lay in front of me, staring at something behind me. I didn't know where the rest of our team was, nor was I able to move enough to find out. The pain I felt was almost unbearable, and as I tried to get my body to move anyway, I heard Tina start talking from behind me.

"Oh, come on, Becks. You of all people should understand what I'm feeling! Humanity is a lost cause, a failure of cataclysmic proportions, a waste of entirely too much time on Heaven's part if we're being blunt. Why they would go through so much to create everything, and everyone is beyond my understanding."

Becks somehow got up on her knees despite the black streaks that were steadily crawling up her neck as she stared at Tina.

"Humans are the most ungrateful lot too, a plague to themselves and everything they touch. Life and prosperity are a joke," Tina spat. "A fucking joke! They go about their insignificant days, destroying themselves and others just because they can, just because they're the *favorites*.

And God loves his experiments so much, yet what have they ever given him, huh? A lot of praise for creating them? Hell no. Try killing each other in his name and calling themselves righteous for it. Why would he create it all in the first place? What could he possibly get out of it?"

She was ranting, clearly holding the impression that she'd won, and I knew the only way that would've been possible would've been if everyone on my team was incapacitated or dead. The ache of that realization tore through me harder than I could've ever prepared for.

"I don't know, Tina," Becks said, sounding utterly exhausted and pissed off. "But I think you're gonna tell me." She was still my little smartass, even with everything that was going on, and I smiled some at her words though the motion caused more pain to slide up my face.

"I've imagined God sometimes as a little redheaded kid with freckles, buck teeth, and glasses," Tina said. "Why redheaded with glasses? No fucking clue, just because."

"Yep, you're gonna tell me," Becks said almost to herself as she made deliberate and subtle attempts at standing up. If I hadn't been staring at her, I don't think I would've even noticed she'd moved at all, but as I watched, I saw the wheels turning in her head.

"The smelly breathed kid on a sidewalk with a magnifying glass who watches all the ants go by, and occasionally, he'll line up the light just right to burn one of them just to say he did. Then that boy laughs and laughs at all the power he holds with his magnifying glass in a throaty, nasally sort of chuckle that only a mother could love." Tina continued, her voice droning on and on when I wanted nothing more than for her to shut up.

"Everyone and everything that exists, humans and hunters alike, are just God's little playthings. It's almost as if he gives some of us the most terrible hands just so he can watch the drama unfold.

It's as if he asks himself questions every day like, 'Ooh, what's this Pegasus going to do if I break one of its wings? How will this woman handle it if she loses that job right after her husband has been laid off?

What kind of life will he lead if I put him in a female body? What's she going to do if her dad suddenly starts being sexually attracted to her? How are they all going to respond if I flood these trolls overnight?

Or, how will Tina take it if I give her a great love, a bunch of kids that love her, a good job and life, only to take all she cares about away in one swift motion by the actions of the very species she's sworn to protect?'"

I knew the story well, as did almost every other hunter in the world. Tina's was a story of legend, told in hushed whispers and talked about with envy by all, simply because of how tragic it had been, and how quickly she'd bounced back afterward.

"Well, I'll tell you now, Becks, I'll react. I'll burn this whole world down! I'll take it apart piece by motherfucking piece, brick by motherfucking brick, if it means putting an end to this torture we call life, if it puts an end to God's sadistic game!

My children were one, three, five, and seven years old! My husband was the greatest husband, father, and hunter that ever lived in my eyes!

What the fuck did they do to deserve being slaughtered in front of each other? In front of *me*, starting with our youngest? Why would he create such a monster that could do something so evil and fucked up? A human, no less!

A *human* learned about us and knew entirely too much. A *human* incapacitated me and made me watch as he killed my family one by one until I was the only one left just because he didn't like the implications of magic and what it could do. And by some twisted sense of fate, that fucker left me alive.

A *human* did this to me as if *I* were human.

As if I wouldn't tear him to shreds and destroy his soul as soon as he gave me the slightest window of opportunity. But it turned out that sending his sick, deprived soul to the Void would in no way bring my family back or ease my heartache. It'll be over a century before I can even have a chance at seeing them again! And that's only if they have the capacity to remember me, or I, them!"

Becks had her mouth hanging open in astonishment as she heard the story for the first time, directly from Tina herself, which even I'd never been privy to. But even as she battled with everything she was feeling physically, and how awed she was over what Tina was telling her, she was still forcing her body to move subtly. She'd already made it to her knees, and with one more big gulp of air, she forced herself to stand, cutting off my ability to see her face.

"We're just a game to him, pawns on a chessboard, cogs. Insignificant and useless. Not anymore, though. I know how to end it all, and I do mean everything," Tina hadn't noticed or didn't care that Becks was standing up, and that made me feel better since the longer she stayed distracted or didn't view Becks as a threat, the better chance Becks had at doing whatever she was planning.

"You'll see. In a way, I'm saving you. I'm saving everyone. Saving them from themselves and from the torture God has in store for them. I'll save them all. Even the fucking ungrateful ass humans. I'll save them by ending them forever," Tina said right before Becks started glowing before me.

A burst of purplish-blue light poured out of her as an enormous burst of power pulsed through me, making my head spin and blackness settle over my eyes.

SOMETIME LATER, all the sunlight had left the forest, which was my only indication that a significant amount of time had already passed, and I could hardly see anything except what was dimly lit by the moon.

My body had done some healing on my wounds while I'd been passed out, but I knew it wouldn't be enough this time. Still in pain, but mostly numb to it by now, I sat up from my spot on the forest floor and saw Tyler's beast a short distance away.

I crawled on my hands and knees over to where he was nipping and biting at the air, lost in a frenzy of not understanding what was going on since, I guessed, his target had disappeared. He was holding his paw up in the air as he turned this way and that, bouncing with the movement, blood dripping off it and staining the grass around him. Looking closer, I noticed there were a bunch of other wounds staining his fur as well. His bright eyes were wide and wild, and every whisper of the wind or groaning of the forest made him bark and howl, slobber foaming from his mouth as he growled and shook in pain and fear.

His rage was palpable, and I knew in his injured and scared state, he probably thought everyone was an enemy, including everyone on our team. He was more dangerous to us now than he'd ever been at that moment.

He scared me on a level I didn't want to accept, and I watched as his anger lashed out at everything around him, my fear stemming from all I'd seen the beast do over the years.

I'd seen its savagery, its ferociousness, its evil side. And not once over the past four years had Tyler's beast regarded me with anything other than contempt and hostility as if he barely tolerated my presence, much less gave a shit about whether I lived or died. That demeanor was how he acted on a good day. Not a day like today where we were literally fighting for our lives.

I didn't have enough energy to use my magic. It was as if I was bleeding out my magical abilities through the wounds those traitorous, bitch ass hunters inflicted, and if I wasn't mistaken, I had even more injuries now than before I'd passed out. But I couldn't dwell on what might have caused them since I could feel my power leaving my body with every drop of blood and bead of sweat that left me. There was nothing I could think of to do that would stop it.

My vision was getting blurry, my head beginning to spin again from the blood loss, and for a moment there, I honestly didn't think I had a chance.

My arms gave out, and I fell face-first to the ground, my weight just too much to carry with everything my body had been put through. As I breathed in the frigid air, my chest working hard to keep oxygen flowing through my lungs, I glanced around at the rest of my team for any sign that they were okay or if they'd be able to help me.

But they weren't faring any better than I was.

Brax was frozen in his stone form, unmoving from where he'd been when he was probably trying to save us all. That little fucker had more heart than any person or creature I'd ever known, but his need to protect made him make rash decisions sometimes, ones that put him in danger in the process, but I had no way of knowing if it was his bottomless heart that had him frozen like he was or if he'd been over-powered. Either way, his statue was lying on its side, mouth still open in what seemed like a scream tearing from his throat.

Adam was lost in a seemingly excruciating vision, one that showed its potency in the clenching of his teeth, the contractions of his muscles, and the tears sliding down his cheeks as his body bent at odd angles in an unstoppable irregular rhythm. The seizing didn't look like it was going to end any time soon, and an unfamiliar pain raced through me at the thought of what my friend must be seeing and feeling.

Then there was Becks. I could see the black poison spreading through her veins just under her tanned skin. It was so much worse now than it'd been before, the speed of the infection moving faster with every passing minute she went untreated. However, the sight of Becks just reinforced what I'd already been thinking: I had to get control of this situation as fast as possible.

If I didn't, Becks was going to die. There was no doubt about it in my mind, incredible powers, or not. There was no time to lose. I had to do something to get us out of here, and if getting Tyler's beast to listen to me was the only way to save my team, so be it if he bit my head off as I tried. I couldn't lay there doing nothing as slowly, but inevitably, life slipped out of my teammates.

"Ralto!" The beast's true name came out of my mouth as more of a cracked gasp of air than an actual word, but he heard me nevertheless.

He turned all that heated and enraged focus on me and started growling low in his throat as he lowered his head, eyes trained on mine, and started slowly inching closer to me as best he could on three working legs.

I could practically feel how much he wanted to tear my throat from my neck, it poured off the beast in waves. His eyes were shifting, body shaking, and I knew Tyler was fighting to take control back over their body, but from what I was seeing, the beast wasn't letting him.

As he got within a foot of me, I used all the energy I had left to reach one hand up and limply push his face in the direction of where Becks was lying. His growl got louder as he whipped his head back in my direction and stepped menacingly toward me.

"Stop, Ralto," I said before I coughed and tasted copper on my tongue. "Killing me won't fix anything. I'm a goner anyway." I shoved at his face again, my vision blacking out for a split second before my hand fell back to the ground. "You love her just as much as I do."

His eyes met mine, and the depth of understanding in them was hard to reconcile. "Save her, Ralto. Please," I said before another cough ripped through me, blood flying from my mouth to land on Ralto's dirty white fur.

He huffed in my face as my body fell limp and wouldn't respond when I told it to move. The only thing I could do was watch through my heavy-lidded eyes and hope that Tyler and his beast would be able to save Becks.

The total loss of control, the inability to help in any way, was a suffocating and infuriating agony.

Ralto's shaking stopped instantly at my words as he stared down at me. Apparently, Tyler had finally given up fighting him, the beast winning over entirely at the worst possible moment. He huffed again, then stepped forward and pushed his muzzle up against my chin roughly.

Once.

Twice.

Three times.

He barked in my face angrily, loud enough to burst my eardrums if he were any closer, and I couldn't understand what he was doing. He did it again, and all I wanted was for him to shut up and get Becks out of here, but the beast, as always, had a mind of his own.

He opened his mouth, teeth gleaming in the moonlight, and I knew he was going for my jugular. It was written all over his canine face.

'This is it. This is how my life's going to end,' I thought.

All I could see at that moment was Becks' smooth features in my mind, laughing from what my dads said to her on the phone, blushing as her hand rushed to cover her mouth, though there was no need to hide that gorgeous smile. The three of them then stood around her, and I knew I was hallucinating, the four people I loved most in this world flashing before my eyes as I felt heat on my neck.

It wasn't as sharp as I thought it might be. In fact, the heat almost felt... good.

It started on my neck, then I felt it spread over my bloody thigh, onto wounds across my back I didn't even realize I had, and then to my foot, which was definitely broken, though I had no recollection of how it'd happened.

The next thing I knew, I got a glimpse of the night sky through the trees after I was roughly rolled onto my back, and the heat started happening over the front of my body where I'd been injured the most.

I looked down as best I could and saw that instead of biting and ripping me to shreds as I thought he would be, Ralto was licking and breathing heavily on each of my wounds, stitching them up right before my eyes.

I stared at him in wonder, all kinds of questions flowing through my mind, but I soon realized, with every lap of his tongue, with every breath he blew over my skin, the better I felt, and the clearer my mind became.

"Thank you," I said as I forced myself to stand up. I knew his actions, as sweet and impressive as they were, weren't going to last for long, my injuries were just too severe for even whatever magic he'd used. I could already feel the wounds on my back opening back up, but I dismissed that pain as my eyes took in everything around me.

"You've got to get us somewhere safe, we can't stay here," I said as I noticed a bunch of dead fairies and pixies lying about the ground as if they'd been trying to help us as well, but didn't make it out alive.

I limped over to Becks and carefully dragged her over to Brax's statue, making sure she was touching him as Tyler's beast did the same thing with Adam despite the convulsions still plaguing his body.

The effort of moving Becks took almost all the strength I had left, and as I fell to the ground beside her, I sighed and shrugged at Ralto.

He came over and fell on top of all of us, his energy levels depleted as well. He made sure we were all touching him so we could teleport with him, his tail landing heavily on my forehead before we started to disappear.

However, as I opened my eyes back up, I knew something was wrong. We'd definitely teleported, but instead of landing somewhere like Binaria West or even the safe house, we'd landed only a few hundred feet away from where we'd been a minute ago, and a whine escaped Tyler's beast as he repositioned himself and tried again.

Next, we landed in a bunch of sand, and I saw the safe house up above us as the morning light of sunrise had begun to shine on it. Tyler's beast hadn't moved since we'd landed, though, and even when I'd pushed at him to make him wake up, he hadn't responded at all. And as the thought of losing that fucker went through my soul with an amount of pain and sadness I just couldn't comprehend, the last of my energy was spent as blackness took over everything I knew for the last time.

CHAPTER 21

BECKS

*I*t was so hot, and the brightness of the sun on my closed eyelids and heated skin made me want to roll over or cover myself with the blanket to get its light off my face. My body was sticky with sweat as if I'd taken a bath in the stuff, and when I tried to roll over because I couldn't feel a blanket anywhere, the feeling only compounded as I felt like I'd rolled into a fresh puddle of wetness.

My thoughts were jumbled as they usually are when I first wake up, but with the agitation that came from all the signals my body was throwing off, I knew I had to open my eyes to figure out what the hell was going on.

The brightness of the sun was just outrageous and completely unnecessary as I opened my eyes. They burned with the light, and it took a bit for them to get acclimated, but once they did and I saw everything around me, they shot open as wide as they could, and I jumped up in alarm.

The puddle I'd initially thought was sweat turned out to be blood. Derrick's blood, specifically, judging by the fact that he was covered in the stuff, his shirt hardly showing an inch of the white it was before we were ambushed.

Instantly, I remembered what'd happened last night, and a gasp tore from my throat as I looked down at my teammates in awe, their safety and survival overpowering my need to reflect.

Brax was in stone form and unmoving, making it seem as if we'd all gotten drunk and passed out around a statue on the beach. I could see that Adam was breathing where he laid beneath Tyler's big wolf, but every now and then, his breath stuttered and shook as if he were having a nightmare. The wolf was breathing too, and though I knew he was injured, I had no way of knowing where his blood ended, and Derrick's began.

I went to Derrick first, seeing as how he seemed to be the most severely injured and checked to see if he was still breathing because I couldn't tell from where I was standing. As I got closer, I still couldn't see a rise and fall in his chest like I could see with the others, and panic started to race through me.

Grabbing him under his arms, I tried to pull him out from under Tyler's wolf, but I wasn't strong enough. Then, mentally face-palming myself for being so dumb, I tapped into my power and tried again. Moving him was much easier then, and after I got him free, I knelt down in the sand and put my ear to his mouth and felt for a pulse with my first two fingers.

His breath was shallow, barely warming my ear at all as he exhaled. His pulse was almost imperceptible, but I could still feel it, so I held out hope that there was still a chance at saving him.

I tore through what was left of his bloodied shirt, exposing a deep and partially closed wound that spread from his left hip bone all the way up and across his chest to his right shoulder. It looked as if the injury had begun to heal, but wasn't for some reason, and though I knew hunters healed faster than humans, something told me if I didn't act quickly enough, Derrick definitely wasn't going to make it.

When I examined the rest of his body, I noticed his foot was laying at a weird and off-putting angle, and that his right thigh had a sizable chunk missing.

Deciding that I needed to inspect all of him, I turned him on his side so I could see his back, and when I saw a bunch of slash marks deeply embedded in his flesh, my breath caught in my throat.

And as if all that wasn't enough for one man to endure, when I looked at the back of his head, I had to fight off dizziness at the image that was quick and powerful. From his hairline on the base of his neck, up to the crown of his head looked like it'd been pried apart, the skin and hair I'd run my hands through in the club the other night separated by nearly an inch-wide gap.

I laid him back on his back and stared down at his face, completely at a loss as to what I was supposed to do next. I had no medical training, and since he wasn't actively bleeding, I didn't know what I could do to help him.

Looking up at the rest of my team, I knew I needed to check them out too, and then figure out what my next moves should be.

Pulling Tyler's wolf off my pile of teammates was way more complicated than moving Derrick had been, even with tapping into my power to get the job done. There was so much fur it was hard to discern where his injuries were at first, but after running my hands all over him, I counted quite a few that were bad enough to cause real concern, especially his left front paw where the skin was torn in a jagged line, and the joint moved in ways it shouldn't.

His breath was steady, though, so I tried to wake him up. However, no amount of calling his name, shaking him where he wasn't injured, or yelling at him woke him up.

As I checked over Adam next, I experienced the same thing. Even though he had a few injuries, they were mostly healed over already, his hunter blood acting normally. However, he wouldn't wake up either, no matter what I tried. It was incredibly infuriating.

Then as a last hope, I reached out and ran my hands over Brax's stone face and called to him. I even tried pulling him to me, pulling on that thread of connection we shared, but again, nothing woke him.

Nothing woke any of them.

I stood and put my hands on my hips, all my teammates laid out before me as I tried to figure out my next move. It didn't take me long to decide. After nodding to myself in acceptance of what I needed to do, I started the slow and agonizing process of dragging each of them up the wooden staircase and inside the safe house, laying them in a row across the floor, categorizing them by the severity of their injuries, and focused on Derrick first.

Once they were all laid out, I pulled Derrick to my bathroom, stripped him down completely, and not so gracefully, put him in the bathtub. I cleaned the sand and dirt from his wounds as best I could, being careful not to reopen any that had started to heal over.

I actively ignored the fact that some had reopened despite my best efforts and the fact that they weren't closing on their own like they should.

I dried him off and wrapped up his wounds with some of the medical supplies I found under the bathroom sink, though there was only gauze and tape, no ointments or stitching needles, not that I would've known how to use them if they had been there.

I clothed him in what he still had in his closet, and eventually, dragged him back to the living room to wait until I'd repeated the process with everyone else on our team.

Washing and cleaning Tyler's wolf was incredibly tricky, but I managed to do it without drowning him in the process somehow, noting a lot of injuries that'd been hidden from me before once he was slopping wet and more of his body was exposed to me. However, Adam turned out to be just as hard to clean as Derrick had been, and I realized as I washed him that I'd missed quite a few of his wounds in my initial assessment, and they, like Derrick's, weren't healing either.

When I finally had them all bandaged up to the best of my ability, I stood there for a second, wondering what I could possibly do next. The guys definitely weren't healing like they should, that was something I was sure of, and it caused me tremendous anxiety and worry. But I lacked any knowledge of how else I could help them.

Brax was still a statue, and as upsetting as that was, I just couldn't let myself worry about what life would be like if he never came back to life. I dismissed that thought as fast as I possibly could and never

ever wanted to think about it again. He was going to wake up eventually if I had anything to do with it. They all were.

I needed help, but my guys were in no position to offer that help like they'd been before.

Thinking of ways I could get in touch with someone, I searched through everyone's discarded clothes hoping to find a cell phone. I knew mine was still packed away at the cabin on Binaria West because it'd been in my duffle when it had magically appeared while I'd slept. However, my hope started depleting fast when I realized there wasn't a phone anywhere in the safe house, nor was there a landline of any kind.

I couldn't teleport like Tyler and Brax could, and there was no one else on this entire island.

As hard as I tried to tell myself they'd all wake up soon and that I'd done everything they required, I knew I was lying to myself. They needed more help than I could possibly give them, and as my thoughts got more and more desperate by the second, I found myself starting to panic.

However, it was seeing the blood beginning to seep through their bandages that really made up my mind about what I needed to do. It was the kick in the ass I'd needed, reassuring me that if I didn't get help soon, no matter where or who that help came from, they were all going to die, and I wasn't willing to live without them. I'd already declared as much in the incubus' lair.

I knew what I needed to do, what someone had already known I *would* do, and as I spoke his name, "Absinthe, Absinthe, Absinthe…" I closed my eyes and prayed to whoever would listen that everything would turn out okay. "Absinthe."

"FINALLY," I heard a smooth male voice say as I opened my eyes and took in my new surroundings, "I knew you'd come."

I was standing in the middle of a cold, snow-filled, sparse forest, my arms unconsciously wrapping themselves around me for warmth as my breath fogged in front of me. There was yet another cave off in the distance a short walk away, and standing in between me and the entrance was something I never expected in all the time I'd known about the jinn named Absinthe.

He was tall with dark tanned skin, which stood out starkly against the snowy backdrop behind him. His head was shaved on the sides. What grew on top was pitch black and smooth, tied back in a man bun at the back of his head. His bright purple eyes were laser-focused on me, running up and down my frame appreciatively as he hesitantly approached me, and I took in his chiseled chin, smooth features, and deadly good looks.

Absinthe was wearing armor over his broad chest made up of a thousand charms that matched the ones I'd found previously. It made him jingle when he moved, but didn't cover his large, tanned, and tatted biceps at all. His legs were clad in what looked like a weird version of black sweatpants, and though it didn't make much sense, I found my eyes drifting over him just as his had drifted over me.

'What the fuck, Becks? Get your mind off his looks, and focus,' I chastised myself as I stood up straighter and leveled the jinn with an expression meant to kill.

"Hello, Absinthe. I need to talk to you, but I think I have to make a deal first since time is of the essence right now," I said, my voice coming out more reliable than I'd thought it could.

Coming to stand right in front of me, so close I could reach out and touch him if I wanted, Absinthe stood over me, staring down into my eyes, and I did everything I could to hold his gaze and not let him intimidate me.

"I knew you'd have questions, and I can't wait to tell you everything. But yes, time is of the essence. We wouldn't want your team to die while you are talking to me," he said before he waved his hand in the air between us, and everything stopped.

There'd been a few natural sounds going on before, but I hadn't noticed them until they stopped entirely. The wind quit blowing, the leaves on the trees froze where they were previously whipping around in the breeze, and even the temperature around me suddenly wasn't so cold anymore.

"You can freeze time?" I asked as I dropped my hands to my sides, leveling him with a glare. Then the jinn smiled a straight white, toothy grin at me, and if I wasn't mistaken, my girly parts jumped at the sight.

"I can do many things, Becks!" he said in a deep baritone that didn't quite match the high level of enthusiasm his words suggested. "Now, ask away. I'm an open book."

Honestly, I hadn't been expecting anything Absinthe was presenting to me; his looks, his overall happy demeanor, nor his willingness to answer any questions I had. It really threw me for a loop for a second as I tried to get my thoughts in order to ask about everything that'd plagued me so far.

Eventually, I did get my mind on track, and after a few seconds of double-checking the words I planned on saying, just in case he wanted to use them against me, I asked, "How were you able to leave pieces of your armor for me to find if you aren't allowed to leave your forest?"

Absinthe reached out a hand to touch my face, but I backed up quickly before he could touch me. "What do you think you're doing?"

As if he were ignoring my question, he said, "Come sit with me."

He turned then, not even bothering to see if I was following, and without any better options, I followed after him and sat down next to him on a downed log that laid across the forest floor that miraculously didn't have a flake of snow on it. Absinthe straddled the trunk, and as I did the same facing him, I sat far enough away to ensure we weren't close enough for him to reach out and touch me again.

However, he didn't seem to care about the distance I wanted to keep between us and scooted so close our knees were touching, but I couldn't back up any farther because the log had a branch blocking any backward movement I might've made. But before I could call him on it, he started speaking, and I wanted answers so bad, I didn't care if he had to touch me to give me the answers I needed.

"It was not hard to get my messages to you," he said. "The people and creatures I'd made deals with were more than willing to do my bidding in exchange for their wishes being granted."

I processed the words he'd said, and they made sense. I knew first-hand how much I wanted my teammates to live and knew without a doubt, I was willing to pay almost any price to see them survive.

"But Ava said the guy that gave her the gem had been crying. Wouldn't he have been happy if his wish was being granted?" I asked, remembering the last conversation I'd had with my friend.

Absinthe smiled a little menacingly as he said, "Sometimes, the people I grant wishes to are of the most despicable breed, and occasionally, I've taken a small amount of joy in scaring them enough to get them to change their ways. He's insignificant and has nothing to do with you, so don't worry about him."

I tried not to read too much into what he said and moved on. "Okay, what did my parents find out that made them want to make a deal with you? Was it that Tina was the traitor in Binaria West?"

Absinthe reached out to take my hand, and as I held my breath waiting for his answer, I realized I didn't mind his touch as much as I'd initially thought I would. It actually had a calming effect on me, slowing my racing heart as I waited for him to tell me everything I needed to know.

"Tina was already well on her own path when your parents showed up to make a deal with me, and though she is a traitor, I know she's being manipulated by someone else. Your parents knew this too. They had also found out that ties have been formed, tethers, if you will, connecting all the realms to the Void. Malcolm and Mandy knew the apocalypse was going to happen within their lifetime if something wasn't done to prevent it," he explained, and it took me a beat to understand what he was saying.

"Tethers?" I asked.

"Yes, tethers. Links from every realm are connecting us to the Void in ways that never should've been created. I do not know what these connections are for or what is being passed between them, but I do know they are being controlled and implemented by someone."

"Who?"

Absinthe started rubbing his thumbs over the back of my hand as he said, "I do not know."

"But aren't you supposed to be this all-knowing genie or something? How do you know everything else, but don't know who's causing it?" I asked, surprised that my anger was still in check despite the subject matter.

Absinthe laughed at that, and the sound made my belly flip, something no one other than my guys had ever been able to accomplish before. Still, before I could dwell on it too much, my worries slowed and quieted, leaving behind a sense that everything was going to be okay in their wake.

"I am most certainly not all-knowing, Becks," he finally said as his laughter died off. "I have some knowledge of the future, but just like with Adam's visions, the future can change," he explained.

"How do you know so much about us then?"

His purple eyes got even more intense if that was something that was even possible, and said, "I have been watching you and your team as if my life depended on it because, in many ways, it does. I know all about you, every person on your team, and even all of Brax's history."

I shook my head some to dislodge the enormity of implications that tidbit of information could entail, and decided to move on to subjects I might actually be able to understand the answers to.

"Okay, I'm going to leave that alone for the time being," I started. Then after taking a deep breath, I asked, "What deal did my parents make with you, exactly?"

With more remorse and emotion in his eyes than I cared to admit, Absinthe said, "In exchange for their lives, the apocalypse would be stopped, and their daughter would live."

I opened my mouth to start screaming or yelling or something, but his eyebrows rose as he tried to explain fast enough to relieve my anger. "A price *had* to be paid for what they were asking, Becks. I told them I couldn't prevent the apocalypse altogether, that I could only set the stage for it to be saved.

The only lives they could offer up were yours or their own, and in the end, they begged me to take theirs instead of yours.

The only things I *can* ensure are made through deals, and that was the deal they wanted desperately: that you would not perish in the apocalypse, and if that wasn't a possibility, that everything would be done to ensure it at least, stayed at bay for as long as possible.

And though I still can't guarantee it will stay at bay or that you will make it through if it does happen, I have given you what you needed to possess *to have a chance."*

The way he accentuated the words he said, the sincerity I heard in his voice, and how his eyes pleaded with me to believe him, had my anger dying off quicker than it could form as I saw my parents' situation through a different lens than I had before.

"What exactly did I need to possess?" I asked as my thoughts swirled.

Absinthe smiled slightly as he said, "I ensured your blood would make you the next hunter queen so that you would have the powers you'd need to prevent the apocalypse. I gave you all the tools you'd need to see the job through. Yes, I killed your parents, but I did it to save you and give you the best chance at life like they wanted."

"Then why did you shred their souls? I don't see how that helped anything," I said, real anger and resentment working its way through my system despite the calmness I'd been feeling before.

"I had nothing to do with that. Those kinds of choices lie outside my realm of expertise. Once a soul dies, I can't touch it, nor do I want to. I've never even tried."

All the negative feelings I'd had slipped away at his words as a small beacon of hope bloomed up in their place. It could very well be that the hunters hadn't found my parents' souls *yet* and that I was holding onto all of this turmoil for no reason.

However, as I continued sifting through his words, a wave of new anger gripped me. "All the tools I'd need? Did I need to be adopted by abusive shitbags? Did I have to grow up in an asylum? Was it absolutely necessary that I get raped? What? Did you just throw that in there for shits and giggles?"

Absinthe brought his hands to my face as tears filled my eyes, and try as I might, I couldn't bring myself to pull away from his soft touch.

"Please don't cry, Becks. As unfortunate and terrible as your upbringing was, it's what's turned you into who you are now, what's made you see the world the way you do. It's what sets you apart from everyone else and makes you the perfect person to rule.

Your flaws, your past, the parts of you that are broken beyond repair, those are the most beautiful parts of you, Becks. I know it hurt, getting the scars you carry on your heart and in your soul, but those scars are what make you, you.

Becks, you haven't taken what happened to you and used it as an excuse to stagnate or regress, and in spite of everything you've been through, you still haven't given up." He paused and smiled sheepishly, "Though I did have to throw in a clause that said you couldn't die by your own hand."

"Wasn't that me giving up?" I asked, confused.

"No, Becks," he said softly as one of his hands threaded through my hair, and the other grasped my hand again. "Those attempts on your life were your cries for help, and there is nothing wrong with that. Everyone needs help. It's why I set up your guys' lives as part of your parents' deal to play out the way they have. So that they could be who you'd need them to be when the time came.

You are perfect, Becks. I hope you know that," Absinthe said, and some part of me cracked at his words and the truth I heard in them. They might not have been true to me, but Absinthe definitely believed everything he said to be the absolute truth, and I couldn't ignore it.

I cleared my throat as my eyes left his for the first time since we'd started talking, and after taking a second, I made sure to pick up where I'd left off in my questions. "Thank you for saying that, Absinthe, but I still need to know more."

His hand left my hair and joined his other one to continue rubbing small circles on the back of my hand. "Go ahead."

"Just to clarify, you can only ensure things through deals, right? What does that mean?"

"Well, I can't make people do anything. I can only put circum-stances in their way to guide their choices in hopes that they make the decisions I want them to make. I can also grant wishes, but that's more of a side gig now, anyway," he smiled at me like I should be in on his joke, but I had no clue what was supposed to be funny about the statement.

Seeming to pick up on this, he explained, "I can't control whether you're going to make it through the gauntlet or not. That, my dear, will be entirely dependent on you. However, I did make your powers possible so that when the time comes, you'll have them at your disposal."

I started to say something, but I forgot it quickly as the next words came from his mouth.

"Oh, and speaking of the gauntlet, you need to go. To be crowned queen of the hunters, which is the only way you're going to be able to prevent the apocalypse, you need to go get the rest of your powers, and *truly* bind yourself to all your kings with your *new* powers."

"Excuse me?" I asked as I tried to wrap my mind around what he'd said. "I know previous queens had kings, but why do I have to have them, and who are they supposed to be?"

He chuckled some at me and said, "Queens must have their magic anchored by others she loves. It could be another female for all it matters, you get to choose who your 'kings' are, but the point is, you can't be crowned unless you have them because your power would consume you without their love grounding you first."

I decided pretty swiftly to revisit that conversation another day and moved on to something else. "If all this is true, then why didn't you just tell Brax what you had planned? It would've relieved a lot of stress for him."

"I know it would have, but it would've also changed the outcome. Brax has every bit to do with this as you do. Remember, he was already your appointed familiar long before I came into the picture. So even with my manipulations in your life, some bigger scheme is afoot as far as what you're expected to do in your life."

"Even so, what's in all this for you? What are you getting out of it?" I asked.

Absinthe sighed with a smile as his eyes closed momentarily.

When he opened them back up, he asked, "Are you ready to make a deal?"

My heart nearly stopped as I remembered everything that still existed and waited for me whenever Absinthe started time back up again. I sighed as I looked at him and nodded my head, assuming I wasn't going to get an answer about his motives. Though I couldn't find it within myself to be mad at him since he'd answered everything else I'd asked.

"Here's the warning I must give you before you enter my cave to make a deal: Whatever you ask for needs to be worded wisely, and there is always a price to pay for what you ask for. There are often unexpected consequences of making a deal with me as well, and there is no way to know what those consequences will be until after the deal has been made. If you step into my cave with me, you can't leave until you've made a deal, so do not enter until you are sure. I leave the choice to you," Absinthe said as he stood from the log and walked toward his cave without looking back.

I sighed heavily as I weighed my options, but again, I had no idea how to save the guys any other way. So, without waiting for longer than it took him to walk in his cave, I followed right behind Absinthe and accepted there'd be consequences I might not like.

THE CAVE WAS BRIGHTLY LIT with candles everywhere, and in the center of the circular shaped space, Absinthe stood in a ring of candles, hands clasped in front of him. If I wasn't mistaken, he breathed a sigh of relief at the sight of me walking in the cave, and I filed the action away in my mind for later examination when I wasn't facing him.

"Please join me in the circle, Becks," he said as I made my way across the cave. "The fairy princess and the pixie prince have already been returned to their homes, by the way," he said confidently as I stepped into the circle without letting my eyes leave his. "They were never harmed, and have gone back to their homes, singing my praises for being such a wonderful host."

I hardly had time to think that matter through before I was standing in front of him and moving right along with the ceremony, and as if he hadn't just solved my first case, he said, "Please state what it is that you wish, and I will then name my price."

Thinking carefully and quickly, I said, "I ask that you save my teammates from dying and ensure that Brax wakes back up from being turned to stone." I didn't know if that was too much to ask since it was technically asking for two things at once, but Brax was just as much a part of my team as anyone else, and I couldn't let his fate rest unaccounted for in my wish.

Smiling down at me proudly, Absinthe said, "My price for this deal is this: You must use the powers I've given you to release me from my prison, binding me to you and your team rather than this cave and forest."

My breath caught in my throat, and shock poured through me. Of course, he would ask to be released from his prison. It's what anyone would do in his case, given the powers he'd assured I would have. But rather than getting angry at him like some part of me told me I should, when I did a deep dive in my gut to see how I really felt, I realized I wanted to bind him to my team and me. Absinthe seemed like the kind of guy you wanted to have around in a tight spot, and even though I had my reservations, something told me I was doing the right thing by agreeing to his deal.

"You have a deal," I said, and as he reached his hand out to shake mine, I smiled and shook it happily.

CHAPTER 22

BRAX

Slowly my limbs came back under my control, and as I stretched and flexed as best I could, the shouting and yelling started to reach my ears. Turning around, I saw we were no longer in the flyer forest, but Derrick, Adam, and Tyler were indeed, still fighting. As whoever they were trying to attack held out his hand to thwart off their blows easily, I got a glimpse of a face I hadn't thought I'd ever see again.

Rage consumed me as I recognized Absinthe, and without thinking, I was launching myself at him with everything I had in me. The other guys joined in on my attack as well, but as if we were children making futile attempts at hurting an adult, he blocked everything we threw at him. He didn't attack back, and all that did was infuriate me even more as I launched myself at him again with renewed effort.

However, before I could even get a few good blows in on the cuntsucker, Becks screamed out an alpha order that stopped even my wings in their tracks, and I fell to the ground with a huff.

"Stop it! I asked him to save you, so you aren't allowed to hurt him!" she'd yelled, and the four of us froze as if we'd been slapped in the face.

"You made a deal with him?" Derrick asked, stepping toward her menacingly, sounding appalled by Becks' words.

"Oh, God, it's actually happening," Adam said as he put his forehead in one hand and wrapped another around his middle.

"What the fuck is going on here?" Tyler asked, skin shaking, evidencing how close his beast was to surfacing.

"Well," Becks said somewhat timidly as she pushed her hair behind her ears. "Yes. I made a deal with him to save your lives. I didn't know what else to do."

Derrick rounded on her without skipping a beat and said, "You let us die! That's what you do!"

Cutting him off in haste, Absinthe said, "Um, we don't need to yell at her," as he placed a hand on Derrick's chest. If looks could kill, Absinthe would've been six feet under instead of standing in our safe house's living room, but alas, I realized then, miracles were lies.

"Don't tell me what to do, you piece of shit!" Derrick said, his temper long gone.

Absinthe just smiled at him and said, "Oh, Derrick. I really wish you knew me as well as I know you. I think you might like me better if you did. The way you got this one's beast to work with you to save everyone? Priceless."

Everyone just kind of stood there without saying anything as we all attempted to process what was going on, but before we could even start, Absinthe kept on talking.

"And Tyler, how you got your beast under control, even when you were in his form, and stopped him from eating Derrick alive, even though you know how much that guy likes to fuck with Derrick. Oh man, that was pure gold.

Adam, man. The way you were just waylaying through motherfuckers, one right after the next till that vision messed you up? How I wish I had your skills!

Oh! And Brax! Hey, man! I haven't seen you in so long!"

Absinthe was all sincere smiles and jovial happiness as he talked to me as if we were old friends, but I couldn't even begin to move, much less think through what was happening before me.

"So, as you might be wondering, part of the deal was that I set Absinthe free and bind him to me and our team instead of his forest and cave," Becks said, distracting us all even further.

We were all at a loss for words, I think, and when Absinthe turned to Becks and placed a hand on the side of her face, I could feel the hate radiating through the room.

"Becks, leave them getting used to this idea to me. You have work to do. I'm going to send you to the gauntlet now," he said, and it was as if time slowed as the next words flowed from his mouth. "It's time for our queen to reign."

Before I could say or do anything, Absinthe waved a hand in front of Becks' wide-eyed stare, and she disappeared right before my eyes.

"No!" Derrick and Tyler shouted simultaneously as they ran forward to where Becks had been standing, mirror images of one another, and Adam pushed his hands through his hair.

My eyes landed on Absinthe as I felt like I was going to explode with all the emotions coursing through me, and I screamed, "What the ever titty-loving fuck, Absinthe?"

To be continued...

ALSO BY CILLA RAVEN

Beholden To Balance

Initiate

Reign

Hunter

Defender

The Fae Bounties

Shameless Fae

Reckless Fae

Lost Savages MC

Wake

Take

Raging Heathens MC

Drifter

Prowler

Hallows

A Date With Death: Part One

Shared Worlds

Sneaky As A Fox

Lexi

REIGN

BEHOLDEN TO BALANCE, BOOK 2

I sincerely hope you loved Reign. If you enjoyed the book, I would really appreciate **an honest review** because they help so much! Thank you!

To get an immediate notification when I have a new release, please **sign up for my mailing list**!

To see the complete reading order for this series and to dive into all of my book worlds, **visit my website**!

ABOUT THE AUTHOR

Cilla Raven is an indie author that lives in Montana with her husband, children, and a few fur babies.

You can find all of Cilla's books, merchandise, and more on her **website**!

Love Cilla's books? **Join her mailing list** to be notified of new releases, giveaways, and more!

She'd love to have you join her **Facebook group**: *The Raven's Nest - A Cilla Raven Reading Group*. You'll get exclusive updates and teasers, live streams with Cilla over coffee, and all the funny memes you can stand. **Join now**.

www.ingramcontent.com/pod-product-compliance
Lightning Source LLC
Chambersburg PA
CBHW031710170626
46808CB00005B/1693